The Shelf Life of Fire

Light Messages

Durham, NC

To Michael

One

"He doesn't want you to know," my mother says. Then she pauses. She's calling from Florida.

I sit in my sunroom in Fayetteville, North Carolina. It's a Friday afternoon in early summer, and she's been telling me about my brother Dennis's colon cancer.

My brother and I stopped talking about a decade ago, after I'd discovered he'd forged checks and had stolen thousands from our mom's bank account.

I had threatened to tell our mother if he didn't confess, something he refused to do.

"Screw you," he'd replied—and these were his last words to me.

Now, street traffic intrudes through the phone line, and I imagine my mother standing on the narrow balcony of the apartment where she lives with my brother and his family.

"Dennis never forgave you for telling me about the checks," she says. "He wants nothing to do with you."

"I get it," I say to her.

Late afternoon sunlight floods the sunroom, and the heat is intense. My husband and I have agreed that next year when we upgrade the HVAC system, we'll install air conditioning in this room.

"He's going for chemo and radiation," my mother says. "Next week."

"What about surgery?"

"Only if they can shrink the cancer. The prognosis isn't good."

I rise from the couch, notice a squirrel eating at our backyard bird-feeder.

"I don't know, Rae," my mother says. "He's got an appointment with a new surgeon on Monday. We'll see what he says."

"Keep me posted," I say. The squirrel is gone; the bird-feeder shakes. "Got to go, Mom. Love you."

"Love you, too."

I walk back into the air-conditioned house, chilly but pleasant. I pet Jake, our old golden retriever, who thumps his tail, and go into the kitchen to begin a salad. For five years, my mother and I didn't speak—having had a falling-out over money—so talking to her now, telling her *I love you,* still doesn't feel right. I turn on our kitchen radio, NPR, and pull salad ingredients from the fridge.

I'm chopping a tomato, watching the sharp knife slice through the skin. The tomato is ripe, and my fingers are wet with juice as I listen to an *All Things Considered* segment about Jimi Hendricks. I don't hear the beginning, but I'm carried back to late April 1969, when I'd come down with mononucleosis right after my fifteenth birthday, at the end of a turbulent year. I stop for a moment, remembering how I'd recovered just in time to finish up the last two weeks of school, to take my state Regents exams before summer break.

The previous fall I'd had an intellectual awakening. I'd read *Walden, Eros and Civilization,* and *The Second Sex,* and I'd met a new group of older, more intellectual kids who became my friends. I finish chopping the tomato, pick up half an onion, and begin to chop that. I turn off the radio so I can concentrate; I want to give this memory attention.

1969—the year I'd also decided to quit modeling, quit shaving my legs, using makeup. I'd stopped accompanying my family on Sunday visits to my grandparents in Brooklyn, joined a student protest movement, and dated "Strike," a college guy I'd met on the Long Island Railroad during my ride home from a Rolling Stones concert at Madison Square Garden.

In October, I'd co-led the Lawrence Junior High walkout with Eugene, friend and Black Power leader. We'd planned our walk-out to coincide with other student protests in the New York area, as five-hundred seventh, eighth, and ninth graders had left their classrooms in the middle of fourth period in an anti-war protest held on the school's football field. Somehow, I'd secured a megaphone, and standing on a table in the cafeteria, I directed my fellow students to leave the building— not out the back door but rather out the front so that they could parade past the principal's office, out the Greco-Roman entryway, down the wide front steps.

That summer—after my year of political protest and illness—would be the wildest of my life. Stuff happened. Stuff that changed, defined me.

The kitchen is full of late afternoon shadows. On the counter, I see that I've chopped tomato, onion, green pepper, walnuts, apple, and have tossed them over our home-grown arugula leaves in a hand-blown glass bowl—a gift from our glass artist son, Will, from when he was still in college. It has deep blue swirls and is, as Will calls it, a "low bowl," a shape more challenging to blow.

Tonight, we'll have warmed-over homemade pizza and fresh salad. Tomorrow, my husband, Nick, leaves for his month-long writing retreat in upstate New York, where he has a fellowship that will allow him to spend a month at Blue Mountain, a retreat center in the Adirondacks for writers and artists. All year he has looked forward to this time. He

3

hasn't been able to write much during the academic year, and although I have written a surprising amount, it's all rough drafts, unfinished stuff that no longer calls to me. But I need the publications, so at some point, I'll have to revise, edit, send this work out.

I've also plotted a new novel—a literary romance set in Fayetteville, NC, my adopted home, where Nick and I, both English professors, have lived for over twenty years. My first novel was a historical novel, based on a woman who had been a slave in Fayetteville. It took me years to research and write, so I'm ready to write something fun, light, and breezy.

The idea makes complete sense. When Nick is on retreat, I'll have the time and the solitude to write. I've already mapped all the major plot points.

Nick and I eat in the sunroom, still hot but now bearable. We have dinner plates on our laps, with extra pizza slices and salad bowl on the coffee table. Jake is with us, begging food, a bad habit, but he's an old dog, easy to forgive.

Packed and serviced, Nick's old Ford pick-up truck waits in the driveway. Nick plans to leave in the early morning, around 5:30. He'll be driving north to upstate New York, but the plan is for him to go west to Asheville first, where he and Will plan to go hiking and camping overnight.

"I'll set the alarm," I tell him.

"You don't have to get up with me. You can go back to sleep."

"I'll get up," I say.

"A month," Nick says, his voice soft, regretful.

"I'll be okay," I assure him as we finish the pizza.

—⁂—

Later, Nick calls out, "Come to bed." I'm on my laptop in my study.

After looking over the notes for my novel, I hit *save.* "Yes," I call back to Nick, turning off the computer. Nick is waiting for me, and the lights are out. We embrace, but too tired for romance, turn over and go to sleep.

Saturday morning—and at 8:42 a.m., it's already hot outside. By now, I think, Nick is halfway to Asheville. In darkness, I'd watched Nick back his old Ranger from our driveway to begin his trip.

Already I miss him. The light in my study is still on, as I've been trying to work. But instead of fiddling with my novel, I'm thinking of yesterday's conversation with my mom about my brother's cancer. I sip tepid coffee and decide to free-write about Dennis, about my half-formed memories of him—my only and difficult sibling.

I take another sip, and as I remember my conversation with my mother, I hear her tentative voice telling me about Dennis's cancer and how he doesn't want me to know. Secrets have defined our family. It was only last summer, after my dad died from Parkinson's—an incomplete diagnosis, for his death was complicated by dementia and other medical issues—that my mother and I reconnected. Not reconciled exactly but got back in touch.

I begin typing, but instead of writing sentences, I find myself typing the words *secret* and *regret* over and over until they almost fill the entire screen. Something inside me wants out. But even after years of therapy and healing, I'm not sure I can find the words to write about my family, especially about my brother and how his actions affected our lives.

I want to discuss this with Nick. On a normal summer morning, he'd be downstairs sipping coffee, working on his laptop in the kitchen. I have a strong urge to see if he's there. But he's not. And I've learned that it's better simply to sit with, not act on, my discomforts. I take a few deep breaths and delete the words on the screen. I close my eyes, breathe, then open them. Haltingly, I write.

two

It's spring, 1959, I begin. Glenn Murmelstein has a large worm in a Dixie cup. I stand near him at the "middle entrance"—a chained-off circle of grass in a sea of parking lot asphalt. We're in front of the cooperative apartment complex where I lived for the first six-and-a-half years of my life—and as Glenn removes his hand, I see a pale, pink earthworm, its thick body squirming. Frightened, my heart races; I gasp, then run from the grassy circle across the parking lot. Upstairs, hanging out the second-floor window, the crazy lady is laughing again. "Ha! Ha! Ha!"—loud slapping sounds that smack the air as I run to the fort at the other end of the complex. My heart hurts. I find my place behind the boulder, the part of the fort my friends and I have dubbed "Freedom Rock." Only when my back is against its cold stone face can I relax. No worm. No Glenn. Branches above shake in light wind; the ground is soft, damp. I fight back tears. *I am Rachel,* I tell myself, digging my fingers into the soil. *I am a girl; soon I will be six years old, and "six" sounds like "sick."*

—∞—

I stop writing, lift my head from the computer and realize that this early memory is connected to Dennis and that memories of him began to haunt me about ten years ago—the same time that my niece Hannah was hospitalized for anal bleeding, and my mom and I had a big fight.

6

At first, the memories were wordless, shadow-like specters that followed me both day and night. When the specters became most threatening, I'd often be upstairs, making love to Nick, husband of thirty-something years by then. He'd touched my mouth, outlining the shape of it with his hand. Round and round his finger circled. My eyes would be closed. I'd feel the suggestion of how he wanted me and turn away from him, his large hand resting on my naked hip. He'd move his face to my neck, his warm breath, a whisper. I'd turn toward him; we'd kiss, our arms around each other. *I am not me*, I'd think. And only then could I relax, feel desire open me.

How can I tell this story? Complicated by gaps of memory, half-remembered images, years of denial, secrets, regrets, I can't piece it together, stitch across the holes.

I minimize the screen, opening another file, one with the notes for my pre-plotted novel. I read them over and try to engage. Do I really want to write this novel? I get up from my desk, decide to take a shower, dress, see what the day brings.

By noon, though, I still haven't left the house. Dressed and ready, I've had nowhere to go. I decide to have some coffee and try to work again. I walk to the kitchen, rinse a cup, and pour the last coffee from the Chemex, our glass, low-tech pot, purchased last year. I wash the pot and turn it upside down in the drainboard.

But instead of going upstairs to my computer, I sit down with my coffee at the kitchen table to gather my thoughts.

Grocery shopping—yes, I could go to Food Lion. We need milk and bread. No, not we, I. But maybe I should go to the campus gym. Or to my school office to answer emails and fill book orders for *Cape Fear Editions*, the small literary press Nick and I run.

Or I could check in with Amanda, my assistant director at the university Writing Center—where I serve as director—and although I don't officially work during the summer, I often check in, see how the center is doing. But then I remember it's Saturday. Amanda won't be in, and the Writing Center is closed. Maybe I'll just do some press stuff and clean my office, purging it of the year's accumulations.

But for now, I sip the coffee, cold and bitter but satisfying. Then a wave of something washes over me—sadness, vulnerability, and I feel six again. No, younger—three or four.

This feeling connects now—as it always does—to a specific scene: the bedroom I shared with my brother in Dunhurst, Queens. I stand up from the kitchen table, refuse the memory. "No, thank you," I say, but then sit back down. The memory insists.

I'm there again. In Queens. In my apartment, in bed. I pull my pink winter quilt with its fresh white duvet cover up to my chin, then over my head, where it's dark and warm. The quilt smells of mothballs, and the duvet cover smells of lemon-scented detergent. The smells mingle as I breathe now, inhaling the odors in my Fayetteville kitchen.

My bed is in one corner of the room, and my brother's bed is in the other so that they're parallel. *Parallel.* It's a word I'd just learned. I like it. I understand how two lines could travel near each other but never touch. When I'd asked my mother to spell it for me, I was thrilled to learn that the word *all* is hidden inside.

I hear my brother toss and turn. This is his signal to me that he's awake. When I lift my face from beneath the covers, the room is dark, but I can see shadows. My face is cool in the air and unprotected.

Dennis, I can feel, is looking at me, seeing what's available, and calculating. He's seven, smart, a sophisticated planner. I'm a dreamer; I take what comes. Dennis is swift; I'm slow. He schemes; I contemplate. Dennis has motives; I trust. He's complicated; I'm naïve.

When Dennis stands over my bed, he cradles my face with his hands. "Sleep," he whispers.

—∾—

Back from memory now, I'm still in the kitchen, sitting on one of the two padded swivel office chairs that flank the table. We bought them so that Nick and I could correct papers at the large table. Jake, who has come to keep me company, naps on the cool floor tiles as I remember an adolescent poem I wrote during the year I had mono. My fever had spiked, and I'd awakened around 3:00 in the morning. I walked from my bedroom—we had moved from our Queens apartment to our suburban home in South Shelburne, Long Island—to the kitchen, where the bay window overlooked Meadowbrook Pond, a small man-made lake that served to drain the area swampland. Wetlands, it's now called, and the creation of a lake like this one would not be permitted.

Looking into the pond, I felt ashamed. I remember how the waters reflected a bright half-moon, how some of the houses had outdoor lights on, how they formed a necklace of star-points rimming the shoreline.

Shame. Why? I'd felt my shame as a piercing needle, a sharp singular stab, making me wince. Sometimes I feel this now, when I make small mistakes in class, misplace my cell phone, or lose door keys. A piercing, self-inflicted stab.

Shame. When I had gotten sick after leading the junior high school walkout, I wasn't there to see that the reforms we'd insisted on were implemented. "Demands," we called them. After the walkout, Eugene and I were invited to the principal's office every day for lunch and a discussion. Eugene wanted Martin Luther King's portrait hung in the library, on the wall above the checkout desk. I wanted girls to be allowed to wear pants to school. We were required to wear skirts, and in the

New York winters, we froze in our stylish mini-skirts and knee socks. Also, I wanted students to be permitted to talk as they made their way down the hallways between classes. No more silence in the halls or cafeteria.

But after I became sick, I fell out of the loop, and felt guilty for not being there. And it wasn't until I returned to school for those last few weeks that I learned that the principal had met all our demands. Girls I'd never known—now wearing their jeans and bellbottoms—would stop me in the cafeteria or between classes to thank me. I'd become a hero.

But during my time at home, sick with mono, I'd felt ashamed. I berated myself for falling ill, for trying to lead, for having the audacity to think that I could accomplish something. I'd felt like my body had found me out, betrayed me.

That morning, in darkness, when I'd been looking out across Meadowbrook Pond, a poem had come—words tumbling forward, insistent. Back then, I didn't revise. Poems, words, ideas came to me like gifts, and I thought they should be written as they had arrived.

I repeat the poem to myself now, at the kitchen table:

Hating the ways of me,
breeding disease in the seas of sorrow,
I turn and lines of destruction
appear on my face—
a place of hate,
a place of hate.

Not really a poem, I think. More a mantra of self-loathing. Yet as I speak it aloud, it surprises me. The words feel so good and right that I repeat them again and again.

three

By afternoon, it's now clear that I've wasted half the day and haven't written anything useable. Today, I decide, will be about something else. Sun pours in from the blind I opened earlier. I rise from the kitchen table, wash out my coffee cup, and think about which of my summer projects I'll tackle.

Organizing. I'll turn my attention there—a closet, a drawer—and that might jumpstart my writing and school work. Order the external world, and the internal one will follow.

Before I begin, I go upstairs to brush my teeth and make the bed. But with the covers in disarray, especially on Nick's side of the bed, I stop.

I'm back in Queens again, in bed, and holding my old heavy pink winter quilt. Shame again washes over me. Then, I'm here, standing by the bed in Fayetteville, on this summer morning, touching the corner of the white top sheet, matching it to the thin summer quilt so as to make up the bed.

As a young girl, I had a ritual I'd follow. First, I'd pull the blanket out from beneath the mattress—all sides. Then, I'd climb onto my bed, gently slip under the covers. Next, I'd gather the ends up to tuck them around my body—lifting my right and my left side, pulling the blanket in tightly so that I was wrapped mummy-like, the blanket becoming my cocoon, my sarcophagus.

I'm back in my Queens apartment. I'm four years old. In two years' time, we will move to our house in South Shelburne, but right now, that neighborhood hasn't been created yet. When I am six, my mother, Dennis, and I will take weekly trips every Saturday morning with my Aunt Em and cousins Ellen and Sheryl from Queens to Long Island to watch our houses and the neighborhood go up in the tidal wetlands. My Aunt, Uncle, and cousins live in the apartment just below ours. They are my favorite relatives. Happily, when we move, they too will move into the same new neighborhood.

But now that future doesn't exist for me. I've just gotten into bed for the night. As I put my head down to complete my cocoon—the only part of me that won't be encased in blanket—something sharp stabs me in the neck. Something inside my pillowcase, on top of my pillow. I have to disturb my cocoon to investigate, removing my arms, turning my body over to find the problem. "Oh," I say aloud. There's a wire coat-hanger inside.

Dennis is still up, watching TV in the living room. His bedtime is an hour later than mine. I can hear the low voices from the set, rhythmic and indistinct.

This coat hanger, I quickly understand, is part of my torture. Because torture, I've realized, often masquerades as a joke.

It's summer, still light outside, still light in the bedroom. Slowly, I remove the black wire hanger from my pillowcase. It's the kind from the dry cleaners. Now, I will need to completely disrupt my cocoon and get out of bed—which I do. I take the hanger and place it in the closet, near the neat line of my jumpers, shirts, skirts, dresses, all arranged by color and season—summer, fall, winter, spring.

The hanger is my reminder that I'm stuck in my brother's universe and must observe his laws. If I don't smile at him during dinner, I'll be punished. If I don't say "please" before I ask Dennis for something, I might be smacked "accidentally on purpose" or hit or tripped when I'm walking. Beneath the surfaces of our family life, there are wild animals and stinging insects. There are rules, customs, tripwires, and minefields. I can be hurt or damaged, and no one can keep me safe.

—◊—

Up now, bed made, memory and its accompanying madness gone, I'm attacking the hall closet, which is currently a mess. Random coats and jackets are hung up on hooks and hangers; some have slipped to the floor. There are two vacuum cleaners stuck there—one working, one not, and a couple of old tennis rackets. On the closet's only shelf, above the hangers, there's a cardboard box of winter hats, gloves, scarves, other winter items.

The box I begin with has *Ajax* written on its side. A decorative box would look better, I think, but I probably won't buy one. I carry the box to the kitchen table.

Inside is the history of our family winters. Children's mittens, woolen scarves, zip-off hoods from jackets we no longer own. A knitted Santa Claus hat—a Christmas gift, I'm thinking—probably belonging to our older son, Cal. Then I find a single black leather glove with a small hole in one fingertip. I try it on. When my parents moved from South Shelburne to Florida, my mom gave me these gloves and a matching scarf.

I stop to think of that move. My mother hated Florida. She loved New York City, never wanted to live anywhere else. It was my father's idea to relocate in Florida when he closed his business. So, they did. Although my mom was still working as a psychotherapist, she gave up her job, and they sold the house.

They left New York in the fall of the 1987. Nick and I were attending graduate school. Cal was six, and we lived in a small house in Endicott, New York. Nick had decided to finish his

PhD in English; I had dropped out of the program in favor of doing an MFA in Writing, a degree that had been suggested by my dean at Empire State College, where I was teaching.

Shame rises again, and I remove the glove. I shouldn't have dropped out the PhD program. I toss the glove into one of the three piles I'm making on the kitchen table—stuff to be trashed, stuff to keep, stuff to be donated.

After almost an hour, the box is empty, and my piles are complete. I put the throwaway pile in a paper Trader Joe's bag, the giveaway pile in small box marked "Goodwill" I've found in the garage, and the keeper-pile I return to the box, which I carry to the closet and re-shelve.

But now my organizing energy is gone. I pull out my mother's glove from the throwaway bag and take it back to the kitchen table, holding it like a talisman or a clue.

—⁓—

My mother slaps my face. I've just gotten off the school bus on a rainy afternoon. I don't have an umbrella or galoshes, and the rain is coming down hard. I spot a large puddle just feet away from where the bus has let me off. I jump into it. I turn around, jump into it again and again. Then, gathering my wits, I realize that I'm now sopping wet and my socks are soggy, squishy. I dash home, which is close, just across the street, bound up the many brick steps to our front door.

And there's my mom, waiting outside on the front landing. She's been observing my antics. But I'm feeling good, empowered by my puddle-jumping, ready to change into dry clothing, eat an after-school snack.

Slap. I get it right across the face. Sharp. On the landing outside the front door.

Quickly, I check to see if anybody has seen. But no one has.

My cheek burns with the sting of her dry hand against my damp face. We go into the hallway. My mother kneels to untie the double knots on my wet shoes.

"Sorry," I say.

"Are you stupid?" she asks.

Tears well up, slide down my cheeks. Huge tears, big as raindrops. I don't sob, but my breath is tight. "Sorry," I say again, pulling off my jacket, leaving it on the floor mat by the door, where unknotted now, I slip off my soggy shoes, and run to my bedroom, leaving my mother kneeling there, my wet things littered around her.

Later, we eat dinner as a family. My father is home early. He and his parents own a furniture store on Queens Boulevard, and it stays open long hours. Most days, my dad comes home late.

Tonight, he's home for dinner, and we're having meatloaf, green salad, and oven fries. Salad is served first. We eat at the kitchen table, in an alcove by the bay window, overlooking Meadowbrook Pond.

"How was school?" my father asks.

Dennis talks about having baseball practice in the gym because of the rain. He pitches for the high school team. He's in tenth grade, wants to play ball in college, perhaps beyond.

I mention an essay about dragonflies that I wrote in English class. Last summer in camp, I made a hobby of catching and releasing them when we canoed on the lake.

Neither my mom nor I mention my puddle-jumping or her slapping me. We discuss the weather, however, and how it's supposed to be a nice day tomorrow—if the weatherman is right for a change. "Good," my father says. "We could use a little foot traffic at the store."

Dennis looks at me. Somehow, he knows that I got slapped, that I cried in my room, that I took off all my wet clothes, dumped them into our hamper in the hall bathroom. He winks at me, and dutifully, I smile.

All this memory I've gotten from my mom's glove.

I take the Trader Joe bag out to the backyard, drop it in trash. The Goodwill box I bring out to the garage, leaving it on an old chair for another day.

I'm done. And too weary to do much else.

four

Early morning, Sunday. My first full day without Nick. I go downstairs to get Jake his breakfast of kibble, a half slice of bread, and low-fat milk. I make coffee, measuring out the grounds, then pouring the boiling water methodically over them.

Quiet. I open the living room blinds to a gray, empty street, nothing moving outside. Then, coffee mug in hand, I ascend the stairs, old Jake behind me, so that I can work.

I pull out the notes for my novel, but I'm not inspired. Again, I give myself permission to write absolutely anything. Free associate, see what comes up. As the Buddhists say, turn off my judging mind.

When I teach creative writing, I tell my students that they should write their passions. If the writer doesn't care, the reader won't. I ask them to open themselves, to be present, discover their hearts, feel everything, judge nothing. No taboos.

I rise from my laptop to stroke Jake, already asleep on my study futon. I think back to when we adopted him. He was about eighteen months old. Will, then around eleven, found him on a Golden Retriever rescue site. We traveled three hours to Charlotte to meet him and his foster family and fell in love. Now he has benign tumors all over his body. A lumpy old dog. I pet his head; Jake wags his tail. Thump, thump against the cushion.

My cell phone rings, and I think about not taking the call. But when I see it's Mom, I answer, sitting down now on my desk chair.

"Dennis has to have surgery," my mother launches in. But the connection isn't good. Her voice crackles, and I lose her next few words. I hear road noise, a truck, a car horn. She's probably walked out of the apartment.

"What happened?" I stare at the Word screen, a rectangle of white pixels.

"They found a small mass in his groin, below his stomach. They've got to go in. His doctor called yesterday, Saturday afternoon, after he received the test results."

"What about the chemo?"

"On hold," she says. If this conversation had happened twenty years ago, I'd hear her drag on a cigarette. But she finally gave them up at sixty-two, after her own cancer scare.

I think of her leather glove with its hole in the finger. The smell of it, the smell of my mother—hair spray, cologne, cigarettes.

"When?" I ask. Jake slowly gets off the couch, heads to the bathroom, where he likes to drink water from the toilet bowl. In moments, I hear his lapping.

"Thursday. Pre-op on Wednesday, bloodwork on Monday or Tuesday, I think. Not sure. Dennis took the call, and I might not be remembering right." I hear her sigh. A truck rattles in the Florida distance. A moving truck, I imagine, and we're silent for a moment until it passes. I invent a Hispanic couple sitting in the front seat. They're in their late twenties, a bit tired, but happy to be leaving their rental apartment and moving into their first house. The woman is pregnant; she wipes her sweaty brow, smiles.

"Rae. You still there? Mom asks.

"Of course," I answer. "Keep me posted about the surgery."

Then I add, "How are you doing? How are *you* holding up?"

"Fine. You know. It's harder on Hannah because she's young." Pause, more traffic, then, "I've got to go. Wanted to let you know. I'll call again soon. Love you."

"Okay. Love you, too, Mom. Remember, call."

"Of course." Click.

I hang up and think of Hannah, Dennis's younger daughter, whom I've never met. She must be twelve or thirteen by now. I've heard she's smart, does well in school, but I don't know much about her.

It's light now but overcast: a steel-colored sky with the promise of rain. In front of me, the computer screen beckons, and I find myself quickly back at work, typing:

Mary Jo left the room after the argument. Sal, who'd become violent, had slammed his fist through the sheetrock wall by the door where she'd stood. He didn't hit her. He never hit her, just broke furniture, damaged walls, shattered Mary Jo's best china, the set her grandmother had given her as a wedding present.

But then I stop. My well-planned novel dissolves. I have no energy for Mary Jo. She was going to work today at the middle school cafeteria, planning to confide in a female co-worker. Eventually, she will leave her abusive husband, find love elsewhere. But I no longer like her nor feel sympathy for her rotten marriage.

What was I thinking? How can I write this story? How can I create this character and write about her life? I delete a sentence, add another. But it's no good. My words stare back at me, stale, dull, mocking, inauthentic. I delete all that I've written.

I get up to pace. Then sit down again and write about my mother. I see her, smell her hair. I think about putting my hand in her glove, then notice it's with me, on my desk. I must have carried it upstairs.

When I return to the keyboard, I'm typing a description of her. She's in her thirties. Her dyed black hair is teased away from her face. It's stiff with hairspray, and I'm not allowed to touch it. She stands in black leather high-heels and wears a well-coordinated outfit: black slacks, a lavender blouse, purple earrings in the shape of small flowers.

Now, I imagine my mother is with me in my study. Her heels tap against the hardwood floor as she crosses the room to pet Jake, who wags his tail at her. She's no longer in her thirties, but ageless—she's all women, and the woman I can never be.

"Mom," I say. But she won't look at me. So, I turn to the keyboard and type her name: Edna Bloom.

A sentence, then two. A paragraph, a page. Words fly from my fingers. I tell my mother to talk to me. She does. I ask her what went wrong, and she begins to tell me.

five

It's Monday. I've just spent about two hours on the computer. I'm done. Between Sunday and today, I've written about five double-spaced pages, but I can't or don't want to look at them.

Late morning now. I shut down the laptop, walk to the bedroom. When I turn on NPR, Diane Rehm's halting voice is welcoming guests to speak about Obamacare.

I'm thinking I'll go to school, check in with Amanda and other staff, then go to the campus gym to work out. So, I open my closet, take out my yoga pants and a tee-shirt, strip off my bathrobe, nightgown. Naked now, I have the urge to look at myself.

In the bathroom, I open the small linen closet, with its full-length mirror on the inside door, stand back to gain perspective.

A woman of fifty-eight—thin, not too out of shape—greets me. But everything's relaxed: skin, breasts, butt. My face is a loose net of wrinkles. I breathe, soften my focus. I turn to the right, to the left. Hold up my breasts to see if that helps.

Now, a memory. I'm fifteen; it's my first time—with Kevin Last. And even back then I recognized the irony of his name. For a quick moment, I'm inclined to return to the computer to write, to describe how I lost my virginity with him one summer afternoon during that important, memorable year of 1969.

Childbirth, too. I want to write about that. I look at my

round belly. Before kids, it was flat. My breasts, how I nursed each of my sons for almost two years. I don't regret it. Nursing offered me calmness, connection with my body. Then, I look at my scar, stitched like an enormous, deformed centipede, across my right rib cage.

Scars are poems, language made flesh, I think. My scar has been with me almost my entire life. A souvenir of the surgery that saved me. A paradox, question, reminder.

—◇◇—

It's 1957. My mother kneels on the floor, pats the warm towel covering me. We're the same height now, her loving face next to mine.

She hugs me. I feel malleable, my body yielding in her arms. When she removes the towel, I'm still warm. First, she helps me into my underpants. One foot lifted, the other...then my undershirt.

"Hands up," she says. Up my arms go.

"Beautiful," she says, kissing my scar. Her soft, warm lips magical.

Now I've forgotten her yelling, how she called me stupid when I spilled my milk on the shaky kitchen table. How her smacks and slaps stung my face, wet from tears.

"No, mommy!" I'd cried. "Don't hit me..."

But that was earlier, when I woke her up with the TV's volume up too high. Dennis and I had been fighting about what to watch: *The Rocky and Bullwinkle Show* or the cartoons with the classical music that I liked so much.

"Sweet girl," Mom is saying. And before pulling my white undershirt completely down, she kisses my scar again.

—◇◇—

I was born with pyloric stenosis, a growth in the pyloric valve that blocks the passage of food to the intestines. Without surgery, babies with this medical problem die. The most significant symptom is projectile vomiting. The problem most often occurs in firstborn male babies. Also, there is a genetic predisposition for this condition, and babies of Jewish ancestry are more likely to have pyloric stenosis. It's rare in female infants and occurs in only about 2.4 out of 1,000 births.

According to my mother, when I was about a week old, I started vomiting and couldn't keep my formula down. A big baby, over eight pounds at birth, by my second week of life, I had lost a pound. By three weeks, I had lost two pounds. My mother was frantic. The pediatrician suggested changing my formula, and when that didn't work, it was changed again. But my mom suspected that the problem was more serious.

My Uncle Ralph, who lived in another building in the same apartment complex, was a general practitioner, or GP as they were called, and he was consulted. It was Uncle Ralph who diagnosed me and saved my life.

I had surgery at three weeks old, with Uncle Ralph attending. My chest was painted with an iodine-based antiseptic that turned my entire middle section yellow-orange, like the sun at daybreak. My mom said the hospital nurses called me "Ray of Sunshine" or just "Sunshine" for short because I was such a happy baby, even after this major surgery.

My pyloromyotomy was made with a vertical rather than a horizontal incision. The surgeon divided the muscle of the pylorus to open up the gastric outlet. It is a mechanical fix associated with few complications or later problems.

If my surgery were to be done today, I might not have any scar, but this was the 1950s. I was lucky back then to have been diagnosed, even luckier to have been born weighing over eight pounds. After my surgery, I weighed less than four.

The ritual kissing of my scar and my mother's words, "It's beautiful," allowed me to think of my scar as lovely, to wear bikinis as a teenager, to feel comfortable when changing in gym class. My scar marked me as different. But I loved it and love it even now.

I think of my scar as I dress. I remind myself: today is my second full day without Nick. I'm not yet lonely, but the house feels empty. My plan is to go to school, walk Jake, then in the afternoon, relax on the couch in the hot sunroom with *Anna Karenina* beneath the whirring ceiling fan. Then, when it gets dark, I'll make myself a salad and a grilled cheese sandwich, retreat to the living room couch, watch *Hit or Miss* on Netflix, and knit slippers for Christmas gifts. Another day will pass.

—⁓—

Nick calls at dinnertime. He'd been camping with Will, and when they were ready to leave, the breaks somehow got hung up on Will's old Tacoma. Will called AAA, but because the Blue Ridge Parkway doesn't allow commercial traffic, the AAA agent couldn't find a tow truck company to come out. The agent, Will later told me, was located in a New Jersey office and didn't have a map with the Parkway on it. She thought Will was inventing it.

"I don't see no Blue Ridge Parkway, sir..." she'd told him. Will imitated her accent for me.

"This is a major highway throughout the Appalachian Mountains. You must have heard of it."

"No sir, if it ain't on my maps, I ain't heard of it. You'll have to find a tow truck company on your own."

So, Will had to find a local service station willing to help— which he did, though it was almost 4:00 by the time the tow truck arrived; they'd been waiting since 10:00 in the morning. Also, he had to pay $150 out-of-pocket, and neither Nick nor he had cash with them. The tow truck driver had to stop at a gas station ATM machine so that Will could withdraw money.

Now Nick was getting a really late start. I tried to talk him into staying the night at Will's and getting an early start the next morning. But he was ready to hit the road.

"Drive carefully," I told him. I was particularly worried because Nick has cataracts in both eyes and can't see clearly at night.

SIX

Tuesday, my third day alone. I make coffee, feed Jake, and head upstairs to my computer. The sun is already out, promising a brutally hot day ahead.

In New York, we'd have hot, very hot summer days, but the humidity was never this bad. Early morning would start out cool, in the low 60s, then reach the 80s by afternoon. Days in the 90s were rare.

I sit at my laptop, turn it on. As the blank, white screen comes up, I start typing. No judgment, just memory.

I'm outside my Queens apartment; the Good Humor truck is parked on Francis Lewis Boulevard alongside the concrete playground that is part of the cooperative complex.

My mother throws a nickel and dime, bundled in a paper napkin and a rubber-band, down from our fourth-floor apartment window.

I see my mother now as she leans out the window, pulls her right arm back, aims the small bundle, throws. I pick it up, in a hurry not to miss the Good Humor truck. But there are ten or so children in front of me, all wanting Fudgsicles, Creamsicles, Italian Ices, which I often get because I like the way the brightly colored ice dyes my lips. Also, I like it that the ice takes a long time to eat.

So, when my turn comes, I order the Italian Ices, my favorite flavor, red-cherry. I lift the lid with the tab, unwrap the wooden spoon, throwing the lid and wrapper away in a nearby metal garbage bin. Once on the playground, I scrape the loose ice off the top, and when the ice has melted a little, turn over the ice mound to eat the gooey syrup on the bottom. I take a seat on the slatted wooden bench by the playground's perimeter. It's been newly painted green; the surface is cool and smooth.

I wear my sun-suit. It's a one-piece jumper, with elastic around the leg openings. The top ties with thin straps at the shoulders. Today, my sun-suit is yellow, with black stripes.

"Bumble bee," Teddy Harris taunts as he sits by me on the bench. He's eating an orange Creamsicle.

"Buzz..." I say, feeling the urge to slap the Creamsicle from his hand. He's wearing dark blue cotton shorts and a plaid shirt tucked into them.

Barbara Goldstein, my best friend, I now see is running up the block to catch the ice-cream man, who is serving the last child.

Barbara has long brown hair that cascades down her back. She also wears thick glasses. Today, she has on a one-piece bathing suit and pedal-pushers.

"I want a Sunday Bar," I hear her say, looking up at the man in white who bends from the window.

In a moment, I realize our gang is all here. Four of us. All with our treats, now sitting on two benches along the chain link fence. A massive oak tree from a small green area outside the playground provides shade. The chain link fence is about four feet high, creating a boundary between the lovely treed, vacant lot where we have our fort and this, the apartment complex's large concrete playground.

Sticky juice runs from Glenn's mouth; he's eating a double Popsicle, the messiest choice because the sticks come apart as it melts.

"Gross," I say.

"Gross," Barbara says.

"Let's play cops and robbers," Glenn suggests. His legs rhythmically pump the air—back and forth, making me crazy.

"Stop!" I yell. But Glenn continues pumping and sucking his Popsicle.

A butterfly dances above us, and Teddy, done with his Creamsicle, puts the wooden stick in his pocket and tries to catch the flying insect with his hands.

In the distance, on the adjoining concrete pad, some older boys play basketball. Their ball thumps the pavement. I look up to see a woman in a plaid housedress open a window, the mechanical kind, and as she cranks the handle, the black steel-framed window opens out.

"Let's find rocks and make-believe we live in a cave," I say.

"And we're married," Barbara adds. She's wiping her sticky fingers on her pedal pushers.

"Okay," Teddy says, beginning to climb the chain link fence behind our bench. Glenn has forgotten about cops and robbers and joins us.

—⁓—

Who was that girl? I ask myself, pulling back from the memory. Do we shed the skins of early childhood? Or grow into them?

Hearing the voices of my childhood friends, I'm feeling my identity slip. Glenn has a speech impediment, a slight lisp, and Barbara's voice slurs and is often high-pitched. Can I hear myself? I lean toward memory again and read aloud the page I've written. But it's my current voice I hear.

Sitting now with my few pages, I think about identity loss or the splitting of self. Then I think about schizophrenia. I had a schizophrenic student once in my advanced poetry class. When Dave was on his meds, his symptoms were controlled, and he was a bright young man. But when Dave decided not to take his meds, thinking that with enough willpower he could control his symptoms, he'd quickly become out of control. Never violent, just inappropriate.

Once, Dave came late to class, put his head down on the large seminar table around which we all sat, and fell asleep. He was one of only two men in the class. One nontraditional student, Greta, who was almost seventy and who had taught high school English for over thirty years but always wanted to write poetry, was in the class that semester. When Dave woke up, we were workshopping Greta's poem about picking vegetables as a child in rural Virginia.

"Wanna dance, Greta?" Dave asked, lifting his head from the table and speaking out of turn.

"We're discussing Greta's poem, Dave," I said, trying to redirect him.

"But Greta likes to dance, and so do her vegetables," Dave said, getting up, beginning to twirl around the room.

I stood and escorted Dave from the classroom. "Back in a minute," I told the class. After that, I didn't let Dave attend class but allowed him to finish the course with me as an independent study. Sometimes his poetic connections were strange, even wonderful. He once wrote a poem about walking across the Arctic Circle and becoming ice.

—⚹—

Now pulling into the present, I realize how disconnected my own thoughts are. Glancing outside the window, I see a woman in running shorts and a sports bra jog by with two German Shepherds. She reminds me of Mary Jo, my novel's would-be protagonist. Is she dead?

Yes, just as I suspected yesterday, I fear that I can't write this book I've so meticulously planned. I find the file with my novel notes, gaze at the plot points, scroll down to a character description of Mary Jo. I don't like what I read. I don't like her. The novel seems trivial. I reread my writing today. I don't like it. I don't like myself.

I remember the line "hating the ways of me...." I close the novel file, remembering that all last semester I'd envisioned writing a simple story, an easy read, light-hearted, perhaps even funny.

I lean back in my study chair, hearing my next-door neighbor's white Ford Explorer pull slowly into the driveway. I hear children's voices, doors slamming.

It's an autobiographical novel I'll write. And even if it's a bad book and makes me feel insane, I must try. Why? Because my brother is dying and my father is dead. Because I'm losing myself and am afraid of that loss.

seven

I'm in the kitchen, an hour later, with a notepad, remembering 2005, a counseling session with Nick and our therapist Dr. Bob Bormann.

We were discussing the ways in which Nick's and my childhoods intruded on our relationship. Nick came from a poor family, Italian Catholic, with parents who were emotionally and physically abusive or, at times, simply inattentive. He had a tendency in our marriage back then to space-out, and when this occurred, I felt insignificant, unworthy—of his or anyone's attention. That was, and still is, my psychological response.

Seeing me upset, Bob turned the conversation to me.

"Remember, if you can, Rachel," Bob began, "a time in your childhood when you felt small, marginalized."

I scanned my mental files for something. I thought about the Queens apartment, about South Shelburne, until I found myself walking along the sidewalk to the neighborhood A & P. But my file didn't have a destination: I just kept walking, walking, walking. The sidewalk was divided into squares— each square, a pace-and-a-half.

Bob and Nick looked at me. But I was still walking, yet had nowhere to go. *Taking too much time,* I thought. *Answer. Say something.*

"We're losing you again," Nick remarked, leaning back in

the upholstered chair.

I realized that it was I, not he, who was the cause of my feelings. I was about to make a connection, perhaps an important one, but then I was back on the sidewalk and couldn't think.

"Dissociation," Bob explained, "is linked to more severe disorders, like schizophrenia. But that's not what we're seeing here." Bob crossed his legs, dangling his right shoe. I noticed his New Balance sneakers with the logo on the sides in bright neon blue.

I looked at Bob and at Nick, now leaning toward me again, who had also crossed his legs. Intentional? Were they colluding against me? I couldn't tell because I can't get off the sidewalk. I couldn't go forward and couldn't turn back. Instead, I took baby-steps to avoid stepping on the lines that divided the pavement.

I'm a piece on a board game, I thought. A Monopoly piece—a top hat, a shoe, a terrier, an iron.

—⁓—

Struggling to write, I'm now at my desk. Afternoon. The sun has moved to the back of the house so that my study is bathed in soft, filtered light. I minimize the pages I've just written, open the novel file—seven pages of notes—and read them once more. No. It's just junk—words that have nothing to do with my life. I take a deep breath and delete the file. Then I take the few pages I'd handwritten earlier and crumple each page into a separate, small, tight paper ball, a satisfying knot of wasted words. I aim, tossing them one by one into the wicker basket by my desk. I sink them all, one shot each. "Score," I say.

I feel alone, wish Nick were here so that I could process this feeling. Dissociated? I ask myself. Yes. Unhooked from the trajectory of my life? Yes.

My head is a balloon filled with helium, lighter than air.

It's floating away, lifting into wind, drifting. Then I'm on the sidewalk, like in therapy, not wanting to step on the cracks.

"Careful," I whisper, as my cell phone rings.

"Hi, Rae, it's Mom," the voice calls out, pitched high, tentative. Something else is wrong.

"What's going on?" I ask. My mind is back inside my body. I'm at the computer; the South Shelburne sidewalk has disappeared.

"You have a minute?"

"Yeah, of course. What's up?" I press.

"It's Dennis," she begins. "He's had his surgery. Early. An emergency." My heart quickens. "He's in ICU. I can't talk much. I'm at the hospital. It didn't go well. They got some of the smaller masses, but the cancer is more widespread than they thought. There are other complications, too. I don't even know, don't want to know. They'll have to go in again. But his heart failed during surgery—twice. So, they revived him, finally closed him up. Not good. No." My mother chokes back tears.

"How long will he be in ICU?" I've turned away from the computer screen and am looking out the window onto a perfect day.

"The oncologist wants to run more tests. He doesn't know when—or if—he can do the other surgery. I don't know how long he'll be in intensive care. We're hoping he'll be out tomorrow, the next day, latest. But he'll stay in the hospital. How long, I don't know."

"Is Dennis conscious? Have you spoken to him?" I'm now drawing concentric circles and geomantic shapes in the margins of a blank legal pad.

"He was awake; then they put him out. He needs to stabilize. He was in lots of pain. I don't have to tell you. Awful. Just awful." My mom's voice wavers, goes up an octave. Then, she sobs. "It's not right that he's suffering."

I let her cry, sweeping the pen across the yellow page so that large circles and a face appear. An animal face? I draw small pointed ears until the face looks like a cat. I draw whiskers.

"Rae, I need a couple of hundred dollars. Please. You have to help me. I need $200 to see us through the week, to pay for groceries, gas."

I should have seen it coming. I take my pencil, turn the cat's mouth into a frown. "Sure, Mom. I'll help. I'll wire the $200 today. But please, no more. I can't do this." The cat has a sitting body. I put it on a zafu; now it's a meditation kitty. "To Tamarac?" I ask.

"Yes, that would be great. I can't thank you enough, Rae. Really." My mom is no longer crying; her voice is pitched normally.

"You have no idea how hard it is for me to ask. No idea."

"Let me go now, Mom. I'll make the transaction. Call me if you don't get the money in an hour or so. Okay?"

"Yes, of course. Thanks again, Rae. This will help tremendously."

"Love you, Mom. Let me know how Dennis is doing."

"Yes, I will. Love you, too, Rae. We all appreciate your help." Click.

I hit the red end-call button on my cell phone, label my cat: Meditating Concentric Kitty.

When I hang up, the house feels particularly silent, and I feel particularly alone. I'm not dressed yet for the day, but I'm very thirsty. I go downstairs to get water, turn on the filtered water valve, fill the red hand-blown glass cup that Will made for me last year. Will, my baby. My second born. My artist. I love this cup.

Soon, I'm upstairs again, ready to get dressed and wire the money—my errand of mercy. But now, with my jeans on, I go to the bathroom closet to pull out a tank top and see myself in the large, framed mirror above the sink vanity. *Can I write about my life?* I ask. A kind of reality show on paper. Is there truth or only the desire for truth? I take a long sip of water, the glass fitting so well in my hand.

—⁂—

Returning home from wiring my mother the money, I climb the stairs to my study, sit down at my desk. Jake joins me and lies down on the rug as I write about my mom—perhaps for my book, I think, and start typing her backstory—the part of it I know:

My mother never felt loved. The fifth child of Solomon and Leah Rosenfeld, immigrants from Bessarabia—a country squeezed between Romania and Russia, that became present-day Moldova—she was born in 1929: six months before the stock market crashed, two months after the infamous Valentine's Day Massacre, two months before the Vatican separated from Italy, and the year of the world's most deadly influenza epidemic.

Married as teenagers, they left with three young children— Lena, Doris, and Bernice. Lena, age five, Bernice, age three, and Doris, an infant.

In America, two children followed: my Uncle Leo, and the youngest, Edna, my mother.

Leo, a thirteen-pound breech baby, was delivered like the others, at home by midwife. But his birth almost killed my grandmother, four-foot, eleven inches tall, and not quite hundred pounds.

A year later, my grandmother became pregnant with my mother. She was distraught, still traumatized by Leo's birth, and she considered having an illegal abortion. She spent the first few months of her pregnancy saving money until my grandfather put his foot down, insisting that to destroy life was to go against God. So, she had the baby against her better judgment and used the money she'd saved to pay for a hospital birth.

A siren screams outside on Ramsey Street, the nearby road that often takes me to Raleigh when I don't want to drive the highway. I think about Uncle Leo, how he was my grandparents' favorite, the only male child. And Dennis, certainly my mother's favorite. I resume the backstory, holding space for the power that memory brings.

At seven, my mom learned that she hadn't been wanted. Why her mother told her, I can't imagine. But, as a consequence, my mother never felt loved. She felt marked, as if a black cloud hovered over her.

The family lived in Williamsburg, Brooklyn, and owned a corner grocery store, above which they resided in a small apartment. The store was almost always open—weekends, holidays, evenings—and the children all took shifts working there.

My mother grew up in that store—shelving inventory, dusting, sweeping the wooden floor, washing the plate glass windows, working the register. She watched kittens being born and caught customers trying to steal.

The grocery store had one of the first phones, and it became the neighborhood phone. My mother would have to go out into the street, yell people's names in the summertime when windows were open, so they could come down to receive their calls. In winter, she'd have to put on her heavy cloth coat and knitted hat, always hand-me-downs from older sisters, and knock on apartment doors to find people.

"Phone for Gertrude..." she'd yell through a closed door. Or, "Irving needs to come down; his sister is on the line...." Or, "Mr. Goldstein, you have an important call from the bank."

Everyone knew everyone's business. The grocery store was a community hub, especially during the Depression, when life was so tough that social boundaries became blurred. But the Rosenfeld family always had enough to eat, and the store kept family members together, allowing them to bond over necessity, grit, and a common goal. Family equaled responsibility, and emotions were repressed.

Love was difficult for my mother. Difficult in her family, difficult in ours.

I stop, pull back my chair and walk around my study and into the bedroom, pausing to remember how when I was a little girl, my mom repeatedly told me that she loved me— almost as if she needed to convince herself. But I'm not being fair.

Returning to my computer, I hit "save," turn off the computer, and move toward the window, where the sun is still bright on this late afternoon, and the clouds have lifted to reveal a penetrating blue sky. No one is out. Jake sleeps on the rug. I watch his lumpy chest rise and fall as he breathes.

I know my mother loves me. She's succeeded in communicating that.

Deciding to go to my school office, I now feel ready to get something done. Check in with the Writing Center. Maybe go to the gym, too. I need to be around people. Make small talk. Be normal, get out of myself.

eight

Wednesday. I'm driving the mile to work in my cherry-red Honda Fit, bought new last year. I've named my car Ruby, and I've bonded with her.

By the time I've arrived at the stop sign at the end of my block, I've changed from NPR to an oldies station. Aretha Franklin belts out "R-E-S-P-E-C-T," and I'm singing joyfully along at the top of my voice.

Turning onto the university's main road, I throw the car into neutral, coast, trying as I've done since I bought Ruby to coax the best mileage from the little engine. EPA suggests that I should get 33 MPG highway, 27 city, but I've gotten as much as 38.3 MPG on the interstate. Even now, though I'm down to 37.3 in the city, that isn't bad. It's a game I play.

At school, I run into a professor from the history department, James, who's organizing and cleaning his office. He's got symphonic music on low, and he's humming along. Stacks of books and papers crowd his desk; a small upright vacuum cleaner leans against the cement block wall. I stop to chat, welcoming conversation. Other than talking to my mom, briefly to Will, and to Nick on the phone, I haven't spoken with anyone for days.

"How's summer going?" I ask, standing in the doorway.

"Good. Going to Philadelphia with Linda next week. NEH conference. Thought I'd get this place cleaned up. Amazing how much junk.... How about you?" James stops as if he's seen something in me or recognized something odd. Standing by the window, a pile of papers in hand, James stares at me—through me—I imagine.

"Yeah, I should clean mine. Not inspired yet," I manage. "Nick's gone to his retreat, so I've been working at home."

"How's he doing?" James, I see now, is wearing plaid Bermuda shorts and a black Grateful Dead tee-shirt with paint splattered on the front.

"Good," I say. But now I want to leave. A shadow has appeared behind James. Maybe it's the sun behind a cloud, but a wave of something has overtaken me. "Well, see you later. Tell Linda hello for me." I walk down the hall, turn onto another corridor, unlock my office door.

It's a mess inside. Stacks of papers on my desk and on the floor. Books are open on the old, defunct radiator I use as a shelf, and my telephone message light is blinking.

Exhausted, I slump down on my chair, close the door. It's hot, I'm hot, and I reach over to yank open two black-framed steel windows rather than turn on the air conditioning.

I catch a glimpse of the empty courtyard outside, where there's a concrete decorative fountain that has never worked. Its two-tiered bowls are empty. Through the courtyard there's a walkway of octagonal stepping stones that few people use.

Now, it all strikes me as sad, very sad. The underutilized path. The paint-stained tee-shirt, my messy office.

I put my head down on my desk and begin to weep. Heavy gasps and tears consume me as I try to quiet the loud noises that characterize my sobs. I raise my head, look out at the courtyard. I understand. Although Dennis is alive, somehow his ghost is with me.

I stop my crying and lean into the chair, realizing that I'm back in 1969, the last day of ninth grade, riding home on the school bus, listening to someone's transistor radio playing "Aquarius." Dennis's ghost is taking me here. "Why?" I ask. But I get no answer.

When I arrive home, humming "Aquarius," my mom isn't there, but Dennis is. Something's happened, and he's in a bad mood. We're in the large kitchen, with its divided areas—one for work space, with stove, refrigerator, countertop, and the other for our large Early American style trestle table. Dennis fixes a sandwich, and our dog Gil intensely watches him. We'd adopted Gil during the summer after we moved to the house. He was a rescue dog, a beagle mix, and we'd driven all the way to Wantagh Point, at the tip of Long Island, to Bide-A-Wee, a no-kill shelter. He was a cute puppy but turned into a rather aggressive adult dog. We all loved him but couldn't trust him around other dogs. His full name, Gadilla, is Yiddish for "big deal" because we all made such a fuss over him when we first got him. We call him Gil for short.

I walk to the kitchen table, inadvertently slamming my thick loose-leaf binder, with the entire year's notes and mimeos from all my classes, onto the table.

"Screw you," Dennis shouts at me from the prep area behind the cabinet divide.

"Whacha making?" I ask but have already seen that it's a tomato and cheese sandwich with French's mustard. We kept a kosher house when we lived in the apartment complex, near my maternal grandparents, but when we moved to our suburban house, that restriction began to gradually change over the years, until we all were eating ham, shrimp, bacon, and mixing meat with dairy.

Dennis bends to look at me; I see his unhappy face above the stove but beneath the overhead cabinets. No reply, just a face. I watch as his hands plate his sandwich and pour orange juice from a carton into a jelly-jar glass with Fred Flintstone on it. Then Dennis leaves the kitchen.

I, too, am hungry and walk to the fridge to check my options—an open cottage cheese container, bread, eggs, milk, deli ham, provolone, etc.—then close it, thinking the pantry will offer better choices.

Here we have cookies—Oreos and chocolate chip. I grab two, one of each, head to my room, first picking up my loose-leaf binder, tucking it underneath my arm.

Gil has followed Dennis into his room. For food, no doubt. I listen at his door. Our bedrooms are at the end of a single long hall—his to the left, mine to the right. Dennis's door is locked shut. I stand outside, thinking that Dennis loves the dog more than he loves me.

The ghost takes me back further. Now, I'm four again; Dennis and I are in our bedroom, the one we shared in our Queens apartment. It's winter, and our father is coming home after 10:00 because it's his night to keep the store open. The room is dark, but for a streetlight from the playground outside. We should be sleeping, but we're not.

"You should pray," Dennis commands.

"I've already said my prayers," I reply.

"But God didn't hear you," Dennis says. "You have to speak louder."

"The man at the shul told me that I should pray quietly, to myself."

"You believed him? Are you stupid, or what?"

"But he said..."

"Are they quiet in synagogue, Rae? Is that what happens there? Yeah, they're all silently praying. Right." Dennis's voice is full of disgust. It's his older-brother voice, the one that's always right, burdened with contempt and suppressed rage.

I stop for a moment. In the background, I hear the TV on in the living room. There's a slice of light beneath our bedroom door. Dennis's bed squeaks, and although I can't see him, I know he is sitting up. I sit up, too.

"Dennis, teach me the prayer again. The whole thing."

"Not ready. You're not ready." Dennis's whisper is loud, thick, throaty. A warning.

"I'll just say what I know, okay?" On some level, I understand that this is a control thing. Dennis must be in charge. He's the one who must have power. I must remain vulnerable, at his mercy. This is our natural order. I must submit. Yet, I also understand that something is wrong. Very wrong. And perhaps that's why I must submit. The fabric of our lives will come unraveled if one family member pulls the wrong thread.

"Sha'ma Yis'ra'eil Adonai Eloheinu Adonai echad." I repeat softly from my bed. "Hear, oh Israel, the Lord is our God; the Lord is one."

"Louder," Dennis insists. "God can't hear you."

"But He's everywhere. He hears everything."

"You have to be deserving first," Dennis's voice is smoke, thicker than air. It lingers in the darkness; it swirls around my head; it smells like my mother's cigarettes. I close my eyes, repeat the partial prayer out loud again. With conviction, with love. But now, suddenly, I'm ashamed. Of Dennis and of myself.

—៱៱៸—

It's rather late when I arrive home from school, and I realize that the air conditioning needs to be lowered. Although it's evening, it's still ninety-something outside, way too hot inside. I turn the thermometer down to 72 degrees and call to Jake, who doesn't respond.

Upstairs now, I find him asleep on the bathroom floor, his eyes sunk so deeply that they roll backward when I try to rouse him. He thumps his tail, as I think ahead to his dying, hoping that we won't have to put him down like we did all our other dogs. I stroke his matted fur, kiss his head, listen to his labored breath.

Sitting on the bathroom's white tiled floor, I see outside the large window to the darkened sky. Not quite sundown yet, the gray sky is cloudy, looking like it might rain. It's been the rainiest summer on record. I sigh, too unmotivated to move.

I see the houses in our planned neighborhood. A deserted street, no one out. The world is shadowless, transparent, blank, generic-looking, as if this gray evening might be a film set that could be reused for a variety of movies.

I'm crying again. For my father, my brother, for Jake—the thought of death hitting me like a hammer blow. "Dennis," I say aloud. "I'm sorry."

For the briefest moment his ghost appears, whispers, "You should be," then disappears.

Jake opens his eyes, wags his tail, a measure of his doggy compassion. I'll take it. I'll take whatever sympathy I can get.

nine

My friend Elizabeth once told me that she sees her life as divided into discernible stages—places she lived while growing up (hers was a military family), her college years, her years teaching school, doing odd jobs, acting in improvisational theater, graduate school, living in New York City, her first college teaching job. Her sixty years blocked out in shifts— places, time, direction.

The philosopher Schopenhauer once said that we finally see our life's big patterns when we're close to death. Before that, our lives appear random, often senseless. Possibly true, I think, but aren't we able to understand some of life's logic, divisions, meaning?

I think these thoughts at my computer now, Thursday morning, working on my autobiographical book and borrowing from Elizabeth's idea, now seeing my life in stages.

When I was young, around five, I would tell people, "I'm a girl now, but I was a boy before I was born." I remember getting into the apartment building elevator with my mother and making this pronouncement to others as we rode from our fourth-floor apartment down to the lobby.

My mother would tug my hand as a rebuke. But she'd say nothing, and I'd add nothing by way of explanation. I'd spoken my piece. The moment etched in my mind: down we go, and I make my pronouncement. With utter certainty. Out loud and in public.

Perhaps it's the same impulse here. It's not so important to know why I need to say something, but very important to say it. Leave understanding to the psychologists and literary critics.

But sometimes I still feel boyish, as if my female body were imprinted on a male template. I don't believe in past lives, and I'm certainly female and heterosexual, but yet, there's something different about me, my gender identity, my sense of my gendered self.

Typing furiously, I'm now ten, in fifth grade, and I've been selected to serve as a safety monitor at Number Six school. It's lunch time; I'm asked to monitor the side door so that when the kids pour out onto the playground, they don't run or get hurt while exiting. I push open the heavy steel door. Outside, it's spring, there's a blue sky above, and the sweet smell of nearby honeysuckle growing by the chain link fence that borders a residential property. On the stone steps, I breathe deeply, stretch out my arms. My thin body is flat and strong. I've been modeling in the city for the past year; I'm a straight-A student. I have friends, and people tell me I'm pretty, though I don't understand that. I run my hands up and down my torso. *I am a girl, and I am a boy,* I think. I have the strength of both genders pulsing within. It's electric; I'm alive with it. This energy defines me. I never want to be *only* male or female. *I was a boy before I was born,* I tell myself again.

In five minutes, a horde of schoolchildren pour into the corridor, make their way out of the building from the side exit I'm tasked to watch. I have the door jamb in place and yell out, "Slow down. Safety monitor on duty. Slow down, please!" The rush of bodies and noise floods the hallway, the nearby staircase, cascading into the playground. *I am losing myself and becoming them*—the pulse, the beat, the energetic throb of noise and impulse. Again, I'm no longer me, myself, nor anyone.

The phone rings and startles me. I grab my cell phone from my bathrobe pocket and find that it's the secretary from Arts and Humanities. She wants to know if I'll be in today; I need to sign some paperwork connected to an invoice, an interdepartmental transfer of funds.

"Yes," I say, immediately regretting the commitment. I'm feeling sad again and want to stay in my world of memory, continue to write. The more solitary I am, the more solitude I seem to need.

But when I look over what I've written only a few moments ago, I feel disconnected to it and to myself. Maybe being out in the world would be good—offer my attention, my focus to an external locus.

There's a Mary Oliver poem, "The Summer Day," that I like, in which the speaker connects with a grasshopper, very particularly, as she enjoys a summer day. But by the poem's end, Oliver challenges the reader to judge her day not as a waste of time but as a perfect employment of her time; her attention to the grasshopper encourages readers by proxy to give their attention to the smallest matters, that in such attention lies the fullness of life.

Before I end my writing, I type out Oliver's lines from memory:

Tell me, what else should I have done?
Doesn't everything die at last, and too soon?
Tell me, what is it you plan to do
with your one wild and precious life?

I save my book—if I can call it that—or document—though the word "document" sounds like something that should be notarized—and turn off my machine. Writing for the day is done.

Summer school is in session, so there are plenty of students and faculty around. I meet Jill, a social work professor, whose office is a few doors down from mine.

"How's it going?" Jill asks. She's petite and has become very thin since her husband left her for another woman last fall. If I remember correctly, he teaches in the math department at a community college in Raleigh. They have two young kids, and Jill is the custodial parent.

"Okay," I answer. But I know Jill really wants to talk about herself. So I ask, "How about you? Teaching this summer?"

Jill sighs, sweeping her blonde hair away from her face. "Yeah, I've picked up an Intro to Social Work course, but after that I'm taking the kids to my folks' farm in Iowa. Horses. Goats. Chickens. Good for them. You know?" Jill has been looking down at her armload of papers, but now she's turned her gaze on me. There are tears in her eyes.

"You okay?" I ask.

Jill looks at her papers again, embarrassed perhaps by her strong emotion. "Got to go," she says. "Catch you later," and walks away.

"If I don't see you, have a good time in Iowa," I call to her, regretting my tone. I watch as she shuffles down the hallway. "Eat some corn or something." Not the smartest thing to say, but the words are already out.

"Yeah," Jill calls back, as I see her turn the corner. I stand there for a moment, realizing that I've failed her.

Before heading to our secretary, Laura, I stop at the faculty lounge to check my mailbox. Nothing. That's good. And when I bump over to her office, Laura's on her cell phone, tapping at her computer, a procurement form on her screen.

"Okay. Tomorrow, I've got another one." Laura lifts her head, nods in my direction, pulling out a piece of paper from a stack and handing me a pen.

I read the paper; there's been a $10.24 charge for supplies that should have come out of the English Department's budget, not the Writing Center's. It's not a lot of money, but I've spent almost my entire Writing Center budget, and I'm not sure that I can afford it—not before July 1, the beginning of the new fiscal year. That said, even if the Writing Center gets charged, the bill will be paid. It's for English department supplies I've purchased at the university store, so the money transfer won't involve the exchange of any currency. Funny money. I sign the form.

"Thanks, Laura," I say. She barely looks up at me. She's got bleached blond shoulder-length hair, and she's wearing a low-cut tight-fitting polyester print dress, with a thick belt around her waist. She's about thirty-five, married to a truck driver, ex-military, and they have four kids.

"No problem," Laura says. But then she does look up, directly at me. "You okay?" And when she says this, I think, I'm not.

"Absolutely," I say. "Why?"

"You know me. Psychic. You sure?" But now her office phone is ringing, so she tells her cell caller, "Hang on," puts the phone on her desk, and wheels around to answer the school landline. "Hello, this is Laura DeAngelo, secretary for Arts and Humanities. How may I help you?"

I'm already out the door.

In my office, tears come again. I've shut the door and opened the windows, deciding against the air conditioning. I look out into the courtyard and notice that the grass is overgrown and weed-filled. There are a few picnic tables off to the side, and I see that one of the Writing Center consultants is meeting with a student. The Writing Center, soon to be relocated in our library, is now located in what used to be the print shop, on the first floor of this, one of the university's original buildings.

I'm thinking about my brother. Thinking that I don't know if I love him. I'm back in 1969 and then, further, back in 1959. My brain isn't honoring boundaries.

Students pour out of morning classes and explode into the hall outside my office. No one will need me or know that I'm here, so I fight the impulse to pull myself together. Instead, I sit, let the tears come, and decide to be with everything—even sorrow. My mind bleeds memories.

"Let go," I say aloud. Then again, louder, "Let go." And there's a perverse strength in relinquishing control. I breathe and turn the air conditioning off. The air quickly becomes hot and real.

I open my laptop but don't check email. Instead, I write. The heat takes me back to my last summer of camp—again 1969. I signed on that year as a CIT—counselor in training—and my job was to teach horseback riding. It was a dude ranch camp designed for city kids, and I'd been a camper there the previous two summers.

But the camp was strange, mostly because there weren't many campers, and it was badly organized. In fact, we had fewer than fifty kids each summer, and the swimming pool was a round concrete hole in the ground filled with unchlorinated water from a nearby stream. The cabins were rundown, the food terrible, and there was little supervision. We had two or three poorly paid counselors, and there was a large lodge-like building that served as our main rec room upstairs and dining hall downstairs. We had no official camp song, not much of a daily schedule, and our horses—mostly quarter horses— were trucked in from the West. The owners—whomever they might have been, because no one ever met them—would hire cowboys from Wyoming and Montana mostly, and they'd caravan in horse trailers with about fifty horses, one for each camper, onto the property. Many of the horses were wild, and the cowboys stayed until they—and some of the campers—broke them. The cowboys were rough, the horses ornery, and nobody seemed concerned with personal liability. I can't imagine the camp was accredited.

It was a late June morning when my parents drove me to meet the camp van in Valley Stream by Green Acres, the outdoor shopping mall. Dennis didn't come with us, but he was going off to another camp the following week. Which camp, I can't remember. But Dennis never liked country life or horses, so he was probably off to a baseball camp held right outside the city limits in Putnam County.

There were five other kids at the van. We stood in an asphalt parking lot, clutching our knapsacks and stuffed animals, said our goodbyes, gave and received hugs, tucked our luggage into the back of the van, and off we went. The driver, an old squat Jewish man, held a dead cigar stub between his teeth, and every time we began to sing, he'd shout, "Knock it off!" which would stop us for a moment, before we'd begin again. After a while, the driver ignored us.

I sat with the teenager who was to be my camp counselor. Her name was, like mine, Rachel, spelled like mine, and her last name, strangely, was Rosenfeld, my mother's maiden name. Rachel had long kinky hair, and as soon as the van was out of parental sight, she lit an unfiltered Camel and offered one to me.

"I don't smoke," I said.

"Good idea," she said. "They're supposed to be bad for you." But she looked unconvinced, took a deep drag, then blew her smoke my way.

I told her that I was a CIT and my job was to provide riding lessons.

"Great," Rachel said. "You can teach me."

"Can't you ride?" I shifted my position and opened the top two buttons of my plaid, Western-style shirt. The van, although air-conditioned, was pretty hot.

"Nope," she replied and opened her own shirt, beneath which was a tight-fitting tee shirt that read, "Get Clean for Gene." I had no idea the message referred to Eugene McCarthy, but it was tie-dyed and looked cool.

"So, why'd you come? Dude ranch and all?" I asked.

"To meet some cowboys." Rachel looked at me and grinned with crooked teeth. I could see something wild in her, just beneath the surface.

"Yeah, but they're not guys to date. I mean they..."

"Watch me. Gonna light their fire..." She laughed, took another drag on her cigarette. I leaned back against the vinyl seat.

—⁂—

A knock on my office door jars me. I say nothing but open it, and Laura is standing there with a small stack of boxes in her arms.

"These are for you," she says. "I was just about to unlock your office and put them here. No room in my office. I knocked but didn't think you were in."

"Yeah, I'm just finishing up. Thought I'd get some work done."

"Hot," she says. Why don't you turn on the a/c?"

"Guess I forgot, but I've got to leave anyway. I'll take these," I say, relieving Laura of the boxes. "Thanks for bringing them."

"No problem," she says. I can see that she really wants to know what's inside them, but I'm not in the mood to indulge her. Two boxes, I already know, contain review copies of texts from publishers. Everyone in the English department receives these and usually sells them to book buyers who come by periodically. But two boxes are small and unmarked—perhaps supplies? Not in the mood to deal with them, I stack all the boxes by my bookcase on the floor.

"Have a good afternoon, Laura. Thanks again," I say through the open doorway. Class in session, the hall is empty now, shadowy as I hear the tap-tap of Laura's high heels grow fainter as she returns to her office.

ten

It's Thursday evening, day five without Nick. Just a few months ago, in spring, we bought a big flat-screen TV, and at night when I'm tired, it's a magnet, and I collapse in front of it. We've given up cable, so now I watch Netflix and a few stations we get with the external antenna Nick installed on our sunroom roof.

Also, I've decided to knit slippers this summer—for Christmas, birthdays, and for charity. We usually do knitting service projects in the School of Arts and Humanities. Dot, at the knitting shop, has offered to help me execute the simple pattern she's found. I'm not a very deft knitter, but I find the repetition of building stitches, row after row, therapeutic, offering me a more productive use of my downtime.

I'm on the couch, watching *Hit and Miss*, with its very appealing transgender hit-man-turned-woman. Again, I'm riveted to the nude shots of her—with her lovely breasts and penis. In fact, I can't take my eyes off of her. She's beautiful, and even her penis looks feminine. I find her attractive.

With the remote in hand, I freeze the frame as she undresses. Jake is asleep on the rug, and the living room is bathed in evening light. I'm on a knit row, making my first pair of slippers.

I think of maleness. A latent masculinity I've always felt was mine. I come to the end of the row, put my knitting on the coffee table, and get up, unzipping my bathrobe, letting it fall to the floor. I close the blinds and turn on our small red lamp, before pulling off my nightgown. Naked, I look at my body, then at the body in transition, so large on the screen. She's telling me something.

Behind the penis resides softness, regret, and seed memory—an opening, a female part, a mouth, a center, a vagina. I look at the screen, the flaccid penis in its bed. I think: *Inhabit me—knife, desire, clock, leaf. Moments are tongues, liquid words. Reduction, boil, refusal, placeholder, voice of exclamation, worry root, dirt and goblet, necklace, solace, thyme.*

Crazy thoughts? Disjunctive? Or creative? I unfreeze the frame. Is the actor transgender? Is the penis fake? But I'm no longer really watching; my attention is elsewhere. Free associating, giving myself permission to think and be whatever comes to mind. A writer's impulse? I put on my nightgown, bathrobe, grab a pen and a pad of scrap paper from the kitchen, where our landline used to be. I write:

I can't remember you,
father, who died four years
ago and, at the end, refused
to see me, although I held
a ticket in my hand.
I feel your leather
arms around me,
your hug, sacrament
and karmic blame.
But there is salt on my sandals
and dirt in my socks.
What did I know of your soiled
grief, its buttons, its elbows?
On my reckoning wheel, childhood
had shovels and spades, and my mouth

was pressed to stone; we had raw
mornings, where windblown prayer
flags mixed with our laundry. Now
I can breathe, but the line grows taut;
shadows press into blurred memories
until the door jamb breaks, and
the door itself becomes unhinged.

Clearly, I've gone over the edge, I think. And now, I can't quite find my way back. I'm still on the couch, watching TV, I remind myself. It's still Thursday evening. I'm still Rae.

I read over my poem and see my father's face. The father of my early childhood. As I grew up, he faded into the background, his presence becoming less and less distinct.

Born Bernard Bloomberg, my father was a good-looking boy who grew to be a handsome man. He was the only child of Bessie and Sam Bloomberg, who were married in the mid-nineteen twenties. They lived in a Bronx apartment, and I have a postcard in my desk drawer with their address. Once I looked up the building on Google maps and found that the building was still standing and that one of the apartments was for rent, so I took a virtual tour. The building, constructed in 1926, must have been new when they moved there. Most of the apartments are two-bedroom, and the one I toured was on the second floor.

256 Walton Avenue, New York City, the postcard reads. No zip codes back then and not even an apartment number. The card is addressed to Master Bernard Bloomberg, with a postal stamp of 8 AM, July 27, 1936. My father would have been seven years old when he received this, with a picture of "American Falls, Illuminated, Niagara Falls, N.Y." on the front and its short, impersonal message on the other side:

Dear Bernard, I hope you are enjoying your vacation. I am enjoying mine.

Remember me to Mother.
Love, M. G. Plunik.

I turn off the TV. I'll feed Jake, then myself—something easy, like eggs, an omelet maybe—but first, I want to pull out our old photo album, the one in which I found the postcard and photos of my dad as a boy and young man. Back when I was a girl, my father was so kind and gentle. Yet I never appreciated him. My mother was the parent in charge, and she got everyone's attention. Even when he was dying, she was the one who stayed front and center.

In the upstairs linen closet, I find an old photo album and page through it, stopping on photos of my dad—baby, young boy, college student, new dad. In one photo, I notice a halo of light around his face, as if the cosmos were gifting him—with kindness, insight, faith. Then I remember that last week in yoga class, we chanted in Sanskrit the words, "I am light." The chant stayed with me. Was my father light? And what would that mean? I make a note to self: *figure it out.*

Behind a plastic box of wrapping paper, I find another album with my dad's childhood photos and locate a photo of my dad's father, my paternal grandfather, as a young boy standing by a tricycle with a huge front wheel. The photo is stuck on a thick cardboard page, and I can't pry it loose to check a date, but it must be circa 1900. I flip to another stiff page where my dad, with thick, wavy hair, smiles in a blurred cream-colored background; it's a professional photograph. The album ends with a photo of my grandfather's semi-pro baseball team. The picture was taken in upstate New York, and this one is also stuck, probably taken around 1920, before he and my grandmother married. Dead now. Both of them. All these young men in uniforms, on a field, about to play baseball. All dead.

I am light, I think as I look out the bathroom window and

see that it's now dark. Everything dies—even the light.

—∞—

When Nick calls, I'm in the bathtub. Quickly, I grab a towel to pick up my cell phone on the sink counter. I'm wet but not cold.

"Hey," he says. "How was your day?"

"Good," I reply, cradling the phone between shoulder and neck, drying myself off. Now I'm chilled. "And it's not over," I say.

"For me neither. We've got some readings tonight and tomorrow, Friday. I'm supposed to read tomorrow, too. Some poems." Silence. I hear voices in the background.

"Nervous?" I ask.

"Not really."

"New work?"

"No. I'll read three published poems, that's all. But I did begin something new today—creative nonfiction. Also, worked on a story and got out a submission."

I hear soft rain, look out the window, and see clouds gathered. And as I walk from the bathroom, Jake sleeps on our king-size bed. Still wrapped in the towel, I sit down to pet him. He thumps his tail and struggles to open his sunken, sleepy eyes.

"Well, that sounds productive. Good you're working," I say.

"Trying to."

"Me too. I did some organizing. Didn't make it to the gym, though." But there's little energy in my words. They're soft like the rain. *Light rain, I think. I am light.* But clearly, it's not true. I'm heavy cotton wool. I'm the old winter mittens in the cardboard box, tucked away on a high shelf in the hall closet.

"Well, I should go," Nick's voice is soft. "Sure you're okay?"

"Absolutely," I say. "You?"

"Absolutely," Nick repeats. We both get it: neither of us is doing well.

"Have a good night. Good luck with your reading. Catch you tomorrow," I say, now lying with Jake on the bed.

"Love you. Be okay. Enjoy your time. Don't work too hard. Chores can wait," Nick says.

"Yeah," I say. "Good night. Love you, too."

I lean back on the bed and remove my towel. Naked again. And depressed.

eleven

It's around 10:00 p.m. when I get into bed to read. But for some reason, I'm still thinking about gender, about *Hit and Miss*, what it means to identify as male or female.

When we were in college together, Nick and I saw an old animated film supposedly made by Walt Disney and shown in the Student Center. I don't recall if the short film, a ten-minute clip, was shown with other films or was part of a series. But I do remember that the film was black and white, very grainy, made perhaps in the 1920s, and featured two characters—a male mouse with such a long penis that he could skip rope with it, and a female mouse, who before she has intercourse with the male mouse, needs to empty her vagina. And as she does, out come old shoes, jewelry, plates, and cups, a car tire— an endless assortment of junk. The male mouse, of course, can't enter her until she's emptied.

The archetypical quality of the clip—the male's exaggerated organ, so long that it facilitates and prohibits movement— becomes mythic and the defining feature to which the male self is subservient. For the female, the vagina becomes the endless repository, the well of self, holder of all things, literal and metaphorical. The vagina is subversive, mysterious, object of fascination, holder of secrets, source of power.

I pick up *Anna Karenina*, the novel I'm reading, and think about Anna's longing for romance. What part does gender play in that? Is romance both giving and receiving equally for men and women? Or are women receiving more than giving—an acting out of our biology?

—⁂—

I awake with my book still open on the bed and my bedside light still on. I check the clock, but the illuminated numbers don't register. It's late Thursday before midnight or early Friday morning. I close the book, careful to place a bookmark between its pages, switch off the light, and fall into a dream—or more accurately, a memory of a dream—where I'm a young girl swimming at Rockaway Beach.

The orange sun illuminates the lower sky and bleeds into the Atlantic. The horizon has surrendered to its magnet and is yanking the sun to some impossible, invisible place. Someone is calling to me, and as I raise my head, I see my mother on the beach sweep her arm toward me, gesturing to get out of the water. I will ride the next wave closer to shore, then the next one, and the next one, until I land on the beach. I duck beneath the approaching foam crest and feel myself forced forward among seaweed and salt. The water is warm, but as I break through the surface into air, I'm cold, very cold.

My bed is wet. I've had a dream. I'm in Queens, it's the middle of the night, and Dennis is snoring in his bed, against the opposite wall. He's a mouth-breather with a deviated septum, so when he tries to breathe through his nose, he makes an awful sound. The cold wet I feel is urine; my bed is soaked.

I get up quietly, feel my tears come. I'm too old to pee my bed. I enter my parents' dark room and go over to my father's side of the bed. "Daddy," I whisper, shaking him gently. He turns toward me, opens his eyes. Everything rests in softest shadow, but for a streak of slanted streetlight entering through the window and marking the wood floor near my mother's bedside.

"What do you need, sweetie? My father's voice is thick, smooth.

"I'm wet," I say. "I need help."

My father nods and swings into action. Covers off, feet on the floor, he wears only his boxer shorts. We walk from the room into Dennis's and my shared bedroom. My father goes to my bed, lifts off all the wet linen and the blanket—which is dry. He puts the blanket on our nearby toy-chest and balls up the wet sheet and stuffs it into the large hamper in our bedroom closet. Next, he opens my dresser drawer and pulls out a fresh nightgown. He lifts off my old nightgown, and, while my arms are still raised, lowers the fresh new one over me. It smells good. I feel soft, dry, comfortable.

Standing by the toy-chest, I feel my pink winter quilt, grateful that it isn't wet. In the hall, my father turns on a light and finds fresh sheets. He also finds a waterproof liner—not a sheet exactly, but it's a rubbery plastic thing, covered in flannel—that he's used before.

I wait on the side as he makes up my bed. He says nothing, but he's not full of judgment. He won't punish me, tell me that I'm a bad girl, or that I'm too old for such accidents. His motions are generous, kind. There's no sharpness, no incriminating shame or subtext to the way he tucks in the sheet corners or opens the closet. Only the soft shadows of my father's gentle love.

"I was swimming at the beach," I whisper, standing by him. "In a dream."

My father lifts me onto the cool, dry bed. He's placed the rubber sheet beneath the fresh cotton one.

"At first, the water was warm, but then Mommy called me, and it happened."

He kisses my forehead. His lips are warm. "Go back to sleep, sweetie. I love you."

I wrap my grateful arms around his neck, put my cheek against his scratchy cheek. "I love you too, Daddy."

In bed after my father leaves, I try to stay awake because every time I close my eyes, I'm swimming at Rockaway Beach. I slip from my lovely bed, the rubber sheet feeling a little stiff, and pad barefoot, quietly to the bathroom, to sit on the toilet to pee. Which I do, and then close the door before I flush. In bed again, I try to have a different dream, but the ocean persists.

I pray to God to keep me dry. If Dennis knows that I have peed my bed, he'll tease me until I cry. My father, I know, will tell my mother not to reprimand me, so it is only Dennis I must worry about.

I sit up in bed, watching the shadow animals on the wall as each passing car on Francis Lewis Boulevard throws shapes against it. They look prehistoric, large crane-necked creatures with huge eyes. They move across the wall, then disappear. I count them, give them names like Jekyll, Star-Face, Mister Monster...

By morning, I'm asleep. It's Saturday. Dennis has rolled the portable TV on its cart from our parents' room into our room. He's set it up by his bed, and the sound is very low.

"Can I watch, too?" I ask, coming awake.

Dennis smiles, pats his bed. I wrap my pink quilt around me, carefully getting up from my bed so as not to crinkle the rubber sheet, and join Dennis. We sit together, backs against the wall, and watch the *Rocky and Bullwinkle Show*.

—⁂—

Morning. Friday. As the memory of my dream starts to fade, I rise, do my morning routine, and go upstairs to my study to write. My dream has taken me to a creative place.

Turning on *Morning Edition* in the bedroom, mostly for some noise in the silent house, I'm now writing about my dream—enjoying myself, fingers tapping out words, the screen filling with gray-black, simple-bodied Calibri.

Then the phone rings. I turn around to see my screen: *Mom;* I think of not taking the call, letting her leave a message, postponing whatever bad news awaits me. *This call will ruin my day,* I think selfishly but then answer.

"Hey, Mom. Good morning. What's up?"

"Caught you at a bad time?" she asks, but this courtesy, I recognize, will likely be the preamble for another request for money.

"Writing, Mom. Just working on stuff." I hit *Control Save* and lean back in my chair, no longer looking at the screen but instead out the window, blinds open, to see the top of our Bradford Pear, a tree we planted as a family when the boys were small.

I drift back. We'd driven Jethro, our large Chevy van, to a commercial nursery in Angier, NC, about forty-five minutes up Ramsey Street, and put this and a second Bradford Pear sapling into the back on a sky-blue tarp. Our two boys sang old Beatles songs on the way home.

"You want me to call you later?" My mother asks. And I realize my silence.

"No," I say, "it's okay. We can talk. What's up?"

"Long story, Rae," my mom begins and pauses.

I don't encourage her; a few seconds follow, perfectly timed for a drag on the cigarette she no longer smokes.

"Dennis," she begins, pauses again. "He went back for his post-op check-up, and they found that his lungs weren't clear. Blood clots—in his lungs. They went in again, had to. I almost can't take it. But it was a procedure rather than surgery. And the good news is that they got them out. Dennis is okay. Recovering at home. On new medication." Pause yet again. I look at the computer screen, distracting myself by looking at the subject, verb, prepositional phrases, and other grammatical elements of the last sentence on the screen.

"You there?" my mother asks.

"Of course."

"I thought I lost you. Dropped call. Anyway, you know that I asked you for money last time, Rae?"

"I remember, Mom."

"Well, it wasn't enough. I hate to ask this. You know I do."

I don't jump in but rather check out a sentence I've typed on the screen: *There the boy slept, unconscious of the scene around him.* "There" is used as an adverb. It can never be the subject of the sentence. I don't like the sentence and tell myself I'll have to revise it. It puts me a bad mood, in fact, suggesting other bad sentences that will need revision.

I get up and begin pacing—first my study, then into the hall to Cal's old bedroom, to Will's old bedroom, and into the master. Jake is on the rug, open-eyed, alert, but not moving.

"I need $500, Rae. We have no money for food, gas. Could you lend us that? Aunt Lena—I've spoken with her—has her own problems. I have no one, no one to ask. I didn't want to make this call, Rae. But I have no one."

"I don't have that kind of money, Mom. I can't help." This is what falls from my mouth. Two simple sentences: subject-verb, with a contracted verb and the adverb "not" used twice. Both sentences are lies.

I've taken off my slippers, and I'm doing a sort of slow Buddhist-style walking meditation, painstakingly planting each foot—toes, balls of the feet, arches, heel—on the hardwood floor. *My walk is like a sentence*, I think.

"But I can't get to work, Rae. You don't understand. I need to buy food and gas to get to work."

I sigh. And quickly in that single breath, relent. "Mom," I say, "I'll wire you $200. You don't have to pay me back. But that's it."

"Make it $300; I'll pay it back," my mother's voice insists.

"No," I say firmly. "$200. No loan. I'll get dressed, go to Western Union. The same deal as last time, yes? Any location in Tamarac—they'll call when the money arrives, yes?"

Silence for a moment. I hear my mother thinking, then, "Thank you. If it's all you can afford. Thanks, Rae. I appreciate your help."

I take a very slow step and struggle to find my balance. "Call me in two hours if you don't receive the money."

"Okay, Rae. I'm sure I'll get the money, and yes, we'll speak again soon. You know I love you. Very much. I always appreciate your help. We all do."

"I love you, too, Mom."

"Goodbye."

"Goodbye." I slow-walk back to my laptop, save without reading over what I've written, and close down the machine. I'm done writing for now. I go to the bathroom for a quick shower, then dress. In a few minutes, I'm backing Ruby out of the driveway, off to the Western Union counter.

Returning within a half-hour—no glitches, money taken off my debit card, forms completed in triplicate, receipt in hand—I realize that I'm pretty beat, even though it's still early. I unlock the front door, Jake greets me, and we both go out into the sunroom, where I collapse on the couch. Jake sprawls on the carpeted floor by me; the morning is cool, but already the day's heat is beginning to intrude. I feel my heart race, a pressure, a tightness in my chest, a shortness of breath. I close my eyes, expecting tears, but nothing comes.

I think of my mother's suffering, her desperation. Why didn't I give her the entire $500? Why did I lie? Yet why did I give her anything when I'd promised myself never again to give her money? I feel horrible, guilty, and there's no one to talk to. So, I just sit.

twelve

My brother started gambling in college when he joined his fraternity, Pi Lambda Phi. At least that's the story my parents told me. I don't remember much because I was so busy with my own crazy adolescence, and neither my mom nor dad ever wanted to talk about Dennis's gambling problem.

I remember once coming home after high school. Dennis had recently been home from college—he attended Drexel University in Philadelphia—for Thanksgiving, and Mom had just discovered that some of her good jewelry was missing from her lingerie drawer. Two detectives sat on the couch in our formal living room. We never entertained there, and for many years, we keep plastic slipcovers over the couch's blue silk upholstery. At some point, however, the plastic was removed, and though the furniture was very outdated, the couches hadn't faded and didn't show wear. My family always relaxed in the den, decorated in Early American style, where we usually sat in front of the large TV console.

I joined the group in the living room and watched my mom's face as she realized that my brother, not a stranger, had stolen from her. No break-in had taken place because there'd been no forced entry. And the thief knew where to look—and had expertly hidden the crime, closed jewelry cases, drawers, stuffed underwear on top of missing things to disguise the theft.

"No, we don't want to press charges," my mom told an overweight detective who sat uncomfortably in his tight uniform.

"Edna," my dad said, "maybe that's not for the best."

But my mom gave my dad a look, and he shut up.

"My wife is right. This is a family matter. We'll talk to our son, detective."

Unable to put two and two together, I asked what was going on, but my dad only turned to me and said, "Later, Rae. Go to your room. This doesn't concern you."

"But…" I began. Then my mom looked up at me, her face stained with tears—mascara and eyeliner bleeding—so I walked first into the kitchen to get a couple of cookies, pour a glass of milk, then retreated to my bedroom.

The next day, a Saturday, my father took me aside during breakfast—my mom still asleep—and told me that Dennis was gambling at college and that this was the second time he'd been caught stealing. He was a political science major, and a group of them had joined a fraternity in September. There was a dog track nearby, and the fraternity brothers would regularly go there to gamble. Dennis had also stolen some of his tuition money they'd put aside in an account to which he had access. How much he had stolen, I wasn't told.

We sat in the sunny kitchen at the table. Outside, I could see that Meadowbrook Pond had partially frozen over. My mom and my brother were late sleepers; usually my dad and I shared breakfast together. When my mom woke, she'd usually eat with *Newsday,* the Long Island daily, as her only companion. If left alone, Dennis would sleep until noon.

My dad worked most Saturdays and always left for the store by 9:15. Typically, I walked to the synagogue for the second Shabbat service at the Orthodox temple. At this point, I considered myself an atheist, but I enjoyed the ritual of attending the service and the community of prayer.

"What did he take?" I wanted to know. I'd made French toast from yesterday's challah, and a mound of slices lay on a plate in the center of the kitchen table. I stabbed my fork into a couple, putting them on my plate. Although we no longer kept a kosher house, vestiges remained: my plate was a dairy, not a meat, plate. The same with the silverware. We had meat and dairy service and kept them separate—long-held habits from our earlier, more religious days.

"I'm not sure. Mom doesn't want to talk about it. She told me not to tell you. Just to say that the incident is over. She'll handle it. It won't happen again." Although my dad was a big eater, he stood up from the table, with many pieces of French toast left on the plate. He wore a pink button-down shirt and a pair of gray wool slacks. He picked up his suit jacket, hung over a side-chair, and carried it to the hall closet in our large foyer, where he put it on, along with his heavy cloth overcoat. "I'm off," he said, buttoning up and walking over to hug me. He bent down, planted a kiss on my cheek. I was wearing my flannel nightgown and wooly sock slippers. "Love you. Don't mention what I've said about Dennis to Mom. She's already upset."

I gave my dad a brief hug. "Have a good day. What time you coming home?"

"Early. Seven. We finished inventory yesterday. No need to stay late. Probably going out with Evelyn and Frank. Dinner, then cards at their house."

I walked over to the front door, feeling the winter chill as I opened it and then again as the storm door slammed shut behind him. I watched my dad walk down the concrete path, then the brick steps that led to the driveway. He unlocked the door, got into his Buick Skylark. I stood in the doorway, looking into the empty suburban street, where, after backing out, my dad put the car in drive. I knew that he'd follow our street to Hungry Harbor Road, which would take him to Sunrise Highway, and then the Van Wyke Expressway to Queens Boulevard in Forest Hills. He'd park the car behind the store next to the delivery truck in the small parking lot and walk through the store's back door to open up.

When we still lived in our Dunhurst apartment, Dennis and I would often accompany our father to the store on Saturdays. We'd get dressed up, me in a frock with white laced bobby socks, Dennis in a suit, often with a bowtie. We'd drive the half hour down Francis Lewis Boulevard and connect to Queens Boulevard. On these days, our mom would get a break from parenting, and our paternal grandparents would have an opportunity for a day-long visit between customers.

In the store's downstairs, Henry, a Black man and the store's only employee, would be responsible for applying gold-leaf to the furniture or for loading the truck for deliveries. Henry also ran errands, cleaned, retagged lamps and sale items. Lamps often went on sale, and when that happened, there'd be an exotic jungle of them clustered together on a large table in the front of the showroom.

On some Saturdays, if the store wasn't busy, our grandmother would take us on the F train to Manhattan. We'd often go to Radio City Music Hall to see the show and movie. We watched *How the West Was Won, Journey to the Center of the Earth,* and *Ben Hur* on the huge screen. I remember sitting in the theater's red-velvet seats, Dennis on one side of my grandmother, me on the other, and excusing myself to go to the bathroom—the expansive white marble steps to the ladies' room seemed grand; the toilets, divided by the same white marble slabs, were large, imposing, like relics from the Roman Empire. Women would gather in front of the entrance mirror in the anteroom, preening themselves like swans, leaning forward to touch up makeup and hair.

The Rockettes, already anachronistic, would lift their legs in their preshow chorus line extravaganza, and I'd listen to the strange clacking of their shoes hitting the wooden stage. They, along with the preening women in the ladies' room, made me feel alienated, genderless—though I couldn't express that. But I'd feel neither female nor male, as if growing up as a woman or man might not be possible.

Even on a Saturday afternoon, even if it wasn't seasonally appropriate, my grandmother would wear her long fur coat. She'd paint her lips bright red and wear a pearl choker. A heavy-set, large-boned woman, she had a complaining voice that suggested: *Beware, this isn't good*. The "this" might refer to her life as a woman or a wife, for I knew at a very young age that she and my grandfather weren't happily married.

Once, I watched my grandfather hit her in the hallway of their Brooklyn apartment. Another time, sitting at her kitchen table, she took my hand, squeezed and kissed it—telling me to watch out for men—a warning that struck me as odd and out of context.

But at the end of our outings together, on the way home from some magnificent Manhattan show, we'd descend into the subway to catch the F train, then emerge from subterranean darkness into afternoon light, to slowly walk the five long blocks from the Queens station to the furniture store. We'd pass a large stone church, where the concrete yard was painted green to resemble a lawn. It was the same shade of green as the walls of the subway stations, and I thought that it was the ugliest color in the world.

thirteen

Jake scratches at the sunroom door, wanting to return to the air-conditioned living room. He's panting. I get up, decide to go inside myself, and as Jake laps water from his bowl, I realize that I'm hungry. I can't remember if I've eaten breakfast.

I assemble a hummus, cucumber, and alfalfa sprout sandwich and sit down at the kitchen table with a recent copy of *The New Yorker*. But I can't focus. I'm thinking about Dennis. How my mother's desperation is a result of his gambling, how his continued stealing from her and the family has destroyed everyone's life—his, our parents', his wife's, his kids'.

I sit down at the kitchen table, recalling how when my parents moved to Florida to retire, my thirty-something brother followed them. He moved into the spare bedroom of their rented condo. For a time in New York, he'd been working as the night manager for a cleaning company at the World Trade Center, but he'd quit. The night schedule had been difficult for him, but it had allowed him to gamble by day. In fact, he'd gotten into so much trouble with some low-level Mafia bookies that he'd left New York to avoid having his legs broken.

Soon after he moved in with my parents, his African American girlfriend, Lydia, joined him. My parents were less than thrilled about Lydia—in large part because she was Black, but also because they felt that she was socio-economically beneath them. She wore tons of makeup, low-cut, tight-fitting clothes, would mispronounce words and snap her gum with her mouth open. But Dennis was in love, and they allowed them both to stay.

Later, when my parents left the condo and purchased a detached townhouse, Dennis left Florida for a job in New Orleans, managing a steak house, and Lydia moved with him. But in less than a year, Dennis had lost that job, and they were back. Lydia confessed to me that he'd been gambling again and was fired because he'd been caught stealing.

Desperate, Dennis and Lydia had moved back into the new townhouse, "temporarily"—or so they promised.

My mother was still working part-time as a psychotherapist. Although she couldn't find an agency like the one in New York to employ her full-time, she hooked up with a group of private practitioners in Coral Springs and began to develop a small clientele base.

Soon, my dad also wanted something more to do than play duplicate bridge every afternoon at the neighborhood bridge club, so he found some partners through a business broker and purchased a small restaurant—a diner, really—and because Dennis was still looking for a job and the business needed a manager, both the partners and my parents agreed to put Dennis in charge. As manager, he had full access to the cash register. After all, Dennis had experience managing a large restaurant in New Orleans. Of course, no one bothered to mention that Dennis had lost that job because he'd been stealing.

I remember visiting my family right before my parents purchased the business. I reminded my mom that they were breaking every business rule possible—buying a business about which they knew nothing, selecting partners about whom they knew nothing, then putting a thief in charge of finances.

But my mom had "good feelings" about these partners, and she thought that the restaurant represented a "closing of the loop"—a fitting end to her life story, which began with her parents' grocery store in Brooklyn.

"Fitting end"—I hear her words now, echoing insidiously because the purchasing of this business was the beginning of the end—the end to my parents' dreams of a comfortable retirement, the end to any possibility that my brother would stop gambling, the end to all semblance of honesty in my family.

When my brother was caught stealing the first, second, and then a third time—my parents failed to give him the tough love he needed. Perhaps they could have forced him into counseling so that he could take responsibility and experience the consequences of his actions. But they didn't. Instead, after each episode of stealing, gambling, loss, and Dennis's many apologies, they always forgave him.

With the best of intentions—and with the most profuse and sincere apologies—Dennis couldn't control his gambling. He stole thousands of dollars from the business, and when the business began failing and the partners found out, they demanded that my family replace the money and sell them their half of the business. But they all couldn't determine how much had been stolen nor how much my parents' share of the business was worth, so they all agreed to sell the restaurant, again through the same business broker who'd sold them the business. I don't think they owned the diner for more than ten months.

When they finally found a buyer, they had to sell the restaurant at a terrible loss—at least that's what I was told. And my parents' share wasn't enough to cover the money they owed to their partners. Dennis's stealing had not only bankrupted the business but also created debt, which my parents had to pay by liquidating some of their investments.

Then, to make matters worse, my parents decided to liquidate even more of their investments and double down. They purchased yet another restaurant—this time, a modest little bagel shop, called The Bagel Nosh, located in a nondescript strip mall near some dumpy-looking businesses and doctors' offices. As neighbors, they had a rundown copy shop, a nail salon, a discount dry cleaner, and a UPS store. Again, my parents hired Dennis, who was still unemployed, to manage their new business and tend the register. Lydia waited tables.

But the walk-in traffic wasn't good, and the small lunch crowd profits couldn't cover the rent on the place. They tried advertising, new menus, but it was soon clear that they'd been badly ripped off, having paid twice as much as the business was worth.

And Dennis, of course, kept stealing—at first small amounts, then emptying larger amounts of cash from the register, taking long lunch breaks, and driving midday to the dog track. Lydia was left in charge, and she'd often fall asleep in the back office.

My mom continued to see clients, and my father now seemed ready to fully retire and spend his afternoons at the bridge club nearby. Often, after a game, he'd stop at the townhouse pool for a dip before heading to the restaurant to help Lydia close up.

There just wasn't enough business. After a flurry of orders at breakfast and lunch from the doctors' offices, Dennis would make early deliveries and cut out to the track. But between the business's low volume and my brother's stealing, The Bagel Nosh soon went belly-up.

Meanwhile, Dennis had gotten in trouble with some bookies, and Lydia had become pregnant. She and Dennis married hastily in the Town Hall, without a formal ceremony. The very next week, two large Italian guys showed up at the townhouse, threatening to break Dennis's knees and throw Lydia down a flight of stairs if they didn't get the money they were owed.

Soon after, my mother called me up and frantically asked Nick and me for a $10,000 loan so that Dennis could pay his debt. It seems that pregnant Lydia, who'd been walking toward her car as she came out of a client's home—she now worked as a CNA, or certified nursing assistant—had had a gun put to her head and was hysterical.

It was early spring. We'd moved to Fayetteville the previous summer. Nick had completed his PhD and had been hired to teach English at a small college here. I'd been pregnant with Will and had given up my faculty position in upstate New York. Also, I was finishing up an MFA and working on a manuscript of poems. Will had been born only a few months earlier, in late October. We had some money saved and earmarked for the purchase of a new house in Fayetteville, so the money we ended up lending my parents to pay Dennis's debts was supposed to be short-term, a few months at most. My mom swore up and down that after the business sold, we'd get repaid. But when the business sold, we were told that they had had to sell at a loss and that there was no money left to pay us back.

Over the years, we did get some of the money—a few thousand at most, in dribs and drabs and after much pleading with my mom. But most of that $10,000 was never repaid and never will be.

Dennis stole from every job he'd ever had, and for the last two decades, gambling had completely overtaken his life. And through all of this—the losses, the devastation, the humiliation of being lied to and stolen from—my parents, or really my mother—continued to support him and his growing family.

Dennis gambled hard, and after each big loss, he'd promise never to do it again, and my parents allowed him, Lydia, and now their new daughter Julia, to continue living in their townhouse until finally Dennis stole so much money from them that they couldn't make their mortgage payment and had to declare bankruptcy. They lost the house and most of their retirement savings.

They began renting but were twice evicted because Dennis kept stealing, and they couldn't make rent. Then, Dennis forged their signatures and cashed in our dad's retirement fund; big chunks of money, saved over a lifetime, were gone. Soon, my parents were nearly indigent. And my mom, the psychotherapist who understood codependency and tough love, allowed this pattern to continue. Every so often, she or my dad would have to call Nick and me to ask for another "loan."

Sitting at the kitchen table, I feel numb. I get up, wash my plate of sandwich crumbs and a few strands of alfalfa sprouts, telling Jake, who's begging for scraps, that there's nothing, nothing left.

I head upstairs, thinking I'll read *Anna*. Jake follows, though he's unsteady on the hardwood treads. I wait for him, offering a little encouragement.

Then, I'm standing in front of my bedroom closet and am strangely inspired to clean or organize again. *Do something productive; you'll feel better,* I tell myself, remembering the hall closet and how good it felt to clean it.

I open my closet's bi-fold doors and the disarray overwhelms me—clothing double-hung, no order, and there are piles of half-folded sweaters on the upper shelf, along with too many pairs of jeans, most of which I no longer wear. I start with them.

I pull out an old faded pair of Wranglers and put them

on—passable but not good enough to wear to school. Possibly okay for yard work. I toss them on the bed, near Jake, now asleep again. I pull on another pair, a sort of cowboy-style jeans, though I'm not sure what exactly makes me think that. Looking at myself in the full-length bathroom mirror, I see the shadow of my teenage self, the one with whom I can neither reconcile nor entirely leave behind.

I plop down on our bed, empty but for a few jeans and Jake, who wags his tail to find me so near.

Then I'm back in jeans and cowboy boots at the dude-ranch summer camp. It's 1969 again, the year that always follows into the nooks and crannies of my adult life.

That summer we had two bunks with four groups of campers. I worked with the head counselor of the ten-year-old girls' group. My job was to teach riding basics to those campers who had never ridden and to gather the girls up in the morning so that they all went to breakfast.

East Jewett, New York, was at the time a sleepy small town resting in the cradle of the Catskill Mountains. The air often smelled of the lovely Rambler Roses, planted in rural gardens widespread across the area, and each summer day began with a cool freshness, dew on the grass, and most often a hazy sky that turned either bright blue or into drizzle.

The other Rachel was assigned the group of older girl campers who shared our bunkhouse but not our bunkroom. A nearby building contained wooden shower stalls, with thick rubber mats placed over the wood floor that, as the summer progressed, would become slimy and slick. The toilets were non-flush, outhouse-style latrines.

Although the bath building was fairly close to the bunkhouse, we needed a flashlight after dark so that we could negotiate the rough stone path. We had a lantern-style one hung on a nail by the bunkhouse front door, a simple wood-frame screen door without a lock, and the two groups of campers shared the lantern.

When we first arrived, there were no horses and no cowboys at camp yet—they arrived mid-week in a caravan of pick-up trucks and horse trailers. Rachel and I—known as the two Rachels—were sitting alone on the wood fence as they all pulled up to the corral. Where the campers were, or why Rachel and I were there, I don't remember. But we were wearing cowboy hats and western boots.

Almost at once, the corral exploded with horses as the large gates opened. Horses backed out of their trailers; cowboys stood, hands raised, whooping them into the corral. They'd driven nonstop from Wyoming, a pack of rough-looking guys right off the range.

Dry dirt rose in clouds of dust, horses whinnied, bit each other, stampeding around the enclosure. By this time, the other Rachel was off the fence, flirting with a couple of the guys. She was clearly having more luck than I, with her swagger and cigarette smoking.

I knew from last year that a few of the more experienced campers would help with breaking the horses, and I was hoping to be among them.

Most of the horses weren't even green broke. And the rest of the week, before the cowboys left, was designated for getting the horses to take bridles and saddles so that they could be ridden by campers. Being chosen by the cowboys immediately offered status, and I wanted to prove myself early.

Johnny, a youngish man, maybe a teenager—I couldn't tell—walked over to me, removed his hat, asked my name. When I told him, he laughed and asked again. He'd never known anyone named Rachel, and now there were two of us.

We walked out by the large, faded red barn, filled with new hay in the empty stalls. The middle area, as is typical in horse barns, had cross ties for grooming, shoeing, hoof picking, and saddling up, though some of that was also done by the corral fence.

"You from around here?" Johnny asked. His thin boyish smile made him look young.

"No," I said. "From the city. Down-state."

"New York City," he said. "New York, New York." He drew out the words, songlike, and I could tell he was impressed.

"Yup," I said, more relaxed now, playing the game with a bit more of an upper-hand.

"You?" I asked. I could hear the cowboys at the corral, trying to get the horses to settle down.

"Outside Cheyenne. Folks own a cattle ranch." Two men walked by us, pulling out hay bales from a stack by the tack-room. Johnny looked at them, nodded, and turned to me. "Gotta go. Ponies need to eat. You around for the social tonight?"

"Yup," I said again.

"See you there, partner." Johnny winked but both his eyes shut for a moment, and I couldn't tell if the facial gesture had been a wink or if he'd gotten hay dust in his eyes.

I gave Johnny a half smile, looked at him from head to toe, nodded back, and left. I walked toward Rachel who was now with her bunk campers, wet from swimming by the waterfall, where they'd gone for the morning with another counselor.

fourteen

Bad dream last night. Nick called late, around 9:00, after the retreat readings. And he upset me too close to bedtime.

He'd listened to a couple of poets read—mixed reviews there—read himself, which went okay, then listened to an opera singer perform an aria from *La Boehme*, and although Nick is not an opera fan, he was moved.

When we spoke, he was low energy, questioning the meaning of everything. Why was he at this retreat? Why did he write the crap he was trying to write? Who needs poetry anyway? He hated having to read his poems. They left a bad taste in his mouth. And nothing was shaking: the creative nonfiction piece he'd begun was going nowhere. He'd only managed to get out one online submission, started a draft of a new poem, deleted it, went for a hike, then a swim. Perhaps he should have studied opera, he told me.

"But you hate opera," I countered.

"Not tonight," he said.

I'd been watching *Hit or Miss* again and knitting a second slipper. I'd tried to listen to the show and to Nick, but ultimately hit the pause button. Then Nick became silent on his end, and the living room went silent.

Jake slept on the floor, stretched out on his side, and I couldn't see him breathing. For a moment, I thought he'd died.

I saw myself in the backyard, digging his grave with the

big D-handled shovel Nick keeps in our shed—its old wood shank and rough metal grip sweaty in my hands as I located a spot, perhaps near the fence, where there's no grass and no large tree roots. I imagined myself struggling to carry Jake's body, deciding to bury him with his dog bed and blanket—and maybe with his old rope tug-toy—a talisman to help set his spirit free. It's a hard job to dig a big hole, and it would take me hours.

I thought all this in a flash. A wave of hopelessness washed over me. Then I heard Nick's voice at my ear.

"You still there?"

"Yeah, I'm here. Sounds like you had a rough day. Anyone say anything about your work?"

"Some good comments, I guess, but I felt like hell."

I paused. "And the singer, where's she from? Have you gotten to know her?"

"Madison, Wisconsin, I think. And no, everyone here keeps a low profile. Weird. Usually people at these places talk. Here, it's just basic chit-chat, but no one talks shop. Or says anything about themselves."

"Maybe that's what's getting you down."

"I just need to write. Get something good going. I guess that woman's voice... beautiful and sad. She's got a gig at Carnegie Hall next week, so she'll be leaving."

Jake opened his eyes, looked at me, then closed them. I felt a pang of guilt, having imagined his death and burial.

"Good dog," I said.

"What?" Nick asked.

"Keep working," I said. "Something will give."

"Yeah," he said. "I'll call you tomorrow." I heard a deep sigh. "Love you."

"Love you, too." And we hung up.

I sat in the half-lit, quiet living room and thought about

opera, which I like, and considered finding *Tosca* in my CD collection and playing it. Frozen on the screen were two people, the transgender Mia and Ryan, the son she'd conceived when she was a man. I thought about penises and how I liked them, not as somebody who wanted one as part of her body, but as a woman who desired them. *I am a woman,* I thought, and decided to continue knitting, finish up watching the show, and get to bed early so as to have a full morning at the computer, working on my book.

At around 10:15, I took Jake out in the backyard for a walk. He has two dog-doors—one in the kitchen's back door, opening into the garage, the other in a garage door, opening into our fenced backyard—so he doesn't need to be walked. But at fifteen, Jake has thick cataracts in both eyes and has gotten senile and fearful, and now insists that I accompany him outside at night.

In bed, I read a few pages of *Anna Karenina* before putting the book on my nightstand, taking off my reading glasses, placing them in their case, shutting off the light, and falling asleep.

At 4:00, however, I awakened with my heart racing, recalling a dream, which propelled me out of bed and to my laptop.

The dream still vivid, I turned on my study light, sat, and wrote:

Dennis and I are living together in a one room, a studio basement apartment, painted battleship gray, with no windows. There's only a small kitchenette—stove, refrigerator, dishwasher, sink, cabinets—and in the living area, doors to a closet and a bathroom, a small kitchen table, two chairs, and two couches that fold open to become beds. We sleep parallel on opposite walls, as we did when we were young children in the Queens apartment. But every time we fall asleep, our ages change: I close my eyes, and when I open them, Dennis is twelve; we sleep, and he's sixty. Sleep again, he's seven. Dennis is fifty-eight; I'm fifty-four. Dennis is nineteen; I'm fifteen; Dennis is twelve; I'm eight; Dennis is seven; I'm three. And so on.

In my dream, Dennis has cancer, no matter how old he is. He can't eat. I prepare healthy meals in our small kitchen: vegetable soup; arugula salad with cranberries, walnuts, goat cheese; organic brown rice casserole with eggplant, zucchini, broccoli. Still Dennis can't eat.

I bring a bowl of food to his bed, but he won't turn to face me.

"Dennis, you must eat," I say. "Please." I sit on the edge of his bed.

"I'm dying," the seven-year-old Dennis says.

Sad and disheartened, I get up and take the bowl over to my bed, where I sit and eat his food. I'm voracious and devour all of the bowl's contents. Then, I get up, put the empty bowl into the dishwasher, go back to bed, and fall into a deep sleep—a dream within a dream.

When I wake again, Dennis is balding, a crown of gray hair in a semi-circle around the back of his head. I have salad for him, mixed with Green Goddess dressing. "Eat," I say.

"I'm dying," Dennis says again. And this pattern repeats many times—with only the food I've prepared and our ages changing.

Finally, at the end of the dream, upset by his inability or unwillingness to eat, I yank Dennis's blue winter quilt, which now covers him completely. And when I do, I discover that he's a child of eight, naked under the blanket. This time, as he turns around and looks at me in surprise and anger, I see that he's bleeding from the stomach; there's a huge hole in his gut, spilling out blood and bile.

"Oh, my God," I say, putting the salad bowl down on the bare wood floor. "Let me help." I find a towel, hold it to the wound, to staunch the outpouring of fluids. But I can't. The more I try, the faster it's all coming out, spilling and soiling the bed linens. Dennis's face is now growing old in front of me, like time-lapse photography of a bud turning into a flower, opening quickly and dying until its petals are all lost. Yet Dennis's body remains the body of an eight-year-old boy.

"It's your fault," Dennis chokes out. "Look what you've done."

His bowels are falling out of him; fluids pour like from a faucet without a value. Then, just as Dennis is about to die, he deflates like a cartoon balloon and is sucked through the black hole of his wound until he's a liquid pool of brown and ochre.

At around 4:15 a.m., as I write down the dream, I'm having a hot flash, and find myself sweaty, almost drenched. The room, my study, is dark, illuminated only by the screen and the streetlight coming through the closed blinds. Jake has followed me and now sleeps on the rug near my desk. I hadn't seen him come in or sensed his presence.

I type one last sentence after I record my dream—*I am killing my brother*—then turn off the computer.

fifteen

I'm in my study now, Saturday morning, maybe 10:00 a.m., having gone back to bed at around 5:00. Jake's been fed, but I feel terribly upset, as if death surrounds me, encroaching on a narrow island on which I'm forced to live. A storm throws sea water across its cliffs and over the shore, as the island seems to be shrinking until there are fewer and fewer places to stand.

I remember 1959, a critical year for our family. But perhaps "critical year" isn't quite right because the whole of 1959 wasn't critical, only one afternoon.

I type out what I recall.

It's early afternoon, and I've been here since morning. My nursery school, a rather informal affair—a classroom in the cooperative apartment basement, run by a teacher hired by the cooperative members. I see the teacher's dress but not her face. I see her hands, hair, shoes. She wears a blue cotton dress, fitted bodice and flaring skirt. The waist is belted with thin braided white leather.

This morning we're executing an arts-and-craft project involving crayons and cutting with plastic scissors. Barbara Goldstein, my best friend, sits next to me. We're the only girls and wear blue plastic smocks that are slipped over our heads and tied at the sides.

I can draw well with both my left and right hand, but I choose to draw with my left one, and the teacher tries to correct me. I won't let her. Instead, I pick up a scissor with my right hand and begin to draw and cut at the same time.

"You're going to be a lefty," the teacher warns. "And it's a righty world."

Later, after we drink our small cartons of cool thick milk, eat our crackers and cheese, we are helped out of our smocks. We walk out the building's side door—up brick steps past the laundry room, with its narrow basement windows, large metal folding tables, machines that make creepy whirring noises, past the damp dryer smells that make me feel a little nauseated—as we take the short-cut to the concrete playground.

Here is a red whirl-a-gig, the old-school type children run beside and power with their feet. And seesaws, six in two groups of three, a couple of commercial-grade swing sets with wide wooden seats—my favorite—and a sprinkler for hot summer days, a basketball court for the older kids, two small rows of baby swings, with seats made of rubber strapping and a chain in front that clips so that babies won't spill out.

I run to claim my favorite swing, knowing that if I sit backward on it, I'll feel like I'm being carried over the chain-link fence and into the "jungle." I pretend I'm Tarzan, never Jane, swinging on rope vines along the rain forest canopy.

Sometimes my teacher corrects me and asks that I face forward like the other children, but today she doesn't. Instead, she sits, relaxing, on the park bench by the fence underneath the overhanging feathery leaves of a mimosa tree.

Barbara sits on the whirl-a-gig while a couple of boys compete to see how fast they can make it spin. She sits crisscross in the center, where a rider is less likely to get dizzy. Her long mousy-brown hair flies about her face.

I swing as high as I can, until the swing's chains skip, buckle, and I become frightened and slow down. When we play alone out here, Glenn and Teddy will jump off their swings, often in unison, and propel themselves over the fence, into the jungle. But that always feels too risky for me, so I've learned to drag my feet to slow the swing, then climb the fence to join them in the wooded area, behind the big boulder, where we have our club meetings.

Today, with our teacher present, however, we don't dare go into the jungle. We swing and play, taking turns on the equipment, shouting, running, getting messy, and finally very tired.

After playtime, we walk noisily, our energy gradually winding down until we reach the nursery room where we take—or are supposed to take—post-play naps on bright, various-colored roll-out mats.

Douglas, a small boy who wears glasses, teases me to take the pink one because my last name is Bloom, and he thinks pink is the color of blooming flowers. Then he calls me "Bloomy Doomy," only because the words rhyme. I often pull his cap over his face to shut him up. But this day, I make it over to the stack of mats early and grab a yellow one, bright as the sun on a summer's day. Bright, I think, as the yellow feathers of Happy, our pet parakeet, the only pet we're allowed to keep in the apartment, though no one has explained to me why Nana and Pop-Pop, my maternal grandparents who lived in the cooperative's other apartment building and are allowed to keep their dog, a terrier mix named Bobo, whom I love very much.

It takes a while for us to settle down, as a few of the children get to their mats late because they need a bathroom break. When they return, they're fidgety, still struggling to buckle a belt, tuck in a shirt, wipe a drippy nose with a sleeve.

By 4:30, our day is over, and when Barbara's mom arrives, I'm told that she will take me home. I hold one of Mrs. Goldstein's hands and Barbara holds the other as we walk around to the Middle Entrance to take the main elevator in my wing of the building up to the fourth floor. Mrs. Goldstein has blonde hair that she wears in a ponytail, and she has on blue jeans with a simple white shirt and flat slip-on shoes. She looks very unlike my own mother, but she is always nice when I come over to Barbara's apartment, where jazz and classical music often play in the background. They don't even own a TV.

On the way up to the apartment, Mrs. Goldstein tells me that my mom is home and that we have visitors. I should be a good girl and listen carefully to what my mom needs me to do. Also, there's a chance that I'll be coming over to their apartment later today for cookies and milk if my mom is too busy to look after me.

I half-listen, although what she says is odd and should focus my attention. When we arrive home, the front door is ajar. Inside, my mom sits at the dining room table with two policemen dressed in dark blue uniforms. Dennis sits in the living room with another man, official-looking, but dressed in a dark business suit. I scan the apartment: some kitchen cabinet drawers are open, and the big silver samovar on top of the sideboard is missing.

My mom rises to greet us.

"Edna, would you like Rachel to stay with us for a few hours? It would be no trouble." Mrs. Goldstein bends toward my mom, gives her a polite hug, then holds her gently by the shoulders.

"No, Gail, not necessary. She'll be fine. Thanks so much for picking her up."

"Anything more I can do?" Mrs. Goldstein asks.

"No, really, you've helped tremendously. I'll call if I need you, though."

"Yes, please do. Don't hesitate." Mrs. Goldstein bends

down and gives me a rather strong hug. It is only then that I notice Barbara, standing too quietly outside the apartment.

"Be a good girl," Mrs. Goldstein admonishes. "A good girl for your mommy."

I'm only home for ten minutes before my Aunt Em—who lives in the apartment directly beneath ours, with my Uncle Leo and my two cousins, Sheryl and Ellen—comes to get me. Aunt Em is my favorite aunt. She has bright red hair, teased high so that light shines through it. She also has a cartoon face, highlighted by cat-eye, rhinestone eyeglasses that glitter when she moves her head. Her head is always in motion. And her thick Brooklyn accent flattens her words so that I love to hear her speak. I also love her hugs, tight and intimate.

Before I leave with Aunt Em, my mom tells me that we have been robbed, that Dennis was home, and that a bad man had tied him up with daddy's work ties, put a pillowcase over his head so that he couldn't witness the robbery. Dennis is fine, but I'm not supposed to mention the robbery to anyone.

Mom takes me in her arms. "Not to anyone," she whispers in my ear.

sixteen

I've been writing. Furiously. Visiting that time, seeing the apartment, with its flocked green wallpaper, remembering its smells of stale cigarettes and coffee—we had an electric pot that often would stay plugged in the entire day. Then, the playground, nursery school. I rise to stretch for a moment, shake off the past; Jake lifts his head and lays it down. I hear his sigh and think that years ending in "9" are somehow powerful, pulling their decades along, numbers with curved, lingering tails.

I sit down, and it's summer 1969—the dude ranch camp again. It's early evening, after dinner, and I'm alone in the rec room, where we're having our first summer social, to include the cowboys, a couple of whom will be leaving tomorrow.

I'm early for the party, but happy to be alone, sitting by the large window, looking out at a group of horses nibbling a bale of hay in the fenced upper pasture. Some campers are resting in their bunks, others finishing up their tooled leather pieces in the craft room. Already there are plates of cookies, paper Dixie-Cups, and pitchers of bug-juice on the wooden tables.

The big juke box by the stone wall doesn't need coins. It's fixed so that campers can select three tunes at a time—by number and by letter—and the selected forty-fives will play. The machine is large and holds over three hundred records— mostly rock-and-roll and country.

Before coming to camp this summer, I cut my hair. A sort of post-Twiggy style, with a dramatic side part, side bangs that cover one eye, and short, almost shaved up the back. I've also taken to wearing makeup, just for summer camp. Rachel Rosenfeld, my inspiration and mentor, has lent me black eye liner, deep blue eye shadow, and pale white ice shimmering lipstick. In fact, I'm now all made up and wearing my tightest jeans, cowboy boots, snap-front red plaid cowboy shirt, and last year's tooled Western belt with an enormous silver-plated oval buckle embossed with a brass-colored horse in a dead run.

Now, it's 7:50; our social begins at 8:00. I lean over the jukebox and play "Light my Fire" by the Doors. The smooth but loud sound fills the room, and I sink into its rolling music—velvety, sexy, penetrating, moody—until I inhabit it. I'm no longer me; I've become elemental, my particles charged, transforming me from girl into heat, sensation, a separation of parts, the song carrying me like the horse I've chosen for the summer, and named today Queen Mab, from *Romeo and Juliet.*

Campers drift in. So do cowboys. My favorite cowboy, who spots me standing by the far wall, saunters toward me, boots clanking on the pine wood floor as "Light my Fire" plays for the second time—someone, appreciating my choice, has selected it again.

"Howdy," Johnny says.

"Howdy yourself," I say.

"Saw the mare you picked out. Nice gal but sort of frisky." Johnny wears a woven straw cowboy hat, and as he removes it, he lifts his other hand and smooths out his wet-looking, dirty-blonde hat hair.

"Think I can handle her?" Leaning against the wall near the juke box, I lift one foot against it, leaving my knee bent toward Johnny.

"Haven't seen you ride."

"You will." And as I say this, I understand that we're no longer talking about horses.

"Me and the boys was wondering how old you are. I guess sixteen."

I give Johnny a small, tight grin as if the subject of my age is to remain a mystery, as if the old adage, *never ask a woman her age,* will save me from a direct answer. I like the idea of being sixteen. It isn't eighteen, the age of consent, but it sounds a lot better than fifteen.

Johnny leans in to kiss me, and I kick off from the wall with my boot. I feel Johnny watch me as I sashay across the rec room, over to my bunkmates sitting at one of the tables. A pitcher of red bug juice and a plate of oatmeal raisin cookies are on the table. I pour juice into a blue swirly Dixie-Cup, remove a cookie from the plate, and sit on a bench built into the wall by the table.

Pamela, a girl from Co-op City in the Bronx, sits by me. She has long blonde hair and cried a lot during the van trip up to camp. She also has a puffy, pink, plastic-covered diary in which she writes every evening after dinner and locks every night with a tiny metal key.

"That your boyfriend?" Pamela asks me.

"Not yet," I reply, though I hate my flippant response. I get up, lean back against the rough wall, take a bite of my cookie and a slug of the juice, which tastes awful, a kind of watered down, over-sweetened Kool-Aid-like drink, dyed with red food coloring.

"Angel of the Morning" plays now on the juke box. Johnny still stands across the room, joined by a friend, but he glances my way, smiling at me every so often. He's placed his hat back on his head—and with his hat, his slender body, Western-style shirt, slim jeans, and tall boots, he creates a kind of romantic cowboy image, fitting, I think, for *Bonanza*, a show that my brother sometimes insists we watch. I hate TV Westerns, but I love the real thing, right in front of me now.

There'll be no strings to bind your hands
Not if my love can't bind your heart
And there's no need to take a stand
For it was I who choose to start
I see no need to take me home
I'm old enough to face the dawn
Just call me angel of the morning, angel
Just touch my cheek before you leave me...

I take a good, long look at Johnny and stare hard. He returns my gaze, nods, and tips his hat ever so slightly. Then he walks down the rear stairs that lead outside.

"Excuse me," I tell Pamela, walk toward the front stairs, and look down the dark well from the narrow alcove that empties into it. Here the music is muted, and the song plays its final soft melody, carrying it to its inevitable end. I find the banister and walk slowly down the stairs to find Johnny.

—⚉—

I save my document, then rise to use the bathroom. When I return, Jake snores lightly, and I hear his troubled breathing add tension to the room.

As I sit down to write, I'm back in 1959—not '69—early summer now, and I give myself permission to be here, to allow connections to emerge. Coherent narratives, I tell myself, are overrated.

I'm at the fort behind the chain link fence by the concrete playground, with Teddy, Glenn, and Barbara—the club's only members—and we're having a disagreement about membership. Teddy wants to disbar Barbara and me because we're girls. Barbara, hair pulled back into a ponytail like her mom wears, and I, with my shoulder length hair pulled into a half-ponytail and fastened away from my face by a metal barrette, stand near the oak tree by the boulder that marks the entrance to our fort. The boys are sitting on the crinkly brown-leaved ground.

"If you throw us out, you'll only have two members," Barbara argues.

"That's right," I add. I'm wearing a seersucker button-down, short sleeve shirt with a bright red balloon stitched into the front pocket and polka-dot pedal pushers that cover my scabby knees. A few days ago, I fell on the concrete playground.

"Girls can't climb," Glenn says, and looks at me. He was the one who helped me when I fell. "And they can't fight and can't keep secrets." Glenn is adamant. Teddy nods in agreement, his deep dimples visible when he talks.

"Can too…" Barbara asserts.

"And they got to go behind the Big Bushy Bush to pee," Teddy adds. "The guys do it outside the fort room." Teddy raises his voice. This last point seems like a slam-dunk, the final argument that will seal his case.

"All right. Listen here," I begin. I put my hands on my hips, begin walking back and forth, gathering my thoughts. "We don't split. We've all taken the oath. Boys and girls alike. We four are together. We're all the same."

The group is silent, and I realize that I've gotten everyone's attention. My time to lead is now. "Girls are as good as boys," I continue. "Sometimes better, sometimes not. We all have good and bad points…"

"But…" Teddy interrupts.

"No, let me finish," I insist, pacing, my voice raised. "We're the same. Boys and girls. Our hair is different. Girls wear it long; boys wear it short. Other than that, we're the same."

"But…" Glenn tries to interject.

"We're the same!" I shout at the group, bending aggressively toward them. "Who tells me that's not the truth? How else are we different? Girls and boys are the same."

Nobody speaks, though I know that what I've just said isn't true. They know, too. The earlier reference to the different bathroom needs of girls and boys indicates that Glenn and Teddy know there are other differences. Also, Barbara has a new baby boy cousin, and I've seen her help her mom change his diapers. I take baths with my brother, and sometimes we pee together—me sitting while Dennis aims between my legs. But my argument holds, nonetheless.

"Rachel is right," Barbara chimes in. "You all know that. So what if we put on dresses sometimes, wear our hair long. Boys and girls are the same."

And with that, the argument is won. The criteria for club membership will remain gender neutral.

—⚍—

It's almost 5:00 p.m. now, on a sultry, August late afternoon in Fayetteville. I'm walking Jake in a field behind the university, where we usually go for our short jaunts. Young male students are tossing a baseball, and two girls jog by, headed toward the nature trails and the Cape Fear River that serves as the eastern border of the university's five-hundred-plus acre campus. There are ticks in those woods, so I never hike the trails in warm weather, but I do like to walk there in winter.

Years ago, however, before the tick problem became bad, Nick and I would often take Cal and Will and our other dogs—first Byron, then Jarrett, and Gandhi—on long nature walks through the elaborate trail system. We've seen eastern rattlesnakes, grouse, black bear, fox, and wild turkey. This geographical region, known as the Sandhills, provides a climatic enclave, where the temperature is warmer and the soil composition is sometimes clay, but mostly sand. Longleaf pine forests once covered the entire coastal plains, but this was during the Miocene Epoch, twenty million years ago. The sea fossils found here indicate that this area was once under water before the sea receded the ninety or so miles to the current coastline.

I've grown to love this landscape, the mixed vegetation, even the stifling blood-thinning summer heat. I love the subtle season changes, short winters, occasional warm January days with their much-needed reprieve from the cold. I've developed an appreciation for Carolina blue skies and for thunderstorms with their sheet or streak lightening, dramatic rain showers, downpours, and wild flash flooding.

What I haven't grown to love are many aspects of Southern culture. And today, as I walk old Jake, who hobbles with an unsteady back hip and has stopped to sniff the borderland between grass and woods, I think about being called ma'am, men who insist on opening doors for women, or who won't swear in "mixed" company, and the million other smalls ways that polite Southern manners irk me.

Why? I wonder. Do other women struggle, or is it just me? I think back to the page I just wrote—how sexualized I seem. And too young. Why, why, why?

I yank Jake, who resists then yields, happy to move next to the big grass clump by the electrical power box near the trailhead. But my cell phone is ringing, I realize. Opening my bag, I hear it more clearly. On the face screen is the word "Nick."

"Hello," I say.

"Hello back," Nick says.

"Good day?" I ask, immediately recognizing his cheerfulness.

"Yeah, went for a hike this morning. Cold here. Then wrote for most of the day."

"What you working on?" I'm by the ballfield and ready to

turn around, head for the car. Jake has just pooped, and he's limping more than usual.

"Poems mostly. But I began a new piece. Sort of a personal essay. Memoir. How about you?"

"I'm good," I say, now crossing the asphalt parking lot and nearing the car.

"Your work, I mean. The novel. How's that going?"

"Sort of. Not really. I'm kind of lost. Writing a little. Just stuff." I press the key fob button, popping the door lock, and open the back door; Jake jumps in.

Nick is quiet for a moment, lets it go. I'm grateful. "Hear from Cal or Will? I'm feeling out of touch," he says.

I'm in the car now, cranking it up and turning on the air. Jake is panting on the backseat.

"No," I say. "I'll give Cal a call during the weekend if I don't hear from him. I think he's got an IBM conference in Chicago. And Will, he's probably fine too, just busy. I'll give him a call..."

"So, you're managing?"

I've decided to drive around the deserted parking lot. I work Ruby into second gear, throw her into neutral and coast in a large circle.

"Yeah, of course," I answer. But then I feel tears well up, a convergence of shame, guilt, sadness, regret...

"Write it," Nick says. "*It*. Everything." But he can't know what I'm feeling. I don't even know.

A car is driving down to the back lot where I'm making my circles, so I decide to put Ruby in gear and head out. "Gotta go," I say.

"Love you. Take good care of yourself. Hear?" Nick replies.

"Love you, too. Speak with you tomorrow."

seventeen

That night, Will calls, as if on cue. He's been busy, he explains, assisting an older glass artist, well-established in the Asheville area, and Will has news.

"Mom," he begins. "Sorry I've been out of touch. I was working, then I went rock climbing on Friday. Took the day off. Went to Chimney Rock with JT."

"Were you safe?"

"Always. We don't take risks, Mom. Really."

It's almost 10:00 at night, and I've muted some PBS nature show that I've been half-watching as I skimmed through a recent issue of *The New Yorker*.

"Be careful," I say. "Extra careful." I don't want to hear too much about his rock-climbing adventure as it makes me nervous to visualize my son on a rock face held only by ropes and clamps. I've sometimes looked at his Facebook and Instagram climbing photos and short videos, and that's been quite enough.

"Listen," Will says, "what I called to tell you is that I've been invited to exhibit my work at a gallery. It's pretty high-end. Yeah, the curator called on Friday, said she saw my work online and that Robert had recommended me...and long story short, I'm in."

I'm immediately happy. It's as if I've won a small but significant prize. I feel my depression lift like someone has taken a large flat stone off my chest.

"I'm hungry, so I can't talk long. Just wanted to tell you. Also, I updated my bio and artist statement. But I think they're okay."

"You want me to look at them?"

"No, Mom. They're good, but thanks. I'm going get take-out with Suzanne. Good news. Just wanted to share."

"Yeah. Very good, congrats, big time. Really great news. Send me your stuff. Say hi to Suzanne and call again soon. I love you."

"Bye, Mom. Love you, too."

I hang up the phone and realize that I'm smiling. I unmute the TV, and a bald eagle calls from a rock ledge, takes off into a powerfully blue sky, and then glides smoothly across the large flat-screen.

—∞—

It's Sunday morning, and I wake up feeling sad again. I think about calling Cal but decide against it. Better wait until I'm more cheerful.

I've fed the dog, made coffee, and now, as I sit down to my laptop, I decide to follow Nick's advice: *write everything.* Turn the faucet on full force, get wet, even drenched.

I start typing to find myself back at 1969, the first evening of my summer vacation, a week before I leave for camp.

My folks have gone out to dinner at Garbadino's, their favorite restaurant, with Evelyn and Frank Schmitt, good friends who live in the neighborhood, and Aunt Em and Uncle Leo, in an adjoining development. Then they're all planning to play bridge at the Schmitt's house. They'd all been taking bridge lessons with Ada, an Israeli expat, who lives in Queens but offers group lessons in people's homes.

Dennis used to babysit me when I was younger, but that stopped when I was about twelve. Now home in the summer after completing his first year at Drexel, he watches TV—a new portable purchased for his dorm room. He has few friends at home because most of them remained in their college towns to work summer jobs. Dennis is a Political Science major and hopes to become a lawyer. He's supposed to look for summer work to help pay his tuition, but he hasn't been out of his room much since he returned from school almost a month ago.

I know Dennis smokes a lot of pot in his room, so I assume that's his plan for this evening, and that's why his bedroom door is closed.

I'm going to my boyfriend Russell's house. Russell is the oldest of three brothers, and he's on duty tonight as his family's babysitter.

Russell lives on the same block as my Aunt Em, Uncle Leo, and cousins Sheryl and Ellen, who having moved near us, remain our favorite relatives. I could walk the three-fourths of a mile to Russell's house but instead I'll ride my bike.

"Dennis," I call past his closed bedroom door.

"What d'you want?

"I'm going out," I yell back. "To Russell's house. On my bike." I'm dressed in my ripped jeans and faded blue work-shirt. My hair is loose, and I'm wearing old tennis shoes.

"Okay," Dennis shouts back. And he turns the TV volume up.

I love Russell, with his blonde hair, green eyes, freckles, and wistful, almost sullen look. I've been dating him for about a year, and although my parents like him, his folks aren't keen on me. I'm too hippy-looking, too free-thinking—and his mom, in particular, thinks of me as trouble. I know all this because Russell confides in me. He calls his mom Rookie—a reference to some family joke. She wants him to date only conservative Jewish girls with excellent grades and promising futures.

My grades over the last two years have been erratic. First

came the junior high walk-out last year—and then my bout with mononucleosis, which laid me low for months. Although I did well on my Regents Exams, my fourth quarter grades weren't good. And this past year, I excelled in History and English but didn't perform well in Chemistry and Algebra. Russell is two years ahead of me, so he's now officially a senior. He's taken his SATs, and I know he's done well. He doesn't want to attend a college in New York but is thinking of George Mason University near Washington, DC. Why this school, I'm not sure.

Russell intends to become a doctor, but he's secretly afraid of blood. He thinks he'll outgrow his fear, however, and he's not about to let it stop him. He recently fainted when he had blood drawn, and we often talk about this issue.

Also, Russell is very Jewish. His faith is strong, and he attends early Saturday morning service at the orthodox temple. And when I go to the dude ranch for summer camp, Russell goes to some conservative Jewish camp, where the boys wear yarmulkes. Russell was bar mitzvahed, and his mother keeps a kosher house.

In fact, Russell's family culture is very different from mine, more rarified, intellectual, and I like that. Russell's home has hardwood floors and imported hand-loomed rugs throughout. His dad, who owns a button factory in Brooklyn, recently purchased a new, beautiful teak high-fidelity stereo system, and all the family members take music seriously. They listen to classical music and jazz. Russell is the one who introduced me to Dave Brubeck's "Take Five," which at first I didn't like but now is my favorite piece—ranking even above the Stones' and Beatles' songs I love.

I leave my bike unlocked against Russell's garage door and hop up the stone front steps, ring the doorbell. Younger brothers Bradley and Phillip both answer in their pajamas.

They let me into the house, a split level, and I can see that Russell is reading in the living room. But I follow the younger brothers into their shared bedroom through the upstairs hallway so that they can show me the model plane they've been working on.

Bradley, the middle brother, explains that I'm looking at a C-130 Hercules, designed for combat troop transport. It's an older aircraft but is used currently in Vietnam because it can take off from hastily-made dirt airstrips. These planes are often equipped, Bradley says, with 20 mm canons and 7.62 millimeter mini-guns.

The glue is drying, and I'm not allowed to touch it. Phillip hugs my waist and stands on my shoes so that I can lift him and walk ploddingly around the room.

"Nice," I say, struggling to lift my feet with Phillip attached to me. He's growing, and carrying him around like this is becoming more difficult. I look at the plane, which seems very generic, nondescript, with its four propellers and typical uplifted tail. "Let's go see what Russell is up to," I say.

"No, walk me more," Phillip insists. Bradley has gone over to his desk, put the plane down carefully over the newspaper spread out over his desk, and is getting out small, square bottles of acrylic modeling paint from his drawer.

"Okay," I say. "A couple more times," and I lift my heavy feet, one, then the other, balancing Phillip's body against mine, as I make two circles around the bedroom.

"This is fun!" Phillip calls out. "We need a sister."

Later, when the boys are asleep, Russell and I kiss and touch each other on the overstuffed living room couch, lying down, rubbing our bodies together, making mock love. Sometimes we watch TV, but more often we listen to music, until we find ourselves necking. Russell loves all things romantic—especially Impressionist paintings and old poetry, which he memorizes and recites for me, as he does this night:

Come live with me and be my Love,
And we will all the pleasures prove
That hills and valleys, dale and field,
And all the craggy mountains yield.

There we will sit upon the rocks
And see the shepherds feed their flocks,
By shallow rivers, to whose falls
Melodious birds sing madrigals.

When no one is around, Russell calls me his "melodious bird," and sometimes his "French milkmaid" after Hardy's *Tess of the d'Urbervilles,* which he just read for Honors English.

By midnight, I leave—his folks usually come home between 1:00 and 2:00 a.m. This night they've gone to Lincoln Center to attend a performance of *Tosca,* and Russell has reported to me that Rookie looked very elegant.

Outside, in front of the garage, Russell kisses me goodbye, tells me to ride home safely, and reminds me that he loves me. After he says that, we kiss one more time, passionately, and I tell him that I love him, too. Then, I'm off.

Russell is my first love. Others will follow, but a first is a first.

—⚬⚬—

I get up briefly to get a glass of cold water, first saving my work. By the time I return, I'm somewhere else...in fact, I'm back in Queens again, in bed, and I'm praying.

I'm four, maybe five, and I'm alone in our bedroom. My favorite babysitter, my cousin Jackie, is watching me. She's in the living room with Dennis, allowed to stay up later, and they have the TV on low. I hear the muffled voices and some road sounds as shadows appear and disappear, traveling along my wall and closet door as cars pass by. I pray in harmony with these shadows, which I believe are important messages from God.

Sh'ma Yisrael Adonai Eloheinu Adonai Ehad. I repeat these words a number of times to correspond with the frequency and duration of the shadows. I've developed a code that, I'm convinced, interprets God's messages to me.

I evoke the She'ma like an incantation. Around it, I have a complex of rituals and repetitive behaviors, developed to keep me safe.

When Dennis is in bed, I try to keep these secret, not because I'm ashamed but rather because I believe God wants me to. It's a private language, after all, and I feel that God requires my obedience.

But Dennis isn't here right now, so I give myself over to God and His communications.

When the wolf shadow appears, I must go under my covers completely and recite the She'ma three times without stop. When I come out of the covers, God approves by sending the carousel shadow slowly across the wall and closet door. This is the slow shadow, and I'm expected to mentally ride one of the shadow carousel horses. Up and down it goes. I repeat the prayer slowly here because if the shadow stops before the prayer does, I lose and must punish myself by getting out of bed, lying on the cold wood floor and reciting the prayer ten times, one for each of my sinful fingers.

Glancing out my study window, I wonder about God and the play of shame, regret, and guilt that trouble me still. Now, I look at my hands, counting my fingers, as I remember the prayer and speak it aloud. Then the heat pump turns on, and I feel a burst of cool air channel through a nearby ceiling vent. When I return to the page, I'm somewhere else again.

—⁓—

I am bad—my brother is right, and I deserve to be

punished. I hate myself because much of what I do is wrong, inadequate, unacceptable.

I'm twelve, in the sixth grade, and my best friends have "dropped" me. Something awful has clearly happened, but I don't know what or why.

Last night we had a sleepover party at my house. Four girls, my best friends—Nancy Gunner, Honey Mazursky, Janie Stein, and Leslie Goldstein—spent the night in my downstairs playroom, spreading their sleeping bags over the multi-colored Linoleum tiled floor. We'd been involved in a game in which we each chose a song to play on my portable record player and then did a dance performance to accompany it. Leslie's was the best; she danced to "You Can't Hurry Love." She did some finger shaking and sexy hip rolling. Leslie has thick straight blonde hair with bangs, and she's very smart but not very nice. She gossips behind the other girls' backs, and she's already caused members of our group to argue.

Honey chose "Born Free" and did a sultry mimed act of loving and then saying goodbye to a lion. Honey has just come out of the full-body scoliosis brace she had to wear for all of last school year. Nancy, my absolute best friend, chose the Beatles' "We Can Work It Out" and did a rather animated dance that included moves from the "The Jerk" and "The Swim," two popular dances we've all mastered.

Janie, who's new to our group and always wears her mousy-brown hair in a ponytail, did a subtle, sort of mime routine to "To Sir with Love," which was corny but heartfelt. She loved the song and the movie, and carried the single 45 to our sleep-over.

My song is the Rolling Stones' "Paint It Black," and I do a weird sexualized dance to it. The other girls laugh at my performance, though it's not intended to be funny. I can't tell what exactly they're all laughing at, and by the end of the night, I feel hurt. We fall asleep gossiping about another group of girls who want to be cheerleaders when they get to junior high next year.

"Stupid," Leslie says. We all agree.

By the next morning, however, my hurt feelings are gone, and my mom, uncharacteristically, has gotten up early enough to prepare breakfast. We come to the kitchen to eat a huge stack of French toast made from yesterday's challah, and it's delicious. We have orange juice, and there's plenty of syrup. We're all chatty and friendly, and everything is fine. Moms are coming in an hour to pick up their daughters, so after breakfast, we go downstairs, turn on the record player—not too loud because Dennis and my dad are sleeping in—roll sleeping bags, put away toothbrushes, and we're done. Then we go out to the front steps to wait for moms.

But on Monday at school, everything is changed. None of my friends will talk to me. In class, in the halls, at lunch—I'm being snubbed.

I sit down at the cafeteria table where we always eat. "Hi," I begin. But Nancy and Honey look at me, pick up their trays, and join the less popular girls at the table on the other side of the room. Leslie and Janie come in later, joining Nancy and Honey as if by earlier arrangement.

"Talk to them," my mother insists when I begin coming home in tears.

"I can't," I say. "They ignore me, Mom. No one will say anything. When Nancy sees me, she walks the other way. If I sit by them, they move away. I saw Honey in the bathroom, and I asked her 'What's wrong?' but she shook her head and left. I ended up shouting at her."

I'm crying again. We're in the kitchen—my mom is preparing to put chicken in the oven, a casserole, and she has a cutting board out, ready to chop lettuce, make a salad.

Potatoes are in the oven already. I'm sitting on the Formica kitchen counter while she works.

"I don't know what to tell you, Rae. You have to talk to them. They can't just shut you out. Did anything happen last Saturday when the girls were here? Everything seemed fine at breakfast."

"Yes," I say. "Everything seemed fine...."

eighteen

Looking back on my adolescence, I don't understand why my parents allowed me so much freedom. Were they philosophically liberal—caught in the spirit of the sixties? Or were they just ignoring what was going on, like they did with Dennis?

I often traveled into the city with friends, bicycled alone to Far Rockaway Beach, attended protests in Greenwich Village, or simply walked alone around Manhattan. Sometimes I'd go to the Museum of Modern Art with Russell or with Henry, another boyfriend. I was permitted to do almost anything I wanted. This was especially perilous during the summer of '69, I now think, remembering Johnny, the young cowboy who stayed an extra week to help break the wild horses and who became my boyfriend after that first social in the rec room.

We never had intercourse, but I willingly took him in my mouth, an act I found repulsive but arousing—and one that made no sense logically. For a week, every night, Johnny and I would go out into the woods by the swimming pond. Our last night together—the day before he and the last of the cowboys left—Johnny told me that I'd better watch it with the boys. That I was dangerous. I liked that idea. In it, I became powerful, not a victim of my desire but a temptress with power to entice, control. Sexual intimacy was no longer an expression of love as it had been with Russell but rather it was power, a political act.

Breaking and riding horses were, similarly, powerful activities for me. I was a naturally good rider and naturally good with animals. I understood their drives and had a nuanced relationship with each of the horses. I could feel a horse's spirit penetrate its physical being.

At the end of that first week, the afternoon before the cowboys left, I'd been riding Queen Mab around the corral. She was a good gal now, long-legged, sort of flirty, mostly quarter horse, but with a touch of thoroughbred, which gave her spunk. Johnny and another cowboy sat on the split rail corral fence, shouting directions at me as I attempted to run barrels with her. Earlier in the week, when I'd broke her for the bridle, the guys had been there, too, giving me directions, cheering me on.

Then, Queenie—the nickname Johnny had given her—skittish and loosely tethered to a fence post, had pranced back and forth as I jump-mounted her by grabbing her mane and wither hair—quickly, decisively sliding over her bare back from the left. She had a rope halter on, and as I slipped the bridle down over her face, Johnny came off the fence and slipped the snaffle bit into her mouth. Then as Johnny backed away, Queenie began to buck and rear. The cowboys shouted instructions: *lean forward, tighten your knees, slacken the reins.* My job had been to hold on until Queenie realized that she had no choice but to accept the bridle and bit. When she'd get ready to rear, pulling back to her hind legs, Johnny would hand me a small but strong paper bag filled with water, and I'd hit Queenie gently between the ears with it. As the bag broke, the water ran down her face, making her uncomfortable but not causing any pain. Who knows if such a method would be considered acceptable today, with horse whisperers and our raised consciousness about animal cruelty.

The day I broke Queenie, I'd been powerful, and I had

only been thrown once. But I'd gotten right back on—a badge of courage. I'd earned respect from Johnny and the other cowboys.

This day, I rode with more ease. Queen Mab was beginning to respond to my neck reining, and Johnny and two other cowboys sat on the split-rail fence, egging me on. Some campers had come to watch me, too. I had the Queen in full gallop around the barrels, even as she bucked a couple of times and, at one point, reared up.

Across the corral I went, taking the barrels close, leaning into the turns, holding my seat with leg pressure. My legs were, and still are, very strong.

"Yippee, gal," Johnny called out with pride, because by now, everyone knew I was his.

"If she can ride that horse, she can ride me next," another cowboy shouted, and he punched Johnny in the arm.

"It's them long legs…" the older cowboy said, referring at once to the horse and to me. He had a weathered but handsome face, and the gossip was that he had once been the Marlboro man and had been on TV commercials and billboards.

After a time, I dismounted. Queen Mab and I were becoming partners, beginning to understand and respond to each other. I walked her a couple of times around the corral with the bridle reins, then took her into the tack room to remove her saddle, blanket, bridle, and put on a halter to brush and curry her before leading her out to pasture.

Queen Mab became my horse that summer. I used the same saddle I'd broken her with. But I'd changed from the snaffle to a curb bit, so I used a different bridle.

That day, the last with the cowboys, after I'd ridden so much, my legs were stiff, almost bowed, as I exited the barn. Evening was coming on; the temperature had dropped a few degrees, and the air was cool and moist. The campers who had watched me were now showering, changing, and getting ready for dinner. My group was going to walk the five miles from camp into town the next morning, so some of them were planning to work their leather projects this evening to finish them up since they would be absent from morning class.

Johnny was waiting for me by the big sliding barn door that we always left open.

"Nice job, Rae." He had his thumbs hooked into his belt. "A real cowgirl."

"Thanks," I said. "I like Queenie. And running the barrels was fun."

"You know what fun I'd like now?" Johnny asked, and slid his thumbs lower.

"Not now. I'm beat." I had stopped in front of Johnny, but because he didn't move, I began to walk around him.

Johnny grabbed my arm.

"I'm tired. Got to get back to the bunk. The girls expect me." I looked at Johnny. I had no fear, no concern.

"We leave tomorrow. Gonna miss me?" Johnny still gripped my arm.

"We'll have time to say goodbye," I said. "Tomorrow, before you leave." I pulled my arm away but stood there, looking out over the pasture where a group of horses galloped across a rolling hill. The sun had dropped, turning the sky magenta and neon orange above the darkening mountains. When I returned my attention to Johnny, he was no longer alone. The two cowboys who'd watched me from the fence had joined him—the Marlboro man and another guy that I recognized as a loner, who rarely interacted with the campers, and worked primarily as the ranch camp farrier.

"Hi, guys," I said causally, though, truth be told, the way they just showed up made my stomach crawl.

Johnny took a step back, and just as one of the guys began

to chuckle—although there was nothing funny—the other Rachel appeared, almost out of nowhere, but I think she'd been grooming one of the horses in a stall and must have come from the barn.

"Let's get cleaned up," she said to me, and looked at Johnny, who dropped his eyes. The other two men exchanged looks and also backed away.

"Yeah," I said. "I feel real dirty." My heart pounded loud and hard in my chest.

"Nothing a good shower won't fix." Rachel linked her arm with mine, and we walked together silently around the barn, past the corral in the direction of the bunks.

I could feel the men's eyes follow us. Rachel must have felt it too because she squeezed my arm and picked up the pace.

At the bunk, Rachel sat down on her bed and said in a throaty whisper, "Close call. Got to watch it. Boys will be boys." She dug under her pillow and found a hard pack of Camels. She knocked them against her palm a few times before removing one.

"Do you think..." I began. I stood by Rachel's bed, leaning against the bunkbed's black metal frame—we were alone, the girls already gone to dinner.

"Yup," she said, and placed the unlit cigarette in her mouth. It bobbed up and down as she spoke. "You got honey, and them bees ain't gonna leave you alone. You're gonna have to watch it. I seen these guys around you, and..." she struck a match, and lifted the tiny flame to her cigarette, inhaling.

"Thanks," I told her. "I mean, if you hadn't shown up...." My words halted. I shifted my weight closer to her and felt tears press from the inside, against my eyes, salty, stinging.

"Yeah," Rachel said, rising from the bed, forcing a smile in my direction but not exactly at me. "Go shower. I'll see you at dinner." She took a deep, long drag that made the tip of her cigarette sparkle. Then, she got up and walked out, the screen door creaking and slamming behind her.

That night I dressed in my oldest jeans and wore a baggy over-shirt. I wore my sneakers, not my dirty, manure-encrusted boots, but I wore my hat low so that it covered my face.

But neither Johnny nor the cowboys showed up for our regular after-dinner get-together. And the rec room was nearly empty, as some of the campers were still in the leather tool room. Sarah, one of the campers who'd finished her project, walked over to the juke box and played "Angel of the Morning." Then she and another camper slow-danced together to it. I sat by myself, hanging out by the window that looked out over the darkening upper pasture.

The next morning, after breakfast, when most of the campers were getting ready for their long hike into town, one of the older counselors announced that all the cowboys had left at dawn.

—ϗ—

On one of my many trips into the city during the spring of '69, I'd gone to MoMA on East 53rd Street, right off 5th Avenue. My mom had driven me to Rosedale Station, where I waited for the Long Island Railroad to take me into Penn Station. There I picked up the F train that let me off across the street from the museum.

Instead of going directly to the museum, however, I'd gone—as I often did—to St. Thomas's Cathedral, located on the corner. That day, the organist was playing Bach. I sat in a pew and breathed in the heavy, cool, incensed air while sun poured through the three blue-stained glass front panels.

The music came from the Great Organ, located in the church's chancel. I'd heard that the organ had been damaged by the construction of the museum, and that it recently had been repaired.

I sat midway up the nave, on a center aisle so that I could more fully feel the force of the organ's enormous sound, more clearly see the stained-glass panels. This was a spiritual practice and a place where body, mind, and soul were welcome.

I sat for almost an hour, listening to a Bach sonata. It had a melodic clarity that moved strangely along the pipes, almost whimsically, unsuited to such a solemn church. Nonetheless, I bowed my head and prayed as the organ flitted up and down the scale, notes colliding, casting vibrating sounds into the stone, troubling the air in resonant but oddly discordant waves.

As a teenager, I'd ceased to have faith, yet prayer felt right—the calling up of one's deeper self to connect with that which was greater.

At the MoMA ticket booth counter, I paid the $2.75 that allowed me to spend the entire day in the museum and to see any film that might be playing. That day, a Saturday, there was an independent short-film festival, and after I saw my favorite paintings, *Guernica* and *The Starry Night*, I decided to watch a few.

The theater was small and located downstairs. I came in during the middle of a film and made myself comfortable near the front, where there weren't as many people. I leaned back so as to see the large screen.

I don't remember many of the films that day, but one has stayed with me and has served as a touchstone for my thinking about God and freewill.

Shot in black and white, and lasting about ten minutes, the film featured two boys tossing a softball back and forth. Wearing baseball mitts, they threw gently and stood perhaps only twenty feet apart, beneath a large, fully leafed tree. The film was shot in summer or late spring, and the boys wore tee-shirts and loose pants. But there was a third boy in the tree, sitting on a thick, extended lower limb. And every time one of the boys tossed the ball, the boy in the tree called out, "I made you do that."

The boys playing catch never responded to the words that the boy in the tree called out to them. It's as if they didn't hear him. The words, "I made you do that," continued throughout the short film, and the ball tossed back and forth was the film's only action. The film began *in medias res*—with the ball in midair—and ended *in medias res*—with the ball in midair.

After the film, I left, although the festival continued. Out of the small dark theater, I emerged as if night had unexpectedly turned to day. Upstairs, I visited the museum's cafeteria and spent seventy-five cents for two wedges of Camembert cheese and two packets of crackers. Lunch. The cafeteria was located near the outdoor sculpture garden, where there were tables and chairs. I sat alone at one table by the side of the garden and looked at a Rodin thinker in bronze on a heavy stone pedestal.

—⚹—

Remembering the short film, I hear the words, "I made you do that," and rising from my desk, I pace my small study. Are we "made" to do what we do? And I think of Dennis and his gambling. Is the short script of our lives already written, or do we have agency?

Jake, on the couch now, lifts his head to see if I'm leaving. *Agency*—I'll go with that.

I sit back down at my desk and write all afternoon.

nineteen

Later, toward evening, after walking and feeding Jake, I retreat to the sunroom to read, relax, perhaps even to nap. I have just shut my eyes when my cell phone rings. It's still light out, and very quickly, I remember that *Anna Karenina* and my reading glasses are beside me. It's very hot here, I think, as I find my book, my glasses, put them safely on the coffee table, and reach for the phone—*mom* appearing on the screen.

"Hi," I say—the greeting seems too informal, even gruff. Then there's a pause and a sigh on the other end. "Are you all right?" I ask, now sitting up and quickly deciding to go inside for the air conditioning.

"No," my mother says. "I'm not. Do you have a few minutes?"

I'm in the living room now. Jake is sleeping on a small area rug by the front window, where the blinds have been pulled up so that he can enjoy the comings and goings on the street. I'm walking around, somewhat aimlessly. "Sure. What's up?" I ask.

"Lydia's car isn't working. The engine seized, and it's too expensive to fix. We're down to Julia's car, and she's staying mostly at Terrell's house." Terrell, I quickly recall, is Julia's boyfriend. He's Jamaican, and the family lives in a large house. Terrell has a younger brother who's still in high school, but Terrell just graduated from community college and is becoming a licensed plumber. Julia works as a pharmacy technician and is planning to go back to college to study nursing when she gets enough money put aside for tuition. They're thinking of getting married.

"Can't Lydia buy another car, Mom?"

"No, she can't afford it. She's still making payments on the car that died." My mother sighs deeply, pauses again.

I also pause. I know what's coming.

"I hate to ask you again." My mother's voice is hard, resolute. "But I need to borrow a few hundred until we get on our feet again. We managed to buy groceries, pay the light bill, but now's there's this stupid car, and our rent is due. Overdue. Lydia sunk some money into a new timing belt because the mechanic thought that was the problem. But he took her money, and the car's not fixed. She's a fool. You know that. She was supposed to pay the rent with that money."

"How's Dennis doing?" I ask. I've walked upstairs, turned on my laptop, and now I'm thinking I'll write a bit before making dinner. Then I remember that I need to go to the grocery store to pick up bread, coffee, and half-and-half. I turn off the computer, open my bedroom closet and slip on my black Birkenstocks.

"Not well. He's tired all the time and in pain." Then another pause. "Rae, I have no one else to ask."

I know this, of course. She's borrowed money from all our relatives to pay Dennis's gambling debts, and, for the most part, she's never paid them back either. "Mom, I can't..." I begin.

"Just three hundred? I'll pay you back when I get my Social Security check. I promise. I don't know what we're going to do." I hear my mom's desperation.

"Mom, I can't. I don't have the money." *Don't have* is so much easier than *won't give.*

"Can't you borrow against a credit card? Get a cash advance?"

"No," I say. I'm sitting on the bed, my heart pumping so hard that I can feel it in my chest. There's something there resisting, resistant. "Nick and I don't do that. I can't use my credit card. Mom, don't ask me to do that." It's the same conversation we've had before.

"Okay, okay." My mom says, fed up with me. "I just don't know what we're going to do. We can't be homeless. Dennis is too sick."

"I'm sorry, Mom," I say. I've walked down the stairs and now sit on the bottom step. Jake has followed me, his companionship steady and welcome.

"All right. I've got to go, Rae. Love you."

"Love you, too, Mom. Sorry."

I sit there for a few minutes, my heart calm again, trying to feel something—guilt, sadness, anger, exhaustion. I can't tell. I certainly don't feel good. But then again, if I gave her the money, I wouldn't feel good either. *I just gave her money,* I tell myself. *I can't keep giving her more.* There's a point at which I feel taken advantage of, abused.

Abused. I sit with the word for a moment. Too harsh? Then I think, *abused by whom?* Not my mom, really. Though I feel bad for her. And angry.

It's Dennis. Lurking ghost-like behind the scenes. A memory stirs, a shadow of a memory that fades before I can grasp it.

Regardless of what Mom says, the mess they're in is Dennis's fault. He's stolen all their money, and even now he's probably gambling somehow—phoning in bets—even sick as he is. But then I wonder, *Where's my compassion? For Dennis? My mom? For my sister-in-law and nieces? If I can alleviate some of their suffering—whatever the cause—shouldn't I?*

"No," I say to Jake, and decide to go back into the sunroom, lie down, calm down. Jake follows me.

Groceries can wait. I slip off my Birks and collapse on the sunroom couch. The heat here is intense. Closing my eyes, I reflect on the Buddhist term "idiot compassion"—used to describe, among many things, those unskillful gifts that enable the addict or offer misguided generosity.

I think about money and what it represents—love, approval, attention, support. I remember back to times when Nick and I needed financial help—when we were first married during a major recession and were desperately broke, unable to find jobs. And again, when we were pregnant with Cal, then poor graduate students—and my parents told us that they couldn't afford financially to help us. Yet they'd managed to help Dennis, always the more needy "child." But wasn't I as deserving? Aimed toward a professional career? Working hard in graduate school? Struggling to keep old cars running, to be good parents, to get ahead? But Dennis was struggling, too, with his compulsive gambling and lying. He, too, was worthy of help, though of another kind. Giving him money and allowing him to steal were never good ideas.

Nonetheless, I feel guilty. In the sunroom now, I lie on the couch and breathe, concentrating on the heat and the breath through the mid-channel of my body, my chakras. I think of the word *aligned*—aligning the breath, the body, our energy, ourselves. Giving money to my mother is giving money to my brother, enabling him as my mom did. And my dad, reluctantly, when he was alive. He couldn't talk to my mother about Dennis's gambling or thieving. She wouldn't hear it, and he knew that she wouldn't or couldn't refuse my brother anything. After my dad died, my mother continued on her own to enable Dennis—even more so, without my dad's silent disapproval to hold her back.

I've lost track of time, and that, I tell myself, is okay, what summer is about. The evening sun is low, and I can't stop feeling bad about saying no to my mom. How can I, a daughter, refuse my desperate mother? How can I live with myself, knowing that she's suffering?

I close my eyes, reflecting on my middle-class childhood. We always had money. Every season, I was allowed to purchase new clothes; there were my summer camps, guitar lessons, trips to the city. I enjoyed a childhood of plenty. Don't I owe her something for that? I blink open my eyes, stare out into the backyard, where a squirrel runs gracefully across the top of our privacy fence. *What balance,* I think.

When my parents first moved to Florida to retire, they had a million dollars in savings. Some of it was the profit they made from selling the South Shelburne house; some of it was my paternal grandfather's legacy. My grandfather, a notorious tightwad, had amassed a small fortune by investing in blue-chip stocks during the Depression, and he'd left most, though not all, to his only child, my dad. Back then, a million dollars was a lot of money. Much of it was well-invested and earning steady interest, which generated a decent, albeit modest, income, but one that along with income from my mom's therapy practice and my dad's Social Security check, offered more than enough money for my parents to live on comfortably. Where did it all go? Bad business decisions. Bad decisions that repeatedly linked their lives with Dennis's gambling problems. Denial masked as optimism.

And, of course, there was the time that Dennis had forged my father's signature to take $50,000 in cash from an IRA. And the time that Dennis had been accepted into a Physician's Assistant program at Nova University but ended up dropping out. By lying that he was still enrolled, however, he'd been able to steal the student loan money that should have paid for his tuition. He gambled away all that money, to the tune of over $100,000, then proceeded to forge checks from our mother's checking account. My mother and father must have known. My mother, in charge of family finances, must have noticed that large amounts of money went missing from her accounts.

That said, Nick and I had often lent my parents money over the years. Small amounts—$500 to $1,500—and we were sometimes paid back, sometimes not. At times, we'd insist that the money was a gift; at other times, we'd tell them it was a loan when we really needed the money returned. Of course, there was the $10,00 loan that wasn't all paid back. But even smaller loans were never repaid on time nor repaid freely; I'd always have to ask or plead.

Often, I'd catch my mother in a lie. She'd say anything to get the money she needed. Although she would never tell me that Dennis's gambling was the real cause of her desperation, Nick and I knew. Once she told me that she had been the victim of a scam—she knew better and was deeply embarrassed, she admitted. But the upshot was that she needed $1,500 to pay the mortgage. Another time she told me—and this happened later when my dad was in decline—that she needed money to pay for an uninsured medical procedure for him. When I offered to make payment directly to the hospital, she said, no, that she wanted the money so that she could pay the bill herself.

"Don't you trust me? she asked

"No, Mom. I don't," I'd said, and she'd hung up. We didn't speak for months.

—〰—

Having fallen asleep, I awake suddenly to Jake's pawing at the sunroom door, wanting to return to the living room. It's steaming out here; I'm sweating intensely—a hot flash, I think. I feel drugged, sluggish, stupid from heat, sleep, worry. But I struggle awake, ready to get out, to walk Jake yet another time before going to the grocery store, then relaxing for the evening. I'm in no mood to write now. Only to forget.

twenty

"I made you do it," the boy on the low tree branch says. I see the ball thrown as the two boys play catch. "I made you do it," and I think of the "it" as a broad pronoun, without clear reference. I'm thinking again of free will. I'm thinking of the crazy way that our lives make sense and then don't. I see myself, a young girl eating Italian Ice by the playground and the young mother working at midnight on a graduate paper at my kitchen table, thinking that I can't go on. Cal had chronic ear infections, and I had a fifteen-page paper due each of the last six weeks of my first semester. What was the force that pushed me to complete the paper, the semester, the degree? What is the thread that connects the young girl to the current me?

After a poor night's sleep, I'm not doing well this morning. I've fed the dog, made coffee, and I'm sitting in my study, at the computer, trying to work on my book. It's Monday, and the house feels empty.

Nothing comes. No words, no ideas, no thoughts.

I look out the window, scan the sky, which appears bright and relentless, summer's oppressive light offering no refuge. Jake sleeps on the rug. And that inspires me, all of a sudden, to get back into bed, read, and nap. Why not? I turn off the computer.

In my bedroom, I yank off my tee-shirt and sweat pants—writing clothes—then lift the corner of the summer quilt.

—ᶬᶬ—

I'm back in school, 1968. And as I see my young teenage self, walking down the hallway where the English classes are taught, I realize that I'm half asleep, caught in a waking dream. I'm dressed in a short blue pleated skirt, a ribbed black sweater, color-coordinated argyle knee socks with saddle shoes. As I walk into a classroom, I spot a large black and white poster of Allen Ginsberg at the back of the room. He's wearing a sandwich board sign that reads "Pot is fun." The poster strikes me as odd but interesting.

Then, I'm at home in South Shelburne, in my bedroom—wearing a work-shirt, low-rise bell-bottom jeans, and sandals—sitting at my desk, trying to write poetry at my typewriter as I listen to the Rolling Stones' "Get Off of My Cloud." I tell myself in the dream to focus on Wayne, and my dream now shifts to include him. He's a new friend this year. With his encouragement, I'm becoming more intellectual and radical.

Wayne is older by a couple of years, and he attends Stuyvesant High School, known at Sty. The school, located in Manhattan, is free but open only to exceptionally smart city kids. How Wayne qualified, I don't know.

Wayne comes from a strange family. His dad is about ninety years old. Once, he'd been a chemist and had actually "discovered" instant coffee during World War I—there was a government-issued plaque in his office, acknowledging his "Contributions to the cause of America's Freedom." The family lived in an old house in Lawrence, the wealthiest of the "Five Towns," in the area we both lived—though the name was anachronistic because even then there were more than five towns.

I first met Wayne through a friend at a party, and we immediately began discussing Freud. I insisted that Freud was phallocentric and that as a female I resented his idea of penis envy, though girls and women, I added, might want the power that a penis represents.

Before long, Wayne and I were reading books together and having regular discussions. Wayne introduced me to Herbert Marcuse's *Eros and Civilization* and Marshall McLuhan's *The Medium is the Message.* We discussed *Walden,* which I'd read earlier. Thoreau had offered me the possibility of a personal freedom unhooked from society's conventions. I found Thoreau's ideas about nonconformity appealing, and I loved his nonmaterialistic views. Someday, I had decided, I'd live away from others, in my own Walden, to develop a deeper understanding of myself before committing to long-term relationship with friends or lovers. Friendships—I now believed, after Nancy, Honey, Leslie, and Jane had dropped me—were over-rated.

—ᴍ—

I'm wide awake. I'm sitting up in bed and willing to give myself over to my lucid dream, which is now a memory.

I'd slammed into adolescence in eighth grade and developed a perverse attitude, in-sync with my generation's counter-culture notions of remaking the world into a kinder, more loving place.

As I walked the halls of Lawrence Junior High that year, moving silently with my classmates, always staying to the right side of the hallway—the rule back then—I'd looked at all the girls with their eye makeup, pretty outfits, and decided to quit modeling completely—a kind of selling of the self, I thought.

When I'd entered junior high to begin seventh grade, my grades had been excellent. I'd placed into all the "smart" classes. By mid-fall of eighth grade, however, I was becoming a more irreverent version of my smart, seventh-grade self. By the spring of that year, I'd become an "out-there" hippy chick, questioning everything—myself, the system that imposed its idiosyncratic, irrational rules, my parents, and the purpose of life. Wayne had played a part in that transformation.

Sitting in bed, I see him: long mousy brown hair tied back in a messy ponytail, big nose, thick lips, thick-set body, and rather short. He approaches me, and I hear his voice again. He's telling me to be careful. "About what?" I ask, but his image fades.

—✿—

When Cal calls, I'm still in bed, thinking about my time at Lawrence Junior High. I'm just settling into my seat at the back of Mr. Lamb's eighth grade Honors English class when my cell phone jolts me back to Monday, today. Cal, an early riser, often calls when he's out buying fresh bagels and cream cheese at Finagle Bagel, just a few blocks away from his apartment in Cambridge, Massachusetts.

"Did I wake you?" Cal asks. There's a lot of background noise, and I think he's probably walking on a busy street.

"Sort of, not really. I was awake but still in bed. How are you? How was your week?"

"Did Dad get to New York okay? Cal asks. "And where's his retreat exactly? North of Binghamton?" I hear wind blow through his cell phone.

"Not really sure, but I think it's more toward the eastern part of the state, nearer Vermont, and very north, near Canada. Anyway, yes, he's there and checking in with me about every day. He's doing fine, getting into the swing of things."

Cal tells me that he was in Chicago last week for a big technology conference and that he arrived home late yesterday, Sunday night. He has the day off, so Jess took the day off as well. Nowadays, he works for an IBM partner company, but he worked for IBM for about five years after graduate school.

"How's Jess?" I ask. She was pregnant in the spring and then miscarried. "Good," Cal says. "She taking a course, Bio-statistics, at night at BU, and now she thinks she'll apply for the Masters of Public Health." I hear a car door slam, and soon I hear voices in the background.

"Where are you?" I ask.

"At the grocery story now. Gonna pick up coffee. Then head to the bagel store. I think Jess and I are going out toward Walden Pond for the day." I hear Cal talk to someone, a clerk maybe, and there's crowd noise.

"Well, you sound busy. I should let you go."

"Are you okay, Mom?"

"Yeah. Of course. Why?"

"I don't know. You seemed weird for a minute. You sure?"

I breathe deeply, realize Cal is right. I'm upset. "I just need to wake up," I say. "I love you. Give my love to Jess."

"Okay. She was asleep when I left. We'll talk again soon. I'm going to be around Boston this week. Maybe you can catch up with Jess next time. Just wanted to check in."

"Yes," I say. "That would be good. Give her my love. And I love you."

"Love you, too, Mom. Tell Dad I say hi."

"I will. Have a great day. Love you."

"Bye."

"Bye."

I'm up now, ready to brush my teeth, wash, make the bed, start the day for the second time. I rise, glancing out the window to find that the sky is dark, clouded over.

But now, I breathe in, breathe out, collapsing onto the rattan chair, where I often read, by the bedroom window. Closing my eyes, hot tears well up, begin falling, until I'm sobbing out loud.

I'm thinking of my brother. I sit on the chair, wipe tears with the bottom of my tee-shirt, which, along with my sweat pants, I've put back on. I stop crying, adjust myself, sit up.

Short vignettes come to mind—fleeting moments, images. Jake is beside me, probably wondering why I don't come downstairs to get him breakfast. But the past is alive within me.

First: Dennis is asking me if I'm "mad" or "glad" at him. He has a face to express each emotion: one with an exaggerated frown, the other with a laughing but silent smile. We're eating dinner at the kitchen table in South Shelburne. Dennis is in seventh grade; I'm in third. He's had a bad day in school—failed a math test and pitched a losing game, his first intramural. He's told me this earlier and made me promise not to tell.

But at the dinner table now, we're talking about school, and our dad, who isn't working late this evening, asks Dennis about his vocabulary words, if he needs any help memorizing them.

"No," Dennis says. "I got them." And he winks at me.

"Any other tests this week?"

"No," Dennis says. "I'm good. Science test next week."

"Games?"

"Yeah, one today. Pitched something fierce, but we lost two to three. I only pitched two innings. Mitch Feldman got to throw."

Dennis is lying. He sneaks a "glad" face at me, and I'm supposed to sneak the same face back at him.

Instead, I'm fixated on my baked potato. I'm thinking I need more butter and should smash the potato with my fork, smother it in butter, then eat it with the skin, which I love. But the butter isn't on the table, and I don't want to get up. It's a problem. Should I look up and give Dennis the grin because I'm not going to contradict his story? Should I just get up, get the butter, but risk Dennis's wrath, without giving him the grin? But I don't want to grin, to collude. On some level, Dennis's code game is offensive; I feel bullied and increasingly unwilling to participate. But his staring eyes pierce me, arrow-like, trained on my face. My features feel loose and disorganized. I put down my fork and make the grin.

Dennis wins. He's more powerful than I, and more needy.

Next: I'm younger, maybe six or seven, and my parents are out on this Friday or Saturday night. Dennis is babysitting me; he's been paid to do so. We're arguing about what to watch on TV, when Dennis picks me up—and I begin to kick and scream—as he ties me up with a belt from his closet, along with twine he's found in the kitchen junk drawer, and then locks me in the hall closet beneath the winter coats. I don't scream now, because if I do, Dennis will gag me as he's done twice before.

I'm cold and uncomfortable. My feelings are hurt, but by offering me a bribe, Dennis will talk me out of telling our parents. So, I think about that. This time, I might get money—as much as two dollars—or Dennis might be my slave for a week, which never quite works because he's the master manipulator, and I can never out-think him. After about half an hour, Dennis comes to the closet door and asks, "Who's the boss?"

"You are," I say.

"I'll let you out, but you can't tell. How about we eat cookies, and I give you two bucks to keep your mouth shut?"

"Yes," I say. "Let me out."

"Deal?" Dennis asks.

"Deal," I say.

"You mad or glad at me?"

"I'll be glad if you let me out."

"Promise?" Dennis insists. "Say it now: You're glad at me."

"I'm glad. I'm glad. Let me out."

The door opens. It's dark in the hall. I scoot out, and Dennis unties me. A few minutes later, we're eating chocolate chip cookies together in the den, and I have another two dollars in my tin-can bank. We're watching *Bewitched* on the couch, milk and cookies spread out on the coffee table. Dennis gives me his glad smile to check in with me. I return a glad smile. We're friends.

Then, it's 1959: I'm in bed, in the apartment, late at night. Much stuff from the apartment has already been moved to the new house. It's the end of first grade, and I'll have to finish the last few weeks in my new school. My mother has told me that this will be best because I'll make new friends before the academic year is out. But I'm anxious and have trouble falling asleep. Every so often, I pray silently for help—with falling and staying asleep, with negotiating my new school, with saying goodbye to friends. I don't want to cry and have to choke back tears when I think of leaving Barbara, Teddy, and Glenn.

"You asleep?" Dennis asks.

"No," I say.

"Can I come over? Rover, rover?"

"Yes," I say.

When Dennis comes to my bed, he lifts the covers and slips in beside me. He puts his warm arms around me, kissing my cheek. We snuggle. Dennis loves me.

As I fall asleep, inhabiting the shadowy place between wakefulness and dream, I feel Dennis's hand run along my body—chest, face, and down. His touch feels good, and I'm floating in gray space, between feathers and air. Dennis's breathing changes ever so slightly, and the pace of his hand on my body quickens. We're in a train now, traveling in darkness toward some faraway destination. When we arrive, Dennis leaves me, and the bed becomes chilly, then warm again. And it's easy now to turn over, fall into the shadow, sleep in God's hands that welcome, hold me.

—⚹—

I'm downstairs. I open the hall closet, the one I've recently reorganized, open the kibble bag we keep on the floor, scoop out a cupful into Jake's bowl, then toss the empty cup back into the bag, catching an unpleasant whiff of the kibble before closing it. I go over to the refrigerator, take out half a slice of rye bread, crumble into the bowl, then pour about a quarter of a cup of nonfat milk over the mix. Jake is intent, following me over to his placemat behind the kitchen table. I put down his bowl, and he hungrily attacks the mixture.

I need coffee to wake up. But I feel like going back to bed again.

Instead, I walk around the quiet house. There's a blankness I'm inhabiting, a large open space with nothing in it. I sit on our odd chair, the mismatched one against the far wall. It's an extra, rarely used sort of Parson's chair from the seventies that we've had reupholstered.

My breathing is shallow, so I try to deepen it. I hear Jake go outside through his dog door.

I sit and think. About childhood. About Dennis. About his cancer and possible death. About Nick being gone. About Cal and Will being grown. About me alone. About the novel I can't write. About my life. My head hurts, especially above my left eye. Coffee. That's what I need. But it will take a tremendous energy to make some.

Jake is out in the backyard and will want a rawhide bone when he comes in. I can get it for him. I muster my energy, rise from the chair, walk into the kitchen, open the lower cabinet where the dog bones are kept, take one, wait for Jake to return.

I feel like I'm three hundred pounds. Maybe I'm getting sick, coming down with a summer cold. But I have no symptoms. Jake returns, and I hand him the bone, which he greedily snatches from my hand. I watch him trot into the living room to eat it.

I head upstairs and lie down in bed again, getting under

the covers. Alone in this house, I can time-travel through my life. Become any age. Bed is bed, I think, and question what that means. Then I let the question go. Not all thoughts have meaning.

Jake is upstairs and joins me on the bed. He won't go there when Nick's home, but he knows he can join me when I'm alone. Jake senses I need him. I close my eyes, try to breathe deeply to counteract the shallow breathes that, I've determined, are making me feel so strange. I fall into another fitful sleep.

twenty-one

I dream about modeling, which I began during the summer between fourth and fifth grade. My father had a customer at the furniture store who wrote a syndicated column called "Taffy's Tips to Teens" that was published, among other places, in the *New York Post*. Her name was Gloria Shifferman, and, at some point, she asked to see photos of my dad's two kids. When he showed her pictures of Dennis and me, she suggested that I try fashion modeling. Then she autographed her book— of the same title—for me.

That night when my dad came home with the book, he asked if I wanted to try modeling. He told me that when I came into the store to thank Mrs. Shifferman in person for the book, she'd tell me more about it. I said yes. That Saturday, when I went to thank Mrs. Shifferman—I'd already written and mailed her a formal thank-you note—she explained that she could give me the names of the top five modeling agencies in New York and that I should start with the top agency and work my way down. My mother was to call and make an appointment for me to go into Manhattan for a group interview. Folks there, she explained, would look at me, and, if they were interested, they'd tell me what to do next.

Mrs. Shifferman was a tall bleached-blonde of late middle age who wore a tailored, dark navy gabardine suit. She thought I was pretty, but more importantly, that I had the "look" that modeling agencies wanted.

"You'll do great," she said, as we sat on a floral print couch together in the furniture store. We were in the display on the front part of the floor, and customers walked past us. Mrs. Shifferman had on high heels and her knees peeked out from the hem of her tight skirt.

I asked Mrs. Shifferman how the agency would determine if they wanted me, and on what basis would that decision be made.

"You never know, sweet-pea. They might have you walk, or not. They'll either see something they think is marketable or else they'll simply pass on you. If that happens, your mom will make an appointment with the next agency down the list. If you go through them all, I'll give you names of some other agencies. Someone will want you."

Mrs. Shifferman opened my copy of *Taffy's Tips to Teens*, which I'd brought with me. It was a hard-covered, slim volume, maybe two hundred pages at most. She found a black and white drawing of a thin, leggy girl in a traditionally waisted dress with a flared skirt. "Wear something like this. Almost to the knees, not too short. And you'll want to wear socks, not stockings. You'll be going into the children's, not the teen's, market."

"Thank you, Mrs. Shifferman. Thank you for all you've done. The book is great. I love it." I crossed my legs. I was wearing a plaid jumper with a cranberry colored jersey underneath, matching knee socks, and new Oxford shoes.

"I can see you're becoming a young lady. I'm sure your dad is very proud of you." Mrs. Shifferman rose and extended her hand.

I rose, too. I thought about curtseying but decided not to. I simply shook her hand. "Thanks again. I really enjoyed meeting you."

"I'll catch your news from your father. I wish you good luck. Remember that young ladies are our future; the civilized world depends on them." She walked into the office where my dad was doing some paperwork. I watched through the glass window as my dad rose politely from his chair and shook her hand before they both sat to do business. As they talked, I felt very excited and ran down the wide staircase to watch Henry apply gold leaf to an end table. Henry usually had a piece of candy for me, and today was no exception. It was a Hershey's kiss that he took from a plastic bag stashed away in a high drawer. I unwrapped the foil and stuck the chocolate into my mouth.

Two weeks later, my mom picked me up early from school, PS #5. I met her in the carpeted office as she was signing me out. She had a change of clothing for me—an old-fashioned cotton dress with a fitted bodice and full skirt—and we planned to drive into the city for my group modeling interview. First, however, I needed to change in the girls' bathroom.

The afternoon sun poured through the high, west-facing side window of the bathroom. My mother and I were alone, standing by the row of white porcelain sinks, low against the tiled wall.

The dress my mom had chosen was one I didn't like, thinking that it made me look like a little girl rather than a young lady upon whom the civilized world could depend. Also, my mom had brought along an itchy crinoline, and I knew I'd have to sit through a long car ride and possibly a subway ride in it.

I yanked the crinoline around, trying unsuccessfully to calm it down so that it would lie a bit flatter. But it didn't cooperate and spread the full skirt out, shortening it inches above my knees. Also, my mom had brought white-laced bobby socks along with patent leather Mary Janes. I looked like a bizarre doll, not a fashion model.

"Mom, I look weird."

"You're beautiful. We've got to go, or we'll be late."

"Can I put the crinoline on in the car? It's itchy. And these socks, I hate them."

"Leave it all alone. I know what I'm doing. You'll be fine." Off we went, down the hall, where, I was grateful, no one saw me. Then we were in my mom's Chevy Malibu, driving down Peninsula Boulevard, out Sunrise Highway to the Van Wyck Expressway, down Queens Boulevard, across the 59th Street Bridge, into Manhattan.

There was little traffic in the middle of the afternoon, and in forty-five minutes we were parking in a small underground garage just a few blocks from the Marge McDermott Modeling Agency, the top one in the city, Mrs. Shifferman's first choice.

We stopped in the ladies' room on the first floor of the large nondescript Manhattan office building, with its marble entranceway, door man, and concierge at a front desk, who directed us to the public bathroom, then to the fifth-floor agency. In the ladies' room, my mom adjusted my crinoline dress and combed my wavy, strawberry blonde hair, which I wore long and pulled back with a hard-plastic, tortoiseshell-colored headband.

Looking into the full-length mirror in the little powder anteroom, I watched my mother as she made me presentable. I looked okay but younger than my years and very un-hip.

"This isn't working, Mom," I tried to complain, but I knew that my objection would fall on deaf ears and that it was too late for any change. "Maybe we should do this thing another day." I tried but failed to smile at myself in the mirror.

"You look great. Trust me." My mom was squatting by me in her tight-fitting burgundy dress and heels. I could smell her perfume and hairspray as she straightened my skirt, pulled up my bobby socks. When I finally managed a smile, trying to project my best self, and looked at myself in the mirror, I saw the hole in the back of my mouth where I'd lost a tooth.

My mom took my hand and calmly said, "Let's go."

We entered a large carpeted room filled with wall-to-wall kids—boys, girls, babies, toddlers, young teens. There were moms to match them. And lots of noise. Some were sitting in upholstered folding chairs arranged around the room's perimeter.

As I walked in, still holding my mom's hand, I noticed that the carpeted area was located in a roped-off section, and beyond the rope—which was red velvet, like the kind that cordon off long lines at fancy movie theaters—a marble tiled area connected two doorways at either end of the room.

No one came out to tell us what to expect. The room felt uncomfortably hot. I looked at my mom with an expression that said, *maybe this was mistake and we should just go home.* My mom smiled back at me as if to reassure me that no, the situation was all right and that we needed to give it some time.

There were no vacant seats. Many people, including us, had to stand. Babies cried, toddlers whined. The large plate glass office window at the side of the room looked out onto the city street, where cars were stalled in traffic and honking—the very beginning of rush hour.

Then an elegant woman appeared, and the crowd hushed as if she were a movie star. She certainly was glamorous, in high patent leather, spiked heels, and a tweed business suit with a yoke collar and pearls. Her hair was done up in a sophisticated high bun, worn at the back of her head. She walked back and forth twice across the marble tile, heels clicking. The room remained quiet, and she glanced over us all, pointing to three children.

"You, you, and you," she said, and at the final *you* had

pointed at me. "The rest can leave. Thanks for considering the Marge McDermott agency." She exited through the door at the opposite end of the hallway. A man came out, exactly on cue, to unhook the velvet rope and to nod the three of us in—a very young girl, maybe three or four years old, me, and another girl, perhaps a few years older.

As if it had been the most natural thing in the world, my mother found my hand, squeezed it, and we walked along with the two other sets of moms and girls into a swanky back room.

"Please, sit down," the woman in the tweed suit said. She was already seated behind a large kidney-shaped dark wood desk. She didn't rise to greet us. The man who had unhooked the rope stood by the now closed door. He was dressed, I noticed, in a black pin-striped suit and had his hands folded together in front like a TV gangster.

"I'm Marge McDermott, and I want to welcome you to our agency," she said.

I sat beside my mom, listening as the woman—Marge, she preferred to be called—explained that she would arrange for a photographer to take photos for our "composites"—a sheet that would contain a sample of photos and our information— and that if they looked good, we'd do photo-modeling as well as fashion shows. But if they didn't, we'd just be doing fashion shows.

Marge offered the moms written contracts to be returned at a later date. There were forms to fill out—so that we could get Social Security cards and working papers. We'd be paid per job, and the rate of pay varied considerably. Much of this information flew by me, and really, I was still in shock that I'd been selected.

There'd been beautiful girls out in that room. Stunning girls and young women whom Marge had passed over. And here I was in my silly white bobby socks, my little-girl dress. I felt like a fool, a pretender, a fraud.

—ᴍᴠ—

I sit in the bedroom, on the wicker reading chair. Awake again, late morning. In front of me is my life.

I can do anything. I can. I can read all day or sleep all day. Eat or starve. Kill myself or write my book. Ambivalence is my middle name. Everything's complicated.

When I was almost thirteen, I attempted suicide. My brother had tied me up earlier in the evening, put me in the closet, but this time I decided to protest and scream. And rather than gag me, he let me out. Rushing, I'd stumbled over winter boots and old umbrellas, the heavy coats like woolen ghosts hanging above, the closet dark and strange, full of damp, unfriendly smells.

Dennis wanted to go out and leave me alone, which was fine with me, but wouldn't be fine with my parents. Letting me out and giving me a piece of chocolate cake was part of his bribe.

"I'll give you a dollar, and I'll be your slave tomorrow." Dennis was dressed in jeans, a button-down shirt, and already had his junior varsity jacket on.

"Where you going?" I sat in the hallway. We'd thrown the boots, umbrellas, and other random items back into the closet. I wore my flannel nightgown but was barefoot. The hall tiles were cold and the front part of the house was dark. My brother hated to leave lights on. He had a kind of quirky fastidiousness. Sometimes he'd go into the bathroom to straighten the towels on the racks or come behind me with a sponge if I left crumbs on the kitchen counter.

"I'm going over to Marlene's for a couple of hours." Marlene and Marc were Evelyn and Frank's kids. In fact, my parents were out with Evelyn and Frank—to dinner and a movie. Usually, after dinner the four of them would go back to our house or theirs to play cards, but tonight they'd wanted to see a recently released movie playing at Central Theater in Cedarhurst. They were going for drinks afterwards. Because their family lived about twenty houses down the block, we kids keep in close contact.

"Let me come too," I said. For years, I had had an on-again-off-again crush on Marc, who was a year older than I.

"You can't see Marc," Dennis said. "He's spending the night at a friend's. Marlene's alone. I want to see her."

"Okay," I said. This was actually the second-best situation. If I couldn't see Marc, I could read a book alone in the house without Dennis teasing me, which he often did when I read or played my music.

"Call if you need me. Be good." Dennis gave me one of his fake, exaggerated winks as he zipped up his jacket and walked to the front door. "Lock it behind me. I've got a key. You can stay up until I come home. Take one piece of cake. One piece. That's it. Mom put it on the top shelf of the pantry. It's still in the box."

"What about my dollar?"

Dennis pulled his wallet from his front pocket, took out a dollar, extended his hand for me to come get it, a sort of passive-aggressive relenting.

"What about tomorrow?" I asked. "You gonna do what I say?"

"Yeah, yeah. We'll see," Dennis said. But I knew the slave part of the bargain was already history.

Then Dennis left. I watched the front door close behind him. I bolted the door, fastened the security chain.

My mood went black. While Dennis was present, I could hate him. But now, I only hated myself. I hated the life I had—my parents, school, home with Dennis. I felt a weight in my chest, an anchor mooring me to some desperate place in a rough sea of powerfully sad, depressing thoughts.

What's the point? I asked myself. *What's the point of anything? Eating? Sleeping? Watching TV? Reading a book? Making friends?* I thought then as I think now, remembering.

I opened the hall closet where I'd been held prisoner and took my winter coat off its hanger. Putting it on, I walked out the back door and into our small yard—a concrete patio mostly, with a little grass around it, beyond which was a chain-link fence that stretched around Meadowbrook Pond, the man-made lake. I sat down on the patio's rear-facing steps, staring into the calm black water. Stars littered the sky, and houselights from across the lake glittered like colored rhinestones.

I hugged my coat around me and began to cry. Cold and alone, I began to pray, muttering the Sha'ma Yisrael. But I couldn't find my faith. I decided there was no God—no heaven, no hell, except the one I was living.

I sat there for a while, then walked inside, deciding to check the medicine cabinet in my parents' bathroom, to see if the valium capsules that my dad took regularly to help with his insomnia were there in sufficient number. Perhaps I could end it all. I found two vials—one completely full, the other partially full. I took eight capsules from each, thinking my dad would probably never notice—stupid logic, of course, because he'd figure it out if I ended up dead.

I put away my coat in the front hall closet, stuffed the sixteen pills into my bathrobe pocket, heading for the kitchen, for a piece of cake, a glass of cold milk. I thought about having myself a little party, and suddenly, I felt liberated, joyful, giddy. I put on my old *Meet the Beatles* album, remembering how as a young girl Joannie, Linda and I—all best friends in early grade school—would dance to it in Linda Freedman's finished basement. We'd spend an entire Saturday playing this record over and over again, dancing with each other, practicing "The Swim," "The Pony," "The Jerk" to "I Saw Her Standing There" and "All My Loving." When "This Boy" came on, we'd get dreamy, maybe even tear up, thinking about boys and romance.

I sat at the kitchen table, devoured my milk and cake, and, after putting my dirty dishes in the dishwasher, I turned the music up even louder and walked to the front foyer, where the large mirror there covered an entire wall. It was "smoked" with streaks of gray and brown, a look that my mother, in particular, liked, for it created a kind of "antique elegance," she'd said.

Now, it became the perfect reflection for my mood. I took off my nightgown, bathrobe, and danced naked. I turned up the volume, made a dramatic entrance into the hall, took a bow, made a courtesy, pretending to lift the hem of my skirt, then began a wild, full-on boogaloo.

After the performance, I apologized to the mirror, my audience, for any inadequacies of my dance routine and left the "stage." I found my nightgown and bathrobe on the floor, dressed, and walked downstairs to the bar to find something with which to wash down the valium.

The bar was an elaborate add-on my parents had constructed during the first year we lived in the house. About twelve feet long, with a Formica countertop and wood-paneled sides, the bar had six black barstools lining the front, with liquor cabinets built into the back. None of the cabinets had locks.

I found a bottle of clear vodka, decided it must be easy to drink, poured out a full glass, and went upstairs. The music still played, loud and crazy. I turned it off, and the new silence changed the whole mood of the house—as if the soundtrack had stopped while the movie continued.

Gil, our dog, slept on my parents' bed, and I walked into

their room to pet him, to say goodbye. I loved him, and it seemed particularly sad to leave him with Dennis.

I walked back into the front foyer, with the valium still in my pocket, the glass of vodka in my hand. Watching myself in the smoky mirror, I stuffed the capsules into my mouth, using the vodka to help swallow them. I had to choke them down. I'd never had alcohol before, and this stuff tasted like liquid electricity. I immediately suppressed coughing the capsules up; my throat burned, my eyes teared.

After I got them all down, I drank the entire tall glass of vodka, although each mouthful fought me. It was awful. I couldn't imagine why adults drank this for pleasure.

My head began to swim. Dizzy and sad, I wanted to return to my bedroom, turn off the light, go to sleep, never to wake up. I thought about my parents finding me the next morning. How they'd probably wake up late for Sunday brunch, with orange juice, fresh bagels and bialys—my favorite—lox, scallion cream cheese, and mounds of tomato-and-onion scrambled eggs. Then, there'd be coffee cake for dessert, with a fresh pot of coffee brewing, its aroma filling the kitchen, bright with morning sun glinting across the lake. They'd open the curtains to the view, spread *The Sunday New York Times* across the table. My favorite were the magazine and book review sections.

Dennis might be in the pool room, shooting with the cue stick he'd been given last year as a birthday present. Perhaps he'd have risen unexpectedly early, had cake for breakfast, and would be now practicing Eight-Ball so as to beat my grandfather the next time they played.

My dad, I imagined, would at some point ask, "Where's Rae?" At first, my mother would reply, "Let her sleep in," but by dessert, she'd suggest that someone wake me. Perhaps my dad would volunteer, go to my bedroom door, knock, call my name. When I didn't answer, he'd call more loudly, "Rae,

Rae. We're having breakfast, sweetie. Come join us." With no answer, he'd open the door, come over to my bed, put his hand on me, gently try to wake me.

Soon, he'd find I was cold, even beneath my blanket, which he'd throw back. Then, he'd see I was dead.

"Ed, Ed, come here!" he'd scream. My mom would dash in, moving gracefully but swiftly down the carpeted hallway to my bedroom.

"What's wrong, Bernie? What's going on?" she'd yell, realizing with horror that something terrible had happened. She'd rush in to find me, throw herself over my limp body, weep like the world had ended.

I thought all this as I lay on the large Linoleum tiles, crafted to look like Greco-Roman stonework. I was, however, unable to move, unable to walk back to my bedroom so that my mom and dad could find me the next morning.

Instead, I fell asleep in the foyer, in front of the smoky mirror. I felt very cold, I remember, before I lost consciousness, wishing I could make it to bed. Then, I felt incredibly stupid and blacked out.

A little after midnight, I woke up. I had puked and found myself in a large puddle of mushy orange-brown vomit. My bathrobe and nightgown were soiled, and neither Dennis nor my parents were home yet.

I got up, and with difficulty, pulled off my clothing, dumping them in the bathtub. Naked, I stumbled into the kitchen, pulled out the roll of paper towels from its dispenser and a paper bag from under the sink so as to clean up my mess. I did my best to scrub the stinky place with an old sponge, tossed it into the paper bag, and sat down in the bathtub to run the shower, wash myself and my vomit-stained clothing before stuffing them wet into the washing machine. Finding an old pair of flannel pajamas, I took the paper bag to the outside trashcan. We had two large trashcans with metal sleeves sunk into the pavement—my parents had paid masons to construct these so that our unsightly garbage cans wouldn't be visible or stink from the patio. I lifted the heavy lid of one of them, folded the bag up tight, put it in.

The night was cold and clear, with stars and the moon out, shining on the still surface of Meadowbrook Pond. My head throbbed something fierce, but I felt clean—amazed and happy to be alive. *I will live,* I decided. God had given me another chance.

I promised myself that I'd study hard, get excellent grades. I'd read important books about the world around me so that I myself could grow smarter, stronger, more powerful. And I'd write—poems about my torture, about how my friends hurt me, about my pains, joys, my private thoughts. Already I felt strong—a girl with resolve, a plan, a purpose.

twenty-two

A little over two weeks have gone by since Nick left. I've been alone, making some progress on my book, but not doing much else. I've gone to school to catch up with a few end-of-semester chores, checked on the Writing Center, etc. Nick has been calling just about every day, but he skipped yesterday, and our conversations are very brief because he doesn't have cell phone service and when he calls he must use the retreat phone, which isn't very private, and others are usually waiting to use it.

It's morning now, a Wednesday; I'm sitting at the computer. Rain is forecast. I'm in my nightgown and bathrobe, feeling off balance.

My novel—I now know—is going to be about a woman who tries to reconcile the pieces of her life—her past and current life—so that she can move forward, become whole. The narrator is a writer, and she can't seem to gain traction toward self-understanding. Yes, the book will be autobiographical, but not completely.

I sit at the computer, begin typing. I work for four hours, until my protagonist is at the grocery store. She's got two tomatoes in her hand as she assesses their ripeness. She chooses one, puts it in her plastic carry basket, and moves to the broccoli crowns. Then she stops. I stop, needing a break.

—∞—

It's afternoon. I'm walking Jake behind the university. Since we can't walk through the lovely woods because of the ticks, we walk again around the baseball field, the football practice field, behind a neighborhood that borders the campus.

Jake limps, and I study him, trying to figure out what exactly is wrong. A hurt paw? His hips? Joints?

Sometimes his hind quarters shake, quiver uncontrollably. Or he'll just sit down like he's taking a short break. "Jake," I'll ask, "What's wrong?"

But right now, he's upright, happy, wagging his tail, sniffing the borderline between the grass and woods, as his back-end quivers momentarily—but then stops. He's just old, it saddens me to think.

Pausing as Jake pees, I realize that I haven't really spoken to my friends in well over a week. My best friend, Sonya, is visiting her sister and nephews in Florida for most of the month, I remember. Also, I remind myself that Nick didn't call last night—okay, but I've grown dependent on his brief check-ins. Hopefully, I'll hear from him today because writing is like listening to ghosts. And without some real voices soon, I might go crazy.

I make the turn around the baseball field as two young men throw a hardball back and forth. They're dressed in shorts, tee-shirts, and they're wearing mitts. I hear the thump of the ball as it's caught. I watch each young man shift his weight and bring back his arm, wind up, then power the ball through the air. *Thump,* it lands in the glove. Very satisfying, deceptively easy. I stand by the chain link fence, Jake's nose buried in a patch of clover, and think *I made you do that.*

As we walk back to the car, Jake is in a slow trot beside me. The hot air is humid, thick, but suddenly, for no reason, I'm feeling good. Then, as I slip into Ruby, a thought occurs: my dad is dead, and like an enormous Atlantic wave, the thought crashes over me. Triggered by the boys playing catch—

something we did when I was a girl—I long for him—the father of my early childhood. Not the dad with dementia, with deafness. Not the one who turned away from the world when his life went bad. Not the South Shelburne or Florida dad who allowed his son to steal from him. Or who watched TV all day. Not the man who lost himself to duplicate bridge and to grade C movies. Not the indecisive dad who had trouble ordering his early bird dinner—the one who'd find everything on the menu so tempting that he'd usually change his order a half-dozen times, driving the waitress crazy.

The last time my parents came to visit us in North Carolina, we took them out for dinner at The Olive Garden—one of their favorite restaurants. They were already nearly broke, so my mom had stopped paying for automobile insurance, and they made the twelve-hour trip up from Florida without any. Somewhere off I-95 in Georgia, she'd backed into a car in a strip mall parking lot by a McDonald's, where they'd stopped for lunch and a restroom break. But without insurance, they basically hit-and-ran. Dennis's older daughter Julia—then about ten—was with them. Will is about eighteen months older than Julia, and with my mom's efforts, the cousins had become friends. Nick and I both liked Julia, a sweet, loveable girl.

Soon after that visit, everything fell apart. Dennis's heavy gambling and stealing bankrupted my parents' businesses, bankrupted them, until they lost everything. There were a series of apartment rentals, evictions for non-payment, and moments of extreme desperation. I never learned everything about those years. Mom never wanted to admit how much Dennis was destroying them.

During that time, my dad had become ill with non-tremor Parkinson's disease, and after many hospitalizations, his health declined until he was placed in a residential hospice in Coral

Springs. They were all living in a duplex, but at some point, Lydia moved out, saying that she couldn't take it anymore.

Lydia rented her own place, a one-bedroom in Tamarac, and lived there alone. But, ultimately, a few weeks before my dad died, they were evicted and all moved temporarily into Lydia's apartment because they had nowhere else to go.

Without the funds to move out, the arrangement held— what was temporary became permanent. Dennis and his estranged wife, my mother, and the two girls continue to live in a six-hundred-square-foot apartment in a working-class area of Tamarac. My mom and Dennis still sleep on the two living room couches—even as Dennis is dying. Lydia sleeps in the bedroom with the two girls on mattresses at either side of her bed.

I'm sitting in Ruby, having loaded up Jake and turned on the air conditioning, when I see my dad's face, once handsome, then not so, projected in the sky, his features in cloud and vapor.

"I'm sorry, Dad," I say. "Sorry that you became so sick, suffered so, and died." But his physical suffering had started earlier, when I was sixteen. My dad was diagnosed with acromegaly, a benign tumor impacting the pituitary gland, causing increased bone and tissue growth. His dentist first found the disease by comparing a recent dental x-ray of his bottom jaw bone with an older x-ray. The dentist could see that the jaw had grown and sent my dad to his doctor.

In the early seventies, the treatment for acromegaly involved spraying radiation at the tumor in the hopes of shrinking it without damaging the brain. My dad had a number of these treatments before a powerful new treatment, involving a linear accelerator, became available at Brookhaven National Laboratories, in Upton, New York, way out on Long Island. Brookhaven, once owned by the National Atomic

Energy Commission, had been taken over by the Department of Energy and began subcontracting its facilities to research institutes and to universities. Cutting edge treatments were being offered there as part of clinical trials to patients with inoperable tumors and advanced cancers.

A short time after my dad was diagnosed, his doctor heard that Brookhaven had recently used its linear accelerator, an atom-smasher that involved a mile-plus circular track that exploded apart atoms, to generate a high-powered, intensely focused beam of radiation that could shrink tumors. The doctor recommended my dad for an experimental clinical trial program specifically designed to treat acromegaly patients. My dad applied, was accepted, and while the scientists in their preliminary examinations of my dad determined that he had not experienced cognitive impairment due to his earlier widespread radiation treatment, my dad, nevertheless, felt that his memory had been compromised.

When I first learned about my dad's medical condition, my mother had just picked me up at Kennedy Airport, after my flight home from college for Thanksgiving break. My mom explained how my dad had been diagnosed, about the old radiation treatment, and about the new treatment he'd just started. We sat together in her old Chevy Malibu, cruising down Sunrise Highway, in mid-afternoon, the road pretty much open.

"He's got six treatments spread out over six weeks," my mom said.

"Then?" I asked.

"It's all experimental, so we don't know. But the doctors' best guess is that after these linear accelerator treatments, he'll be able to live normally." Even though it was late November, my mom had her window partly open as she smoked a cigarette, flicking the ash outside.

"Is he damaged?" I had my knapsack, the only luggage I'd brought, on my lap. I unbuttoned my sheepskin coat, shifted my gaze downward to make sure I'd remembered *Crime and Punishment*, which I needed to read over break.

"When you see him, you tell me," she said. Soon we pulled into the driveway.

—∞—

I sit now in the hot car; the a/c won't really work until the car moves. "Dad," I call out like I might have as a child. "I love you."

Jake pants, drools, so I crank up the engine, feel the a/c kick in, and drive in circles around the empty parking lot, putting Ruby in gear, then in neutral, seeing how long I can coast, how many circles I can make before having to step on the gas pedal. After a few circles, I take off for home.

Opening the front door, I walk with Jake into the lovely cool air, collapsing onto the living room couch, arranging the throw pillows comfortably behind my head. I'm not sure if it's a headache coming on or the effect of the heat, but I'm very tired.

Now inside, the air has almost no humidity, a welcome change from the intense thick afternoon air outside. Jake pants on the front rug by the window, looking drowsy, ready for a nap.

I think that perhaps I'm just lonely. If Nick doesn't call, it will be two days since we last spoke. I close my eyes, continue thinking about my dad.

Yes, I definitely saw changes in him on that trip home. His face seemed gaunt, but his high cheekbones looked thick, almost ape-like. At some point, I picked up my guitar—to do a duet like we used to—and tried "More," one of his favorite songs, which started with a G chord. But the smooth tone and impressive range of his voice were gone. It hurt me to hear him struggle, clearing his throat as he tried to hit the high notes. We sat in the kitchen, where the ceramic tiles offered the potential for lovely sound, but never made it through the first verse. It was the last time we sang together.

That trip home marked the beginning of the end of my relationship with my dad. For as he started to experience his losses—which continued over two decades—my father became oddly detached—from me and from everyone.

Once, on a weekend trip home from the University of Bridgeport, where I finally received my undergraduate degree, he sat with me on a Saturday morning at the kitchen table, over bagels and coffee cake, and told me he couldn't understand me anymore. With tears in his eyes, he rose from his seat to hug me. I could smell his aftershave, see the thatch of dark hair in his right ear, hear his constrained breathing. "I love you," he whispered, and I hugged him, feeling our lost connection.

On the couch, I say, "Goodbye, Dad," and again, "I love you," as tears come—fast, faster, until I'm sobbing. I remove an old tissue from my pocket, blow my nose. But as I sit up, a wave of deep grief knocks me back.

My dad's face appears again, this time as a memory—his handsome, young face, the one I've really only known through photographs. On the magnetic board in my study, I have an old black and white photo of him, half-smiling, his young body forward-leaning, impatient. My mother sits behind him on a park bench. Perhaps they're on the Brooklyn College campus or maybe in Prospect Park. Their adult lives are spread invisibly before them, the molecules of their future already coalescing.

Then I remember back to a dinner Nick and I had with my parents in the South Shelburne house. We were newly married, and Nick made a comment about needing to protect his inner life.

"What's an inner life?" My dad wanted to know. Nick

thought he was making a joke, turned to me to laugh. But I wasn't smiling and had to explain the concept to my dad, who replied quite matter-of-factly that he didn't think he'd ever had one.

twenty-three

How did I get here? To this emotional place? To Fayetteville? To motherhood? To this book? Why did I marry? Who are my children, now grown men? And my dying brother? Mother? Father?

Thought loops—carrying me in circles. I can't stop.

I'm in bed, early morning, drifting into a dream in which I'm in my study, but there's no exit in the room. Bookshelves line all the walls, and there's no door. Random books lie open on the floor. I try to skim their pages, thinking clues to my escape can be found in them. I'm wild, frantic. Then I read: *Karma lives on Flatbush Avenue. Her shoulders are hunched, and she walks with Zen, her golden retriever, on a retractable leash.* Is this woman me?

"No," she says, trying to become real, to emerge from the book, to stand beside me.

I say to her, "You're just psychic trash. Go back to the page."

Then she speaks, as if reciting an incantation, "Ghosts and dandelions, cotton lace and dirty maps with missing continents. Oxen and mountain paths. A floor smelling of incest. Words can rip you in half. Chaos, blue water. Vertigo and snow. Apologies on cardboard." Next, she yells, "I could fit my hand inside your mouth, so lick the salt off my shoes, breathe the nitrogen until my eyes melt your face."

When I wake, I'm sweating, and Jake is on the bed, licking

my face, wagging his tail.

It's Saturday morning, and Nick hasn't called for three days now. I shouldn't worry; I told him he didn't have to call every day. But then again, I can't call him. It's weird that there's no cell phone service there. The number at the retreat center is just for emergencies, and I don't think I'm having one.

I'm sitting at my desk now, having made coffee, fed Jake. And I've just written two pages. As I read over the work, I'm thinking that it doesn't make sense, that it mirrors back to me my incoherency, failures, uncertainties, issues. Which makes me crazy. I now have about fifty pages, counting my two newest pages, which I've just saved. Turning off my laptop, I let the screen go black.

I feel dull, disorganized, as I walk downstairs to the kitchen, sit at the table with my coffee, a bag of pretzels, and *Anna.* Jake appears, after coming in from outside, laying his head on my lap, then collapsing at my feet. I reach my hand down and offer him a broken pretzel ring, which he gobbles up.

Anna needs Vronsky. But the more she expresses her need, the less interested Vronksy is. Push and pull, pull and push. I think of Nick. Maybe my need of him—*do I need him?*—is driving him away.

I close the pretzel bag—empty calories—giving Jake one last broken ring, and *push-pull,* I'm back to college.

I met Nick when he and I attended the University of Bridgeport—a full decade before Sun Myung Moon, founder of the Unification Church and his followers, called "Moonies," bought the entire Bridgeport campus, turning it into what many suspected was an indoctrination center. Back then, UB was an above-average university with a few strong programs, among them the creative writing program run almost single-handedly by a little-known but well-published poet with a strong personality and a wonderful ability to nurture talent.

I'd heard about UB and its creative writing program at Nassau Community College, where I was taking a Spanish class one summer, and where my mother was enrolled as a nontraditional student, a rarity back then. She'd always wanted to go back to college, to become a professional woman, so she started at the community college the year I left for Shimer College.

In high school, I'd accelerated my academic program. By tenth grade, I decided that I wanted more academic challenge. I longed to read philosophy and literature, to have important discussions about the nature of art and culture. I'd been reading, studying on my own, and my high school classes had failed to engage me.

So, during tenth grade, I came up with a plan for the summer: I would go to C. W. Post College, part of Long Island University out in Brookville, New York—way out on the Island—live on campus and take all my eleventh-grade classes on the college level so that I could return to high school as a senior. I'm not sure how I convinced my parents or Lawrence High School administrators that this was a good idea, because it had never been done before, but I did.

That summer of 1971, with a roommate named Sandy Sondheim, I lived in Riggs Hall, enrolled in Sociology, Cultural Anthropology, American History I and II, and a basic English/Comp class. I had to petition the dean because, as a non-matriculated student, I was taking an overload, which was against the standard academic policy. Somehow, though, I made it all happen—though other stuff happened, too.

I did a lot of drugs that summer—pot, cocaine, psychedelics. Many of the students at C. W. Post came from wealthy families, drove fancy cars, did recreational drugs. One student, a diplomat's son from Brazil, owned a Lamborghini, and he took me for an incredibly fast ride down the narrow rural roads that connected the far reaches of the North Shore fishing villages all the way out to the tip of the Island. The sixties had ended, but the word wasn't out.

One night, Sandy drove me in her royal blue Mustang convertible to a mansion in Greenvale for an all-night party. The house was on the beach, and we swam naked under a full moon. Some of the guys were professional musicians and had just scored a large amount of cocaine. We snorted it, rubbed it into our gums, listened to the guitars, the lovely male voices accompanying them, then dove into the warm waters of Long Island Sound.

The next afternoon, I had a sociology exam; despite staying up all night and arriving back in my dorm at dawn, I managed to get sober enough to study and pass. And ultimately, I kept my grades up enough that summer so that when I returned to high school, I was, as planned, a senior.

But by then, I felt myself to be a full-fledged college student, no longer interested in completing high school. So, when I heard about Shimer College—a small liberal arts school that accepted "early entrants"—bright young students, capable of college work but who hadn't yet completed high school—I applied and was quickly accepted.

I dropped out of high school in November, and by spring semester, which began in January, I arrived in Mount Carroll, Illinois, about a hundred thirty miles due west of Chicago. My high school principal had agreed to award me a diploma after I completed a certain number of college courses, but to this day, I don't know in which year I officially graduated. I think my mother picked up my diploma, but somehow it got lost in the shuffle of moves.

I loved Shimer. It had a Great Books curriculum, so we read and discussed important primary texts in translation. All courses were five credit hours; students enrolled in three per term. Classes were conducted as seminars, and students were expected to read between five hundred to a thousand pages per week. The school used a New Critical approach, and we read the works without ever researching their historical or critical context. In fact, the Shimer library was very small, and students were discouraged from doing any supplemental reading outside of class. We were supposed to think deeply— on our own—about the texts we read. Also, the courses, Humanities I, Social Science I, Natural Science I, were all deliberately linked, so historical and philosophical contexts were actually embedded.

I loved the assigned readings, the discussions. At the end of my first semester, I met Sonya, who I now consider my best friend, my sister of choice. We cemented our friendship during the summer after that first semester by traveling across Europe together.

After Europe, I returned to Shimer for another semester— my last. Sonya also returned but was losing interest in her studies there as well. Then, after my second semester, I'd decided that I wanted to study creative writing, but there was no way to do that at Shimer.

So, I enrolled at Campus Free College—an unaccredited college "without walls," where students invented their own curriculum. I decided that I'd live in Manhattan to study writing. Somehow this decision was okay with my parents, and through an apartment-sharing agency, I found Diane McCain and moved into an extra room in her flat on East 81st Street between East End and York Avenues, a block from the East River.

Diane was twenty-eight; I was still seventeen. She'd had a daughter out of wedlock and had sent the child to live with her aunt in Jersey City. Diane was depressed—about her daughter, about her derailed life, about her parents' recent divorce, about her chronic unemployment and low income, and about her failed attempt to complete a college degree in sociology at City College of New York.

But we immediately clicked. Diane loved my intellectual curiosity, my courage to take on this unusual course of study, what she called my bravery. I was to pay her $75 a week to live in her small apartment and agreed to sleep on a mattress in an alcove between her bedroom and living room. My sleeping area had no doors, no privacy. After Sonya and I had returned from Europe in the summer, I had worked my old high school job as a dental assistant and saved about $1,000 to pay for rent and living expenses for my year in New York. My folks paid the modest tuition.

The semester's curriculum—which I had designed myself—involved studying drama and theater with Arthur Stein, a playwright and theater critic for the *Village Voice*; studying poetry with Helen Burstein, a Bank Street Cooperative poet; taking Existentialism, a 300-level undergraduate course offered at The New School for Social Research and taught by Paul Edwards, a well-known contemporary philosopher; and studying modern dance with Barbara Gardner's Construction Company, a small performance group in the upper East Village.

Two weeks into the semester, however, I arrived home late one evening to find Diane unconscious, sprawled out at the foot of her bed, with pills dumped around her and a notebook open with "Please forgive me. Mother Mary, please forgive me," scribbled over and over on its pages.

I remember walking the apartment's one narrow hallway to call 911. The operator asked me if Diane had a pulse, and I had to walk back down the hallway to find out. Holding Diane's arm and concentrating, yes, I recognized a weak one. Time became distorted; my legs felt like rubber-bands. When I returned to speak to the operator, I couldn't find my voice.

I opened my mouth to say, "Yes, there's a pulse," but nothing came out. I had to struggle to find my voice. I did, but barely.

When the ambulance came, two medics carried Diane's almost lifeless body on a stretcher down multiple flights of narrow stairs. The dimly lit hallway recalled a Grade B film noir movie, in which I had a small supporting role. I rode with Diane in the back of the ambulance to Lenox Hill Hospital, where she had her stomach pumped and finally revived. The doctor in charge came out to the small ante room where I waited alone and told me that had I arrived home fifteen minutes later, Diane would be dead.

I spent the winter helping Diane recover. I also hooked up with Marty, a man in his 30s who ended up raping me. After Diane's attempted suicide, I'd become unable to sleep and found myself in a downward spiral. I'd met Marty in Washington Square after class, and we became friends.

Then one night when I was feeling particularly depressed and isolated, I went to Marty's apartment, and he raped me. I never reported the incident because I felt I'd been to blame. But also, there'd been something familiar about the experience, as if Marty knew, expected my complicity. And weirdly, after many years, I found Marty's photo in *Newsweek*, running along the story of how he had raped hundreds of young women in New York over decades. Most never reported, but finally two women had, and Marty had confessed and was convicted.

Suffice it to say that after this experience and Diane's attempted suicide, I gave up my studies at Campus Free College. I returned home to live with my parents, took Introduction to Spanish at Nassau Community College, and commuted to campus with my mother, meeting her basic general education requirements while studying psychology. It was there that I connected with an English professor who recommended the University of Bridgeport for its Creative

Writing program. I was tired of nontraditional approaches to education, just wanting now to complete my undergraduate studies in Writing as quickly and painlessly as possible. I applied, was accepted, and by the spring semester, in the middle of January, found myself in Bridgeport, Connecticut.

It was during that spring semester that I met Nick in my first official creative writing class. I loved his short story, "Headed for Canad'y," about a couple of draft dodgers headed north to escape induction and a tour in Vietnam.

I approached him after class, asked if we could get together to discuss his story. Nick thought I was coming on to him when I invited him up to my dorm room, where he tried kiss me, and I insisted that he leave.

"Are you throwing me out?" he'd asked.

"Guess so," I'd said by the open doorway. "Time for dinner, anyway."

"Can I see you again?"

"Maybe. Perhaps. I'll see you in class on Wednesday." I'd gotten my sneakers and jacket on.

"No. You know what I mean."

"I'll walk you down."

Later that week, however, I agreed to see Nick again. On our first "date" we walked out to Seaside Park, a long stretch of beach that opened up to the Connecticut side of Long Island Sound. And that stretch eventually turned into the city landfill, where we continued to walk. Somehow, it was all romantic— and we continued our stroll—even around mounds of garbage, broken appliances, and feeding seagulls that squawked as they fed, and we took in the mixed smells of brine and rotting food pungent in the air as we talked philosophy and finally sat, at one point, on a concrete bench together near the sea.

We continued to see each other. I liked him, but certainly felt nothing stronger. He, on the other hand, by the fourth time we got together, insisted that one day I'd marry him.

"Yeah, right," I'd said. I was still seventeen—even after my four months in New York City—and marriage was the furthest thing from my mind.

After a rather rocky beginning—I dated other boys even as Nick continued to pursue me—we finally became a couple and pretty much inseparable.

For my eighteenth birthday, we went drinking—the legal age then—with a bunch of our college friends at the Sportsmen's Pub, a working-man's bar on the outskirts of campus, near the docks of Long Island Sound. I got drunk on Rum and Coke. Looking back, I remember only small moments from that night: walking into the bar, insisting that we sit at one of the round tables by the window where the Sound stretched mirror-like into the night, Nick by my side, proposing a toast to the girl he'd one day marry.

So, it's Saturday. Saturday, Saturday, Saturday. My thoughts are chaotic, even paranoid. I imagine that Nick has found a young woman writer or artist with whom he's having an affair. Maybe there's no woman but only a newfound freedom with which he's fallen in love.

Afternoon now, but I'm not hungry. I need to get out of the house. Perhaps some retail therapy. I offer myself a bargain: take the clothing I'd previously identified as unwanted, sort it into throwaways and giveaways, bag it all, and bring it to the garage so that it's ready for Goodwill. Then I'll treat myself to a modest shopping spree. I've spent the morning trying to write then reading on the sunroom couch, but now, motivated, I go upstairs to make good on my bargain.

In my bedroom, I turn on NPR, the "Talk of the Nation" as background to my purging. Obama is fighting with Congress, and the Tea Party is fighting to repeal Obamacare. In Afghanistan, car bombers have blown up a van near a marketplace—thirteen dead.

Holding in my hand a thrift-store blouse I'd bought but never worn, I feel saddened as I sit by Jake on the edge of my bed. It's in the "keep pile," but now its polyester fabric and muted paisley design strike me as very out of fashion. Why did I buy it? Why, during my first sorting, did I decide to keep it? It's all very sad. I weep over the shirt, but really, I'm weeping for our broken government, our divided country and violent world, my potentially broken marriage, the mess of my life, my dead father, my dying brother.

By 2:00, my clothing is bagged, my crying jag is over, and I'm feeling better. Bags in hand, I descend the stairs, go to the garage, and find a good spot to leave them until I can give them away.

I feed Jake an early dinner in case I'm late getting home, change into my North Face roll-up pants, a black tight-ribbed tank top, and a button-down cotton over-shirt. I've retrieved the two garbage bags full of clothing I no longer want and now plan to drop them off at the Goodwill on Raeford Road before I hit some clothing stores.

My plan is to go to T. J. Maxx, then Talbots. This way, I'll avoid the mall, which isn't pleasant, though it's been recently remodeled with high-end marble tile and a new food court.

I'm thinking that I'll shop for school outfits—new stuff to teach in, wear to meetings, etc. Maybe I'll even try on shoes. I have foot issues, and for the last twenty years have only been able to wear Birkenstocks. My podiatrist has told me that Birks are a great solution and that if my Morton's Neuroma were to act up again, I'd definitely need surgery. My feet are also flat, and the Birks with their high arches correct my pronation.

At T. J. Maxx, I start combing the racks—first sale, then clearance. But I'm not having much luck. Nothing school-appropriate, nothing out for fall yet. I meander over to the shoes to find a pair of clogs—which I love and slip on—but they immediately hurt my feet. I'm discouraged but then, returning to the pants rack, I find a pair of black skinny jeans on sale, along with a heather-gray cotton sweater and a sleeveless hot pink knit shirt. Might lift my spirits, I think, as I decide to try them on. But in the dressing room, as I pull off my clothes, stand in front of the full-length mirror in underpants and camisole, I look at myself, immediately getting depressed. My breasts are soft, stomach no longer flat, my butt, well...not good. My young body has abandoned me. There's no escaping death. "Don't get so dramatic," I tell myself, and thinking of my brother, I say aloud, "Sorry, sorry." And I'm filled with remorse.

With that, I close my eyes, sit on the tiny corner bench seat in the dressing room, breathe deeply, exhale, fight back tears.

Then, I flash back to my suicide attempt. I see the middle-aged woman I am and the young girl I was. I imagine a glass of vodka in my hand. I taste the clear, sharp liquid.

Now, I'm no longer interested in the clothes I've taken into the dressing room. I pull on my shirt, pants, return my three items to the rack outside the dressing room, and leave the crowded store.

I'm off to Talbots now, more upscale, and maybe the attention from the sales women will give me the human connection I need.

But before leaving the parking lot, I sit in my little Honda Fit, weeping again. Ruby's interior is brutally hot, but I rest my forehead down on the steering wheel, try to pull myself together.

I've wasted my life. I should have completed my PhD. I should have stayed in New York. I should have moved to Iowa when I was wait-listed for the Iowa Writing Workshop MFA program. Perhaps I should have reconciled with my brother before it was too late. Should've, should've, should've.

I find myself praying. Then, I berate myself. To whom is my prayer directed? I think of my youthful prayers to an anthropomorphic god. I think about George Bush calling himself "the decider," and now, I'm imagining God—my present image of him *or her*—as the decider.

A woman with a shopping cart walks over to the white Lexis next to me. She glitters—her silver hair is pulled into a knot at the back of her head. Her shirt is studded with small rhinestones and a bizarre pattern of pink and red swirls. She's my age, but about forty pounds overweight, and stuffed into her clothes. She lifts two large T. J. Maxx bags from the cart into her back seat. She feels me looking at her and turns to me through my car's closed window, smiles briefly—a warm, unexpectedly genuine smile. I smile back, a human connection. Then she's in her car, starting the engine, backing out, leaving the parking space empty by Ruby's passenger side.

I'm unraveling. I don't know who I am. I have no center of gravity.

Also, I'm suffering in the hot car, so it's time to move. I crank up Ruby, and hot air blows through the a/c vent. I back out of my spot, heading to Talbots, a five-minute drive. The tears have stopped, and I feel okay, better in control. I decide to stop first at the nearby Burger King, to use the bathroom, splash cool water on my face, comb my hair, straighten my clothes.

The bathroom is empty. And alone there, before I leave, I take off my glasses, and washing in cold water, I splash my face. At the paper-towel dispenser, I pump out a few sheets to dry myself before looking into the mirror—which feels dangerous. An older woman stares back at me, in disarray. Removing a comb from my bag, I run it through my hair, short, gray, not attractively cut. Oh, well.

I stand there and, for a moment, think back to Bush, "the

decider," and begin to chuckle. I lean against the tile wall of the bathroom, now laughing out loud, almost hysterically, almost enjoying myself.

In the mirror, I see that my face appears a little swollen. I feel punch-drunk and decide to shop for a few minutes in Roses, a very low-end discount store across the parking lot from Talbots and Burger King. *Get your shit together*, I tell myself.

As the bathroom door swings shut, my cell phone rings. Quickly, I open my bag to find that my phone isn't in its little side pouch, so I have to root around until I locate it, which I do, without looking at its face to determine who's calling.

"Hello," I call out, rather loudly, my back to the Burger King side exit, pushing it open.

"Hey, Mom," I hear, recognizing Will's voice.

"Hey, good to hear from you." I'm walking to the car.

"Good news. Just wanted to let you know. I'm at the Glass Center. Can't talk for long."

"Great," I say, sitting in the driver's seat with my feet out the side, car door open because it must be 100 out.

"Sold a set of my wobbly whiskey glasses, with a decanter, then a set of glasses, and a bowl. Also, got a check today for $500. So anyway, just wanted to share the news."

I can hear noise in the background, and Will's voice is loud, shouting above it. "That's wonderful. Really good."

"Yeah, and Dad called yesterday. He's having a great time. Sounded really good. Met some artists or something. Another writer. We didn't talk for long. Anyway, got to go, Mom. You okay?"

"When did he call—Dad, I mean?"

"I don't know. Yesterday. Afternoon. Late. Maybe five or six. I was on my way home...talked for a few minutes. He had people waiting to use the phone."

Before I can ask Will anything more, I hear someone call his name.

"Gotta go, Mom. Speak with you again soon."

"Yeah. Great news, sweetie. Really good. Be careful. I love you. Call when you can talk. Love you." I've blurted all this out, tears welling up again. I end the call, try mindfully breathing in and out to stop another meltdown.

In Roses, I walk around the circular display of women's jeans, Wranglers, old-fashioned high-waisted seconds. I tap them, thinking that I might look for my size, but I'm not really interested. I'm having trouble swallowing and feel short of breath. Also, I'm hungry, and my stomach feels hollow.

A young Black woman walks by with a toddler in tow. She's wearing a tight tee-shirt with the words "NEW YORK, THE BIG APPLE," written in glitter across the front. Her young son—I'm assuming he's her son—dawdles, walking with his hand extended, trying to touch as much merchandise as possible. He has a lollypop in his mouth.

An older White woman in an electric wheelchair passes down the wide center aisle. She's about sixty, with one foot wrapped in a black plastic immobilizer with Velcro straps. She holds an oversized purple cloth purse on her lap, and she's moving rather quickly toward the back of the store. She must be with someone, I think, looking around for that person, following the wheelchair with my eyes. But then the wheelchair turns by the shoe aisle, and the woman vanishes.

I'm standing by the scarf display, so I rifle through them, thinking I might find an all-cotton one I like. But I don't.

I leave through the automated door between the two security poles. Outside, the late afternoon is still scorching, and the parking lot wavers in heat that rises from the asphalt. I don't want to speak to Nick. Or anyone. I'm no longer in the mood for Talbots, with its attentive saleswomen, its orderly racks of tailored, well-designed clothing.

Outside, there's a full-length mirror by the display window. I glance at it, shaded by overhead cloud cover, and see myself— my pants hang, too baggy, unflattering, my dark cami too revealing, my unbuttoned over-shirt too loose, like an aging hippie or someone who's fighting mental illness.

I hit the key fob, unlock the door of my little red car, my Ruby. Inside, her black upholstery is again very hot, as is the dashboard and steering wheel. Nonetheless, I get in, turn on the ignition, the air conditioning , drive from the parking lot, out to Morganton Road, which will connect to Skibo, which will turn into Pamalee, then Country Club, where I'll turn left onto Ramsey Street, head north until I turn left onto Ridgeway, which will take me to my street. A fifteen-minute drive if I hit the lights right.

A psychologist I used to see once told me to watch myself for times when I remove or detach myself, feel unhooked from my surroundings. "Those moments of dissociation are psychologically dangerous," he warned me.

As I drive, I feel like a cartoon version of myself, like I'm floating rather than driving. At a light, I look to the left at the Dollar General lot to see four antique cars—restored Model As or Ts—parked with a group of people gathered around them. Then, traffic backs up. I turn on NPR to hear something about global warming—which feels very real this summer—then, I'm on Ramsey Street, and soon, I'm pulling onto Ridgeway, then onto my street, into my driveway. I turn off the engine, get out of the car— mindfully, I might add, bringing attention to every small action. I check my mailbox—four pieces of junk mail and a bill from Nationwide, either for house or car insurance.

Inside, Jake lies by the front living room window. He doesn't get up to greet me but thumps his tail. I go over, bend to pet him, then sit on the floor to stroke him lengthwise along his lumpy body.

Rising, I hang my purse on a kitchen chair, then go back to the living room, collapse on the couch, close my eyes. Tears gather. I'm a mess again.

Soft pinkish light spreads behind my eyelids—transparent, soothing, mixed with tears. It's evening now, Saturday; I've fed Jake again but not walked him—too hot out there, and I'm too beat. Sprawled on the couch, grateful to relax, I fall into a sort of trance, remembering an experience I had many years ago during college, in a sensory deprivation tank.

Nick and I had heard of the tank from a psychology student at UB. It was designed by a professor who was doing experiments with it—although I'm not sure about the nature of those—the tank was made available for students and faculty to use free of charge.

Nick and I walk down concrete stairs into the basement of an old building. There are lockers where we can change and clean towels that we can use to wrap ourselves once we undress.

A grad student, a man in his thirties with black hair and tortoiseshell eyeglasses, asks to see our student IDs, takes down information about our academic majors, and records it in a log.

When I ask him if there are any dangers involved with using the tank, he turns to me and says, "If you're going to go bananas, it's in the cards."

Nick and I exchange looks. Bananas? In the cards? Not very professional language. And what is he implying? That the tendency to go insane is predetermined?

Nick decides to go first. I wait in the locker room, sitting on a bench, reading *Pride and Prejudice* for a Brit Lit survey class while Nick is in the tank. The Psych Department's policy is that no one is to remain longer than a half hour.

When Nick's time is up, the grad student walks into the room, and, a few minutes later, Nick returns, wet, wrapped in his white towel.

"How was it?" I ask.

"Sort of boring," Nick replies and sits down by his clothes on the bench near me.

"Is that it?" I stand up, put my book in an empty locker, indicating to the grad student that I need to get undressed.

"I'll leave you alone for a moment. Call when you're ready," the student says as he leaves.

"Don't expect much," Nick warns. He's back in his chinos and pocket tee-shirt. He, too, has brought along a book.

Wrapped in my towel, I call the student, who comes, then leads me to the back room, which is very dark.

The tank is located on a wooden platform in the middle of a small room. When the door opens, I see the platform, the tank, and the concrete-block walls, all painted black. The student awkwardly tells me that I'll have to be naked for a moment with him as he gets me situated in the tank; then he'll close the lid and return after the half hour. If I panic, he assures me, I can simply push open the lid and call for help. Otherwise, he'll see me in thirty minutes.

Taking my towel, he explains that he's placing it on the platform, near the lid. Just in case.

"In you go," he says.

"Yup," I agree. In I go.

The water, exactly body temperature, requires almost no adjusting to—unlike getting into a hot bath, a swimming pool, or the ocean. I hear the water lap gently against the tank's sides. It's rectangular, like an over-sized coffin, large enough to stretch out my arms, not touch its sides, and long enough so that I can float effortlessly.

After I'm in, the student asks if I'm okay and if he can close the lid. I tell him yes.

The tank is rather shallow, I quickly realize, but the water is so saline that I float with ease. I hear the tank hinges creak a little, feel the lid close, and there I am.

"Cool," I say aloud in the tiny chamber. I like my voice, so I hum a few bars of "Amazing Grace." I don't hear him, but I assume the student has left the room. I begin reciting Hamlet: "To be or not to be: that is the question. Whether 'tis nobler in the mind to suffer the slings and arrows of outrageous fortune..."

I open and close my eyes to see if there's any difference. There isn't. Then I think about how much time has passed. I don't know. I settle down, thinking that I should just "be" with myself. A Zen idea, a pretty good one, so I tune into my body, listen to my heartbeat, think that perhaps I can even hear my blood coursing through my body. But no, I'm not hearing that. Just the occasional lapping of the water if I move and the feeling of my body swaying.

I begin to relax, not that I'm tired exactly, but my brain is letting go. By now, I'm not interested in thinking anything, so I don't. Then, I feel sad. Not sadness connected with any particular thought, but body-sad, as if all of me were rising and falling in a full-body breath. No thoughts. The clarity is nonverbal. Tears well up in my eyes, rolling from my cheeks into the water. I feel sad, yet whole, nourished, with a soul, an essence.

I don't know how long I stay in this state. I feel on the brink of a comfortable death, on some edge of consciousness, drifting in a place touched by sadness, softness, deep acceptance.

When the student comes into the room, he says, "Time's up. I'm coming in, about to lift the lid. I have your towel."

"Not ready," I manage, finding my voice.

"Time's up. Got to get you out." As he lifts the lid, I see dark light. He extends a towel, which I take from him, wrapping it around my torso, stepping from the tank.

By the doorway, he hands me the clipboard, asks that I sign my name on the log by the time slot, where he's written the exact times I entered and exited the tank.

In the locker room, Nick asks, "Well, how was it?" I can't answer. No words come out of my mouth. I simply nod.

"You okay?" he asks. I nod again, begin to dress.

—∞—

On the couch, the experience strikes me as perfect therapy—healing, oneness with self. Far better than the talking and cognitive therapies I've tried.

I hold myself back from tears. Triggered by my memory of the tank or just generalized weepiness? Maybe it's that Nick hasn't called. Or my isolation. Am I falling apart?

I'm in the kitchen now, preparing my new dinner favorite: two grilled cheese sandwiches and a salad. Jake, who's been sleeping on the front rug, trots into the kitchen to check his blue ceramic dog bowl that I see needs to be washed. I scour it with hot, soapy water, dry it with a paper towel, then remind Jake that he's eaten. Regardless, he expects something, so I crumble some bread, settle his bowl down, and he begins to eat. I start on my grilled cheese sandwiches with the same bread that Jake's having for dinner.

It's quiet now in the house, too quiet. I turn on the kitchen radio, catch a snippet of a news report—a woman has been raped and murdered by a gang of ordinary young men on a public bus. I miss where she's from, but only hear that she was a university student. A female lawyer for the victim's family explains that violence against women is common and underreported. She calls for immediate action, and an NPR interviewer asks how this issue has impacted public awareness. But now, I turn the radio off. Not good company for my black mood.

Silence again as I make my sandwiches, pan frying them in a combination of olive oil and butter. I use organic cheddar cheese, and as the sandwiches sizzle, I make a small salad.

I'm out in the sunroom with Jake, eating my dinner and reading my novel. At the end of *Anna Karenina,* Anna goes crazy. Not crazy-crazy, but she loses perspective, becomes paranoid. In this frame of mind, Anna kills herself. Attentive readers already know where the story is going; in the book's beginning, Anna witnesses a man commit suicide by throwing himself in front of a train. The foreshadowing might seem a little too obvious, but most readers have forgotten that scene because it occurs so early in a very long book.

Like so many of my favorite books, I've read *Anna Karenina* probably a half-dozen times. Rereading a beloved book is like sitting down to eat comfort food—it delivers the satisfying tastes, textures I expect and love. Yet there are surprises as well—while the recipe is the same, each time it cooks up differently so that the experience yields something new.

I'm on the last hundred pages; I've been taking my time, savoring, paying close attention to the narrative's pace, the sense of inevitability.

Tolstoy, with his great omniscience, drills deep into his characters' hearts. I understand how Anna gets crazy, why Vronsky can't see Anna's desperation and instead feels trapped by her needs. But has Tolstoy shortchanged his female protagonist? Perhaps Anna would be more sympathetic, especially to the contemporary reader, had she left her passionless marriage as an assertion of her independence, a refusal to conform to social norms. But she leaves Karenin and her son, Seryozha, whom she loves, for a romance with a man who doesn't know himself.

Of course, Anna doesn't know herself either and when she begins to suspect that Vronksy has found another woman, she decides to punish him by taking her own life. This is a version of the adolescent who attempts suicide to punish the inattentive parent. But perhaps most suicides involve desire for punishment. In a flash, I'm brought back to my own suicide attempt, my own inattentive parents, my need for self-punishment. "Anna," I say aloud, "I'm with you."

twenty-four

It's the next evening; I've taken Jake for his walk, fed him, and eaten some spicy garlic broccoli from the Chinese take-out place near Food Lion. Nick tried calling me yesterday, but I missed him. I was in the shower, didn't hear the phone, and couldn't call him back. Frustrating.

I've taken *Anna Karenina* out to the sunroom again. Anna is fighting with Vronsky, who's doing his best to minimize the argument. Convinced that Vronsky is being unfaithful, Anna suffers. Vronsky, disappointed that Anna's husband won't give her the divorce that will allow him to marry Anna, just wants to leave the house, to do something pleasant, like play cards with his soldier friends. Anna's position as a mistress preys more on Vronsky than it does on her. Anna insists that marriage is not, and should not be, important, while Vronsky believes that normalizing their union through marriage will help his career and their relationship. But her status as a marginalized woman impacts Anna's mental health more than she knows.

I turn pages, lying on the couch, ceiling fan whirring above, Jake panting on the floor, trying to nap in the evening heat. As much as I don't like Anna for mistaking her thoughts and feelings for reality, I continue to empathize with her.

Sleepy now, I rest the heavy book, spine open, across my belly, allowing Anna mystical and direct access to me. I drift off.

—◊—

I'm walking a muddy trail in my dream, near the summer camp dude ranch I attended so many years ago. I'm barefoot and slipping constantly. I grab a branch for balance, and as I pull myself up a particularly steep incline, the branch comes alive—transforming into a human hand. A bright sun radiates through the woods, blinding me; I can't see who's helping me.

The moment, perhaps, takes fifteen seconds, but my dreamtime is playing in slow mo, perhaps 120 frames per second. My right foot slips downward, sinking into soft mud while my left foot, my lead foot, catches on a large rock embedded into the ground. The woman's hand I'm holding so tightly—for the branch is clearly a woman's hand now— is sweaty, slippery, so the dream is characterized by losing ground, grip, clarity.

Slowly, the hand pulls me up, and I feel like I weigh three-hundred pounds or that I'm carrying a backpack filled with bricks, inhibiting my climb upward. "Help," I whisper, sensing that I'm both on the sunroom couch speaking these words while in the dream speaking them. I think: *This is my life. I can't lift myself; something is weighing me, holding me down; I'm stuck.*

I exist in two realms, on two planes—one involves my younger self, the other involves my current self, and they're both exerting equal pressure, occupying the same space-time continuum. The woman's hand loosens for a second, then re-grips, now more strongly connected to my hand. Her strength pulls me forward, upward. My right foot lands next to my left on the boulder; I'm no longer floundering. And the sun has moved so that I see a mountain top, where there's a flat plateau and a trail that continues.

I hear horses, as if people are waiting for me. Then I hear a loud whistle and the sound of a long train rattling across tracks.

Suddenly, I'm not sure if I should trust the hand I'm

gripping. The train whistle frightens me. I think of Anna. I don't want to climb the up to the trail. But I can't relinquish the woman's hand because I'll fall.

The sun shifts position again; I look up to see my mother's face to realize that it's her hand I hold. Yet, her face looks so much like my own that I wonder if I've become my mother.

After one strong yank, I stand on the rock, balanced, my muddy feet firm, and because I actually do have on a heavy backpack, I take it off, releasing my mother's hand. She lets go reluctantly. The heavy pack rests on the rock beside me, and my mother has climbed up on a clump of birch trees, similar to the clump located in the yard of our South Shelburne home.

"Rae," she says in an authoritative voice, "Come with me. Now." My mother is in her late thirties, with raven-black hair, red lips; she wears a brown polyester pants suit from the seventies, with matching four-inch heels. *How she got up there in those shoes,* I think, *is a miracle.*

"I can't, Mom. I just can't come. I need to get down to the valley, to camp. The horses need to be broken." I look into the stand of birch trees, the white parchment-like bark creating a rural Russian forest, one that Anna might recognize.

"But you'll miss the train. And your brother is dying." My mother hops down from the birch trees, brushes off her clothing, smoothing her suit jacket like she's ready to leave. "You're going to regret not seeing him, and your brother is going to be disappointed." She shakes her head, admonishing me. "You never listen."

"But Mom," I insist. "Anna is about to kill herself."

"I know, Rae. But we all have to die."

I shoot awake with bullet-like force. Jake breathes heavily, asleep by me. I'm sweating, dripping, and as I sit up, the novel slips from my belly to the floor. The room is dark, so it's got to be past 9:00.

I get up. Jake comes with me. In the kitchen, I check my phone for missed calls. Nothing.

The a/c feels great, and I think I'll change into my nightgown, bathrobe, watch another episode of *Hit and Miss,* though I don't have many left.

Upstairs now, I feel inclined to write, even though it's late. Yes, the book. I'm writing two to five pages every day. What began as an exercise—to write organically, without a plot, specific characters, conflict—has become a novel.

For a couple of hours I sit, typing away—Jake on the futon near me. I write about a childhood memory of spilling my milk all over the wobbly Queen's apartment kitchen table.

The story is painful: I get blamed for intentionally spilling my milk, for making a mess on purpose.

"Accident," I insist. I'm two, maybe three years old, in my pajamas, barefoot at the table. My mother yells, threatening to hit me.

"Clumsy!" she yells, grabbing a sponge, wiping the spill.

The memory moves to my dad. I awoke from my late afternoon nap with thoughts of him just beneath consciousness. I switch from writing about the spilled milk to writing about him, remembering that before he died last year, I wanted very much to see him, to say goodbye. My mom agreed that I should come down to Florida, to the residential hospice facility where he was placed after he could no longer live at home and his doctors couldn't do anything for him. I hadn't seen him for years, and I wanted to touch him, see his face, tell him that I loved him.

I bought a round-trip ticket to Fort Lauderdale, booked a hotel near the hospice, rented a car. I was supposed to leave from the Raleigh airport on a Friday, when I had no classes, return on that Sunday afternoon. It was mid-April; my dad died in early June. He was still conscious most of the time, although with his dementia, he wasn't always coherent. I agreed to take my chances. This visit was for me as much as for him; I needed closure; I wanted to say goodbye.

Then, less than a week before I was supposed to leave, I received a snail-mail letter from my mom, telling me not to come. My visit would be "too difficult for the family during this tension-filled time."

My mom went on to write, "I have to ask that you don't come. I can't explain myself right now, but I hope that you'll understand and trust me."

I never went. Instead, I canceled all my reservations.

I still have the letter, written in my mom's distinctive hand, its regular, even script with large upper and lower loops, very pleasing to the eye. I loved my mother's handwriting. When I was a young girl, I would trace it by taping a sheet of blank paper over it, then taping both sheets to a window, where the light made her letters distinct through the top paper. Her hand suggested control, strength, regularity. No matter what happened in our lives, my mom's handwriting was always the same.

On one occasion, I took an absence note she had written to excuse me from school after a brief illness, traced her note completely and handed in my forgery, keeping her original note. My forgery was never detected.

Her letter to me was also well-written—as all her documents are. My mom's grammar, sentence structure, paragraphing, organization, transitional language are as lovely as her penmanship.

I think about my mom, her handwriting, and realize how much I'm digressing. *No worries,* I tell myself, *life is all digression.* I write.

At some point, I discovered her high school yearbook in her night-table drawer. I sneaked it out of her bedroom and put it between my mattress and box-spring, an illicit book with photos of my mom taken before I was born. In her senior portrait, her young brilliant face is caught in its frame, alphabetized in a neat row along with other black and white faces. So many lives.

I'd take that book out at night sometimes and would dream about my mother. Not night dreams, but fantasies in which I might bump into her in the hallway of her old Brooklyn high school. Or I might watch her as she found her seat in English class. Or I might hear her laugh with her girlfriends in the school yard or open the girls' bathroom door as she brushed her hair.

On page fifty-two, my mom had a short essay on "rain," with another student's artwork adorning the margins around the piece. I'd read and reread that piece, paying close attention to every word, how her sentences were put together, how tightly she paragraphed them. Her vocabulary, her word choice struck me as superb. I'd speak the piece out loud sometimes, trying various inflections so that I could bring her essay fully to life, to thereby better understand my mother.

After I'd slipped the book back in the drawer, one day I followed my mom into her bedroom as she was making the big king bed in which she and my dad slept. I sat on the floor by her closet, near the nightstand, opened up the drawer, pretended to find the yearbook for the first time.

"Oh, what's this, Mom?" I asked, quickly leafing through the volume to find her piece.

"Nothing. Really. Just my old high school yearbook."

"Look, Mom. You have a piece in here. Can I read it? Wow." Without waiting for an answer, I stood up, began to read the piece aloud in my best practiced way. She wore a pink gingham duster with snaps down the front. Her hair, always teased and set, formed a little hair helmet around her face. I seldom saw that face without makeup, but this morning it was washed clean. I had the piece almost memorized, and my inflection, I thought, was just about perfect. It began:

Rain. I have seen the rain fall all my life. I have heard raindrops beat against my windowpane, in a fury, as they spoke to me—about today and tomorrow, the unwritten future for which I long...

I don't remember more. But there was a descriptive part when she sits down near the fire escape, opening her window to listen to the rain. As she does, she thinks about escaping her own life, until she climbs out of the window, sits on the metal grill, allowing herself to get soaked. She's alone in the scene. As she gets soaked, she reflects that this is what life is about—being part of it, getting wet, angry, happy, or disappointed. Always saturated with life.

I'm sure I fail here to do the piece justice. And yet if I read it today, I'm sure I wouldn't be quite as impressed as I was then. But I was about twelve years old and felt incredibly honored to stand in front of her, to speak her words aloud. I had fallen in love with those words and I stood in the bedroom—window shades halfway drawn as they always were, day or night—offering my mom a gift: my best dramatic reading of her essay.

The last word in the piece was "rain," capitalized and punctuated as a sentence. An intentional, effective use of a fragment and a repeat of the fragment with which the piece began. Cohesive, coherent, so smart. Yes, I was full of admiration.

"What do you think, Mom?" I asked, the book still open like a hymnal in my hands.

"What do *you* think, Rae?" she retorted, never looking up at me or stopping her bed-making, pillow fluffing.

"I think it's beautiful. Perfect. You never told me that you liked to write."

"I wrote it for senior English, and my teacher, Mrs. Shapiro, wanted to put it in the yearbook. I didn't like it then and still don't." She hesitated, the bed with its blue duvet and matching pillow shams had been made so firmly that the bed was completely tight, smooth. My mother's touch always so exacting.

"I love it. I wish I could write like that."

"No, you don't. Put it away. I ought to throw it out. That and everything else in the drawer. It's all clutter. Old junk. Really, Rae." My mom forced a smile, then retreated to her walk in closet.

I tucked the book back in the stuffed drawer, realizing that there might be other things there that would be equally as interesting, things that I should definitely look at before my mom makes good on her threat.

Soon, my mom emerged from the dark closet with a pair of slacks and a sweater in her hands. "I need to get dressed now," she said. So, I left, closing the bedroom door respectfully behind me.

My mother's letter to me, written in that lovely regular hand, so careful, with so much attention to how she weighed her language—what she said and didn't say—left me with admiration similar to that which I had felt so long ago for her piece on rain. Here, her grammatically perfect sentences, with intentional fragments for emphasis, read like a song, a painful song: "...too difficult during this tension-filled time"—all the lovely hard consonant sounds, conspiring against me. The song of *done, don't do, don't come, don't be*.

With that, I'm done writing. I'll watch TV, those last episodes of *Hit and Miss*. Try not to think about my mom, dad, brother...who I am, or the stuff the transgender protagonist brings up for me. Instead, as I watch, I'll turn to my knitting, the rhythmic knotting of yarn.

twenty-five

I wake to a ringing phone. Actually, I was awake but not up. Although it's Monday, not Saturday, when Cal usually calls, I immediately know it's him. Like the last time we talked—on a Monday. At thirty-one, he's an early riser, though I remember as a teenager, he could sleep, if I let him, until 2:00 in the afternoon.

I find the phone in my darkened bedroom, catching the call before the ringing stops.

"Hello." My first word of the day.

"Hi, Mom. Were you up?"

"Just lying in bed. How are you? What's doing?" I rise from bed, walk downstairs to fix Jake's breakfast, make a pot of coffee. I can use the bathroom and brush my teeth in the hall bathroom by the kitchen, where I have an extra toothbrush and toothpaste stashed.

"Nothing much, just thought I'd call. I'm back from Chicago and have the morning off. Work in town this afternoon, then tomorrow I'll be driving down to Albany. Got stuff with the state for the rest of the week."

"Great. How was Chicago and how are you? Jess at work?"

"I'm good. Chicago was good. Everything's good. Jess is at work and definitely applying to Boston U's Masters of Public Health program. She found out that she can basically do it for free." I hear a plane roar overhead and wait until it passes before speaking.

"Will the bio-statistics class she's taking count?" Jake now has his food, the pot's heating on the stove, and I'm quietly brushing my teeth.

"Oh, yeah. She'll have that out of the way and then take another summer class."

"It's a lot to manage with her job, yes?" But my real concern is the subtextual message I'm hearing: they won't try to get pregnant again. Commitment to a demanding academic program suggests that they've given up trying for now.

"I told her that, but she wants to do it. One or two courses a semester. Hang on, Mom."

I hear Cal talking to someone, background voices. I hear someone say "Grande."

In a moment, however, he's out on the street. I hear the exaggerated sound of wind through the phone.

"Okay," Cal says.

"Where you off to now?" I ask.

"Headed back home, do some work there. I have a 1:00 appointment at MIT. Walking distance."

"How's the weather?" I ask.

"Overcast today, and it's chilly, actually. How are you? Heard from Dad?"

"Fine," I say. "I'm good. But no, I missed Dad's calls a few times," I lie. "So we haven't caught up lately." I'm now pouring boiling water into the Chemex.

"You lonely? What you been doing?" The wind is gone, and Cal's voice is clear.

"I've been writing. I'm fine."

"Well, I should go, get to work. Just wanted to say hello."

"Sounds good," I say. "Appreciate the call." Now, sitting on the sunroom couch, coffee in hand, I'm feeling deflated, a balloon with a loose knot, air escaping. "I love you," I say.

"Yeah, Mom. Love you, too."

I hit the end-call button, put my cell phone on the low table. The morning cool is quite lovely, and Jake now joins me. But I'm feeling lost again. I was feeling good with Cal on the phone, but that energy has dissipated.

Outside, two blue jays bathe in our little poured concrete bird bath. I imagine that they're a couple. One stands on the ledge, like he or she is in charge. The other stands in the middle of the bowl, preening itself, fluffing its wings. A squirrel runs along our privacy fence and jumps up to a longleaf pine branch by the back shed. The limb sways, shakes. The squirrel is gone. A summer day. I think again of Mary Oliver's "The Summer Day," this time focusing on her remark that although she doesn't "know what prayer is," she does "know how to pay attention, how to fall down on the grass." I agree. The world closely observed offers us grace.

Then remember another Oliver poem, "The Journey," remembering its first lines:

One day you finally knew
what you had to do, and began,
though the voices around you
kept shouting their bad advice—

I think of all the bad advice bombarding me now—from the dead and the living. They're no longer whispering but rather shouting.

Oliver goes on to write:

though the whole house
began to tremble
and you felt the old tug
at your ankles.
"Mend my life!"
Each voice cried.

But you didn't stop.
You knew what you had to do...

But do I? Can I mend my mother's life with money? Or my brother's with forgiveness? Or my own?

I watch the blue jays, still in the birth bath, and breathe deeply. Do birds have lives that need mending? I look closely at them. One is much larger than the other and is more deeply colored. The smaller bird has a wider, shorter beak and now stares at the larger one on the ledge. One chirps; the other remains silent. Then, as if on cue, they take flight together, rising into blue sky. No mending. Just flight.

I'm going to have a good day, I tell myself.

Upstairs, I write. Three hours, without interruption. I'm feeling better. I've completely abandoned the earlier novel I had planned during the semester and had worked so hard to outline. It's all okay. Just good that I'm writing....

About remembering—stuff from childhood, adolescence. Now, with six new pages, I'm feeling satisfied, ready to stop. I think, in fact, I'll reward myself with a trip to the outlet mall in Smithfield, about fifty miles up I-95. A little retail therapy in some new places. I'm feeling better about myself for the first time in days. I deserve a reward for my six pages.

Soon, I'm in Ruby, traveling on the interstate, listening to NPR. A female host is discussing something with a male guest. He's a soldier who's written a book, and although I can tell he's got something important to say, I'm not in the mood. The hot bright sun penetrates the windshield as I cruise past the Wade exit. The Carolina blue sky overhead is cloudless, open, inviting. Everything is possible.

I hit the tuner, scale up and down the FM dial until I find an oldies station. Yes. There's Mick Jagger singing "Satisfaction." Yes, yes, yes. I blast up the volume as Ruby's interior vibrates to Jagger singing me back to 1969. I lock in the cruise control at seventy-three.

I-95 is a straight shot; there's little traffic. In the left lane, I shoot past a gaggle of slower moving vehicles—a UPS truck, a Walmart semi, an old white Cadillac—and the road opens.

I can't get no...satisfaction...I can't get no girl-reaction, 'cause I try, and I try, and I try, and I try...I can't get no, I can't get no...

—∞—

I'm on the Island Railroad now, rattling through Queens on my way to Penn Station, where the Stones will be playing at 9:00 tonight. It's late November. I've fought with my parents to let me attend this concert—and won—mostly because there'd be no subway ride late at night as I'd only need to get from Penn Station downstairs to Madison Square Garden upstairs.

Three-fourths of the train commuters this evening are concert goers, so I've purchased a one-way ticket, suspecting that the train will be packed on the return trip, that the conductor won't ask for tickets.

At the concert, Tina Turner struts onto stage: the first warm-up act. She's done up with a spectacular Motown hairdo, a tight leather mini-skirt. But the audience isn't pleased. A Black guy with a bandana across his forehead sits next to me, shouting out that she looks like one of the whores working 42nd Street. She dances around, singing a few songs; then she's gone.

Next, B. B. King comes on—warm-up act number two. He's completely fabulous, but no one is really in the mood for his slow rhythm, his electric blues. He sits on a chair center-stage, a relic from some other time. The audience listens politely, though still impatient.

After King, the stage goes empty. The crowd, having waited long enough, begins to chant like an oversized tribe of hungry cannibals. I'd been sitting in the far back of the center mezzanine, close to the aisle, having bought a relatively cheap seat. But when someone off-stage finally yells, "And here they are, the Rolling Stones," the crowd surges forward in a wave of mad energy. I'm lifted by the crowd, carried to the center, directly in front of the stage. We all stand on top of the theater-style seats, on the flat wooden arm panels, bodies raised, everybody screaming.

When we'd surged forward, the guy next to me almost got trampled, but now I see that he's gotten to his feet. One woman, I notice, has climbed onto another guy's shoulders, standing up as if she's performing some weird cheerleading routine.

Then, Mick Jagger dances onto the stage as the crowd shouts, "Mick! Mick! Mick!" Jagger launches into "You Can't Always Get What You Want" while everyone goes absolutely crazy. I too am caught up in the frenzy, the chaotic madness. The new guy next to me wears a tie-dyed tee-shirt, ripped low-rise bellbottoms. He's extremely hairy, and as he lifts his arms, his belly hair and chest hair are so thick that I think—yes, we're definitely descended from apes.

The concert continues, song after song, a frenzy of energy and magic, until the final couple of encores.

After the concert, I'm electrified as hordes of young people pour onto the escalators that carry them into Penn Station, onto LIRR trains, back to our homes and beds so that tonight we may sleep, and tomorrow resume our uneventful lives.

The conductor, as I predicted, doesn't collect tickets in the standing-room only train, leaving the station well past 1:00 a.m. I stand next to a burly guy with a full beard and long hair. He introduces himself with a joint, which is being passed around to all riders. In fact, lots and lots of drugs, most visibly pot, are being consumed.

The guy tells me that he's a college student, that his name is Strike. I like him. He asks for my phone number, which I give to him. I tell him to call me Ramona, my new nickname, and that I'm eighteen, a high school senior, planning to graduate in spring.

Even now, riding in Ruby on this stellar morning, I can see Strike's face, feel his large sweaty body next to mine as we balance, our hands holding the same pole as the train leaves the Garden, rattling down the tracks to one of its first stops, Laurelton station, where Strike gets off. He's wearing a red plaid flannel shirt, blue jeans, and a thick black leather belt with a huge silver fish buckle. He's got on hiking boots, no jacket. A large-faced Timex is strapped onto a studded black leather watchband. His hand, eye-level with my face, grips the pole as the train shakes to a stop. I look at it, see that it is rough, grizzled but clean, and that moment—as I stare at Strike's hand—becomes a short video clip that I replay now, as I've replayed it so many times before, although it is unimportant.

"Satisfaction," is over. My thinking has taken me far away. I feel my hands on Ruby's hot, black leatherette steering wheel. Tears well up. I pull the visor down, hoping the culprit is the strong sun, not the memories. Why can't I escape my past? But maybe that's the wrong question.

I near my exit, move to the right lane, turning on my blinker. The mall is actually a collection of strip malls with gaping black parking lots in between. The spaces closest to the stores are filled with vehicles, and I drive around the two main areas to get the lay of the land. I've only been here a few times before, with Nick, when we purchased some baskets and a wicker papasan chair for the sunroom at Carolina Pottery.

I park out a way, but in the lot closest to Banana Republic and Talbots. I wander in to Talbots first, and a saleswoman asks, "What can I help you with today?" Startled, I look at her, an older woman with teased, well-coiffured dyed-blonde hair, a wrinkled and made-up face, and wearing black slacks that make her butt appear strangely flattened.

"Just looking," I reply, and touch a rack of blouses.

"We have some excellent sales today," she continues and walks, assuming I'll follow, down a twisted trail between round and linear racks to one against the back wall, where a sign reads "75% off lowest ticket price." She stops, opens the palm of her hand, like a magician. "Our lowest prices of the season." And steps back.

"Thank you," I say, moving toward the two racks—one high, one low—beginning to riffle through the shirts. I find a blue button-down one, check the label to see the fiber content. The shirt feels like a cotton blend, but it's mostly polyester, so I return its hanger to the rack.

Ultimately, I do buy a few things: a light blue cotton sweater, something I know I'll enjoy wearing to work, along with a deep pink tee-shirt that fits well-enough and can be worn either under a jacket to school or with jeans.

The day passes swiftly; at some point, I realize I'm enjoying myself. I speak to other women shoppers in dressing rooms—a sort of instant camaraderie, as we offer opinions about the success or failure of the pants, the shirts, the sweaters, the skirts we try on. When I come out of the dressing room in Chico's with a beige, classically designed pencil skirt, one woman looks me over. "I like that," she says, to which I ask, "Not too short?" to which she replies, "Perhaps." I nod, telling her, "No knees," and point to them. The stranger laughs. "I know what you mean," she says.

I love this dressing-room intimacy. How a strange woman's opinion, offered at the right moment, seems so sisterly, so connecting. I feel oddly solid, a physical feminine presence.

My secret: I am in disguise as a real woman. I look the part, and everyone reacts to me as if I am the real deal. Have I fooled them? But I am a woman, aren't I?

At the register, just as I'm putting away my credit card, offering my last smile to the nice saleswoman who has helped in my selection, my cell phone rings. "Thanks again," I say, exiting quickly with my purchase folded neatly in white tissue paper, packed so nicely in a shiny white plastic bag with the store's signature ribbon curled around the handles. Outside, I open my messenger bag and say "Hello," trying to glance at the name appearing on my screen.

"Hey," I hear. "How have you been? Sorry I haven't been calling. Can you speak?" I recognize Nick's voice and trot out to Ruby, where I plan to sit with the driver's side door open— in relative privacy.

"Yeah, good to hear from you. I've been a little worried." I cross the parking lot, the asphalt wavering in the late afternoon heat.

"Nothing to report, really. I'm fine. Writing every day. Finally got to meet some of the other writers here, so that's good."

"Oh," I say. I click open Ruby's doors, throw my few purchases onto the backseat, then fit myself behind the wheel so that I face the open door, legs and feet dangling. The car's interior, however, must be well over a hundred degrees, and I'm immediately sweaty. I sit down anyway.

"How about you? You doing okay? What's new?" A long pause.

I decide not to tell him that I'm out shopping although I can't think why. Suddenly, I have little or nothing to say. "Everything's fine. It's just good to hear from you." I feel my face grow super-hot as heat spreads through my entire body until I'm experiencing a full-blown hot flash. I'm melting, and now something more—tears again. I strain to hold back sobs, sitting miserably on Ruby's black interior cloth, just wanting to get off the phone.

Nick is quiet for a long time. Then he says, "You don't sound okay. What's up?"

"Nothing," I insist. I'm angry, but I can't tell if I'm angry at Nick or at myself. A young mom carrying a baby in a chest papoose walks by. The baby, I see, is sound asleep, head jostling loosely as the mom walks by—a paper bag in her hand, an enormous blue diaper bag slung across her shoulder. I think of myself—*my self*—in young motherhood, twice—each time a life-changing experience in which my idea of self was altered.

"You still there?" Nick asks. "What's going on, Rae?"

Instead of lying, I tell him. "I'm shopping at the outlet mall in Smithfield. I'm in the car. It's very hot."

"That's all?" he asks. "You sound upset."

"Nothing. Just hot. Hot and tired. End of the day." I'm fighting many strong emotions, and it's urgent now that I hang up the phone. "I guess you didn't catch me at a good time." Immediately, I regret my words. I really do want to speak to him. So, I say, "Tell me about your friends there, what you're doing. What you're working on." But as I ask, I realize that I don't want to know. I'm just asking for the sake of keeping him on the phone. Though I'm not even sure I want to talk.

"Look," Nick says, "I'll call you later," a note of dissatisfaction in his voice. "Anyway, I got to go; someone needs the phone."

"Okay. Call me again. I love you," I say, grasping, wanting something but not sure what.

"Yeah. Love you, too. Take care. Take care of *yourself*," Nick adds.

"Right. You too." I hit the end-call button, lean back on the seat. Tears fall as I ready myself for the big cry I've been holding back. But then, in a second, the feeling is gone.

I slam the driver's side door closed, start the engine, turn up the a/c, buckle myself in, and off I go. Home? Right now, I'm not sure.

—ɷ—

Does Nick love me? I turn onto the I-95 entrance ramp and descend into rather heavy but fast-moving traffic. I merge into the left lane, increasing my speed until I'm going 70 in the 65-mph zone, and hit the cruise control.

Well? I ask myself. When he's with me, yes. But connections need to be immediate; neurons need to fire all the time for love to stay. I think about my father—who was my original model for the man I married.

In some sense, my father abandoned me late in his life. But no, I think, that's not fair. I try to remember the last time I saw my dad. I can't. Was it during a visit to Florida? Or the time my parents drove up to North Carolina for a weekend visit?

As I think back, I switch to the right lane so that I can float behind a huge mail truck and drive a little less mindfully. I begin to craft memory from small moments. Ordering dinner—where were we? Yes, I remember, the trip to the Georgia coast.

That was our last time together. My father was becoming deaf but wouldn't acknowledge it. Instead, he insisted that it was we who didn't speak loudly enough. Or he'd blame the TV stations that broadcast at too low a volume. He'd turn up the sound until the room reverberated with a laugh track or until the roar of some football game. Our hotel rooms adjoined, and the TV sound kept me up at night, as he'd usually fall asleep in front of the set, like a dead man in a room full of shouting voices.

The heavy traffic is now stop and go, as Highway 301 merges onto I-95, and I'm carried back to South Shelburne, remembering that when my brother's gambling first became an obvious problem, my dad wanted to throw Dennis out of the house. Tough love, he insisted. Later, after another gambling crisis, after Dennis had moved into their Florida condo, my dad again wanted Dennis to move out. But my mother wouldn't hear of it. When my father threatened to leave her, she told him, "Yes, go."

But he wouldn't, of course, ever leave her. My mom made the big decisions in their marriage, and my dad responded by falling further into deafness, then dementia—perhaps both, successful strategies for absenting himself.

Ultimately, my dad turned against me. I lived too far from him geographically and had separated from my family of origin in a way that Dennis, with all his problems, hadn't.

I sigh, approaching my exit, which I dutifully take. *Duty.* I am a dutiful teacher. A dutiful mother. A dutiful wife. But not a dutiful daughter. I'm stung by my own accusation. Tears come again, blurring my vision as I follow the exit's curve onto the I-295 connector that will take me to Ramsey Street, approximately two miles from my home. Jake awaits me, I tell myself. Duty.

—⚊—

At home this evening, in the sunroom, I read *Anna* rather than watch TV, stopping at around 9:00 when I've lost the light. I put down the book, thinking about Anna's desperation, which leads me to think of my mom's desperation, about our family's falling-out five years ago, my father, his move to hospice and death last year.

Five years ago, they'd all been in that duplex, renting from the Cuban family who lived next door. At some point, Lydia had moved to her one-bedroom in Tamarac and was barely in contact with Dennis or the girls. I don't know the formal custody arrangement—or if there was one—but Dennis had the girls, was gambling heavily, and they were always on the verge of being evicted.

My mom and I had a bad argument that year, and she insisted that she couldn't in good faith continue our relationship. Like Lydia had, she felt Nick and I were abandoning the family. They'd fallen behind on their rent and been threatened with eviction.

"Rae, what are we going to do? Live on the streets? Is that what you want?" Mom asked. She needed $1,500 and promised to pay me back as soon as she received my dad's social security check.

"Mom, I can only give you $500. Not as a loan, a gift."

"Rae, thanks. Thank you. But it's not enough. I need $1,500. Can't you wire it to me?" My mom's voice, stressed, became loud, demanding—but carefully demanding.

"Mom, I don't have that kind of money." At the time, we were paying off Cal's college loans, had a mortgage, car payment, Will's college tuition, and our living expenses.

"Can't you borrow against your credit card? We'll pay you back, plus interest." She'd breathe, pause, exhaling her ghost cigarette.

"Mom, no. We won't do that. The fees are ridiculous. Anyway, you're not going to be able to pay us back." I sat in my bedroom on the wicker armchair.

"What do you want, Rae?" she asked. "That a mother should have to beg? Would that make you feel better?"

I didn't give her the $1,500. I knew that Dennis would keep gambling and that whatever amount I gave to her would never be enough.

"Mom, tell me where to send the $500. You don't have to pay us back."

"Use Western Union. Tell them Tamarac." Weary, she knew she'd lost the battle, but she'd take what she could.

"You need it tonight? Or can I wait until morning?"

"No, I need it now, tonight. I have to give something to the landlady. She's such a bitch, Rae. Then she starts shouting in Spanish. Really. I just hope it's enough. Some people. Give me a call after you wire the money."

I agreed.

And after this call to say that I'd wired the money, she broke ties. Nick and I figured that we probably gave my parents more than $20,000 before the break. The $10,000 was the largest single amount. But there were many, many smaller amounts throughout the years—some loaned and repaid, but many given as gifts. This was my therapist's suggestion. Give what you can comfortably give but don't "loan" because you can't control the outcome. You won't be tied to an expectation.

My therapist was right: because when the $10,000 was never completely repaid, I felt betrayed, lied to, hurt, angry. On some level, I knew my parents could never pay back a loan of this size, but I felt that I had to believe them; they're my parents and wouldn't let me down.

Then my mom would get testy if I'd bring up the money she owed. "You think I forgot, Rae? You think a day doesn't go by when I don't remember what I owe you?"

"I don't know, Mom. If you never mention it, I can't read your mind."

Once, Nick got mixed up in one of these loan requests. I'd been out grocery shopping when my parents called, and my dad ended up speaking to Nick. My dad wanted to borrow another $1,500—the standard request amount. My dad probably already had some dementia at the time, but it was undiagnosed and his responses were erratic—sometimes clear, sometimes appropriate, other times not.

Nick had tried to explain to my dad how the loans and non-repayment made me feel—that when I trusted my parents to pay back loans and they didn't, I felt betrayed, like a trust had been broken. At this point, perhaps in a moment of candor, desperation, or as a consequence of dementia and his filters not working, my dad simply said, "We just need the money; I don't care about Rae's feelings."

After my dad said that, Nick hung up on him. Later, my mom wrote one of her famous letters to me in which she recalled the conversation differently, faulting Nick for being so disrespectful as to hang up on his father-in-law. Nick became very angry, and to this day, curses whenever he recalls the episode, which probably contributed to my mom's decision to sever the relationship.

All of this I think about, sitting in the darkening sunroom. Then about not seeing my dad before he died. When he was transferred to hospice, my mom had called me to say that my dad was dying. She wanted me to know and for the family to reconnect. I agreed, and we both apologized. I made my plans to fly to Florida, but then my mom wrote me the letter, telling me not to come.

"To hell with what she thinks. Go see him anyway." Nick had said. "He's your dad! She doesn't get to call that shot. You do." With that, Nick had walked out of the house and into the garage, where he often paced.

I followed him out, shouting, "If I'm not wanted, I don't think I should go."

"She's only taking care of herself," Nick yelled. We stood alone in the cluttered garage, then walked back into the house to talk. Cal had moved out, lived in Boston with Jess, who was still in nursing school, and Will lived in Cleveland, attending art college. Jake, sensitive soul, had put his tail between his legs and had scurried upstairs, where he'd be away from our yelling. I took the letter back from Nick, who'd been waving it around. "Let me read it again."

But ultimately, I went upstairs to my office and called Expedia, who held my reservations. After hearing my story, the woman agent helped me cancel all my tickets and absolved me of most of my financial responsibilities connected with the trip. I think there were some minor penalties, but these came to less than $50.

After a few days, I called my mother. She apologized but was firm about me not coming. I quickly understood that Dennis was behind the decision.

So, I imagined my father in hospice. I pieced together details from my mother's description. I'd asked my mom lots of questions: What does the hospice look like? Is it a free-standing building? Is it located on a busy street? What does dad see from his window? Is he in a private room? What's on his night-table? Is there a TV in the room? Where is it located? Where do you sit when you visit? Does Dad get out of bed? Is he taken to a day-room? Does he walk or is he in a wheelchair? Who are the other residents? How many of them live there? When you visit, with whom do you speak? Is there a social worker? Are there aides whom you've gotten to know, who know Dad? What are their names?

I needed to visualize everything, to form a kind of mental diorama so that I could place myself there. I even asked my mom to describe my dad's blanket, to tell me specifically if it was tucked in with hospital corners, and if the bed had a metal side-bar that could be raised and lowered. In this way I was able to construct an imagined vision of the place where my father died.

—⚬⚬—

The building is brick and free-standing. The social worker in charge of my dad's case is a French-Canadian Buddhist nun. She's completely bald and has always been so, having been born with some congenital condition. She likes my mom and willingly engages her in philosophical conversations about life's meaning, the nature of suffering. She tells my mom "to accept," and "to love the man by letting him go."

I see her lanky figure as a shadow—everything but her face, which I imagine as having high cheekbones, a pronounced nose, gray eyes. Her name is Agnes, a German name, and she speaks with a slight French accent although her English is perfect. My mother loves to hear her voice, with its softened consonants, perfect grammar.

My dad has a private room at the end of a hall. The building is a single story, accommodating twelve residents. My dad's window opens to a courtyard with a lush garden, brick-paved walkways. My dad is wheeled out during his first two weeks, but he's bedridden after that. Every afternoon after work, my mom visits him; her new telephone sales job consists of selling greeting cards made by handicapped artists to businesses throughout the country. So, she talks to lots of people and actually enjoys these conversations during which she charms, cajoles, sells. In fact, my mom is already the second highest producer in her sales group of ten.

twenty-six

This is what I know—pieced together and imagined.

It's late in the day at the hospice; the intense South Florida sun is low but still saturates the sky. My father lies on his side, stares out his open bedroom door to the hallway, watching people walk by. The TV is tuned to *Wheel of Fortune,* the old game show he's enjoyed for years. Today, as my mom comes into the room, my father recognizes her, the love of his life, the only woman he has ever desired.

"Ed," he says. "Take my hand." My mother sits on an upholstered side chair that's been pulled up to my dad's bed.

"Bernie," she says, "oh, Bernie," forcing a smile, for his sake.

"Where am I?" he asks, shifting his emaciated body to indicate that the room is unfamiliar.

"You're here, in this facility, where you need to eat and get strong so you can come home." She squeezes his hand, large-boned after the acromegaly.

"I'm thirsty, Ed. Could you get me some juice? I'm sick of water." My mom gently strokes my dad's head, smoothing his comb-over so it lies nicely over his mostly bare scalp. My dad smiles. His dentures are white and clean, his smile is genuine, his expression grateful.

With a plastic cup of apple juice and a bent straw, my mother returns to the room. But by now, my dad has closed his eyes.

"Bernie?" my mom questions. No answer. She places the cup on a tissue in case the cup sweats on the wooden night-stand.

And she sits, waits with him.

An aide brings him dinner—a slice of roast beef, a small mound of mashed potatoes, a tablespoon of peas, a wedge of iceberg lettuce.

"Bernie," the aide says, "Blue cheese with that?" My dad opens his eyes, smiles.

"Yes, honey." He turns to my mother, who has stood up, placed her chair back against the wall, picked up her purse, is about to leave.

"She knows how I like it," he says to my mom and winks.

"Bernie, I'd better go. You've got your dinner. Eat. Get strong."

The roast beef is one of his last meals. His dying begins at the Sabbath, or Shabbos—Friday at sundown—and ends on a Saturday, before Shabbos is over. It's a Yiddish word; in Hebrew, it's Shabbat, but at our home, we used Yiddish. My mom and dad grew up speaking English and Yiddish; both of them were fluent. Around the dinner table when my parents didn't want Dennis and me to understand, they spoke Yiddish, which, with effort, I did learn enough to understand, although I never could speak it. When my friend Sonya and I hitchhiked across Europe after our first semester of college, we traveled through Germany—much to my family's dismay—and I understood German because many of the words are so close to Yiddish.

According to the Old Testament, God made the world in six days, and on the seventh day, Shabbat—the noun form of shavat, a Hebrew verb meaning "to rest"—He rested. It felt appropriate that my dad's dying began at sundown on the beginning of Shabbos and that his death occurred before the

Sabbath was over.

After dinner that day, my father becomes mostly unresponsive, then comatose. What happened, what precipitated his decline at this particular moment, no one knows.

The next day, a Saturday, my mom visits, stays the entire day. Dad sleeps, no longer waking in intervals as he usually does. His breathing is labored.

My mother later reports to me that she speaks to him, but he never responds.

"Bernie, I love you," she says.

She holds his hand; he slightly squeezes hers back.

"I know you can hear me," she whispers, bending so that her face is near his. His warm breath is precious to her.

The aides and staff hang back, coming to the doorway to check if anything is needed but not entering the room.

My mother tells me how the sun enters the room through the slats of the closed blinds. How all that last day she sits by my dad's bedside, listening to the heavy traffic on Commercial Boulevard.

My mother weeps. She retells the stories of their youth— and I take a moment to recall a couple of the stories she's told me.

My mom and dad met through a friend at Brooklyn College, at a dance in the gymnasium. Mom was nineteen; Dad was twenty. But even before they were introduced, my mom had noticed my dad—a handsome young man and wonderful dancer, as he let go across the wooden floor, doing a wild version the Lindy Hop with a partner who couldn't keep up. After the song ended, Mom's friend Belinda, noticing Mom's interest, took her over for an introduction.

"Bernard," Belinda began, "this is Edna. Edna, Bernard."

"Bernie," my father had responded, offering to shake hands

as the next song began. And when Mom took his hand, the introductory handshake became an invitation to dance, which they did. And they danced together for the rest of the night.

Coupled with this memory is their proposal story—how Dad had proposed to her at the Brooklyn Botanical Gardens, where they'd gone on a date. It was an unusually warm March Saturday, and they held hands, strolling through the outdoor gardens, barely in bud. Then, they went inside to the extensive hot house, where exotic flowers were kept in bloom all year. Mom admired the aisle filled with "Birds of Paradise," and Dad suggested they sit on a nearby bench. Then, Dad got down on one knee as a small crowd gathered to watch. Almost a cliché—albeit a romantic one—Dad had said, "Eddy, you're the love of my life. Will you marry me?" Mom had told him "yes," thrown her arms around him, and the group had applauded.

Shifting back to my imagined death scene, I hear Mom remind Dad how handsome he was back then, with his thick wavy dark hair, regular features, his shining brown eyes, expressing both mischief and passion.

She doesn't tell him that he has lived the wrong life, that he wasted his talent for math and engineering when he appeased his parents by going into business with them. She doesn't tell him how his love for her subjected him to an inauthentic life—how he gave her what she wanted, how he sacrificed himself.

I think about how many times my father wanted to throw Dennis out of the house: when Dennis would borrow money from bookies or from low-level Mafioso, when he'd lose a bet or lose at the track, when he'd steal.

Once, when we still lived in South Shelburne, I'd come home from college to hear my parents fighting about Dennis, who was out for the night but had recently stolen my mom's diamond necklace, a valuable piece of jewelry she'd inherited from her mother.

"Ed," my dad began. "A little tough love. Dennis needs consequences." He stood by his clothes closet, getting dressed for a formal dinner.

"Never," my mother said in her best definitive voice. She could command an army with that voice; soldiers would walk into active fire and die because of that voice. I, certainly, was afraid of it.

"Ed, when will it end?" my dad asked, knotting his tie, even before his pants were on. He looked at himself in the closet's mirror, as I walked into the room with them: my dad's handsome figure, standing in his boxer shorts and white shirt, my mom in the master bathroom, fully dressed in a black sequined dress, fooling with her hair, finalizing her makeup.

"I'd rather die than send Dennis away. Do you understand? He needs us. He'll get over this. This gambling is just a phase. Would you send me away if I had a problem? Would you? Is that who I married?" Her voice was stern, dictating exactly what could and couldn't be said.

"This isn't the time. We'll talk again," Dad said as he noticed me there in the room, then pulled his pants on, neatly tucked in his starched white shirt, and put on his suit jacket before slipping on his black patent shoes. He approached my mom, who brushed him away until he insisted, and gently hugged her.

I had watched them, stood there like a shadow, a hollow shell of a person, embarrassed in front of such love, such devotion. I realized then that my dad adored my mom. She completed him.

—◊—

I've been lying in the sunroom for over an hour. Thinking that the past is like looking down a deep well. Yet I keep looking, drawn by its cool darkness and dank magnetic pull.

I sit up, hungry, deciding to make myself a cheese omelet

and toast for dinner.

Jake trots with me into the kitchen, reminding me that he, too, is hungry, so I get his bowl, fix his meal, place it on his mat. But now, suddenly, I have no energy for the omelet, so I sit at the kitchen table. "Dad," I call aloud. And he appears.

I'm back in South Shelburne, where Cal, still a toddler, and I are visiting my parents. Nick, having a long paper to write for a graduate class this weekend, has remained at home in Endicott, grateful for the time to work. We're both in graduate school at SUNY Binghamton, now Binghamton University.

When I come upstairs, having put Cal to bed in his port-a-crib, I join my parents at the kitchen table, where we talk mostly about their upcoming move to Florida. They've signed with a realtor and must empty, clean, and paint the house over the next month. They're hoping the house sells quickly as they've found a luxury condo they'd like to rent, possibly purchase, in Lauderhill, a suburb of Fort Lauderdale.

Dennis, a night manager for a commercial cleaning company located in World Trade Tower II, is working tonight and won't return until almost 9:00 tomorrow, Saturday morning. This visit to my old South Shelburne house might be my last.

For some reason, the conversation shifts to Dennis as my mom explains that he's gambling again and what little good jewelry she has left has been locked in their safety deposit box. She bows her head, hands folded on the table as if in prayer. Then she stands up, walks over to the prep area, nearby but enclosed by overhead cabinets, with only the pass-through connecting the table and the working part of the kitchen.

But just as I think of how odd her action is, my father clears his throat. "We need to tell you something, Rae. Something important. Something we should have told you years ago."

My mom opens the dishwasher and unloads. I hear

the clanking of plates and silverware, ordinary household sounds, but carefully muted so as not to wake Cal perhaps, or perhaps so that she can distract herself but hear the difficult conversation she knows will follow.

"What?" I ask. My father lowers his head, plays with a paper napkin on the table, folding it, then tearing it along the creases into neat geometrical shapes, squares and rectangles.

"Do you remember when we were robbed in the apartment, Rae? When Mrs. Goldstein brought you home from nursery school that day?"

"Of course," I say, staring at him, slumping now, mechanically dividing the last half of the napkin.

"Well, what we didn't tell you, because you were too young, because we needed to protect you, because we loved you..."

"What?" I ask. "What else happened?" But I already know.

My dad takes a deep breath, lifts his gaze from the napkin, looks at me, his eyes saddened, wearied. "The assailant forced Dennis to perform oral sex on him. At gun point. I mean the guy held a gun to Dennis's head and made him do this."

My mother appears by the table. "We should have told you a long time ago. But we could never find the right moment." I see her standing in her pink zippered duster. "We're sorry. I'm sorry."

Perhaps I should get up, go over to hug her. Reassure her that not telling me for all these years was the right thing to do. But I don't. The moment is not about her. It's about secrets. How they reveal themselves. It's about impact. Collusion. About things too awful to talk about. Also, it's about Dennis tying me up. Dennis's "mad" and "glad." His lying, his gambling. Perhaps more.

"Why tell me now?" I ask.

"Mom and I wanted you to know why we've helped Dennis so much, how responsible we've felt for him, his problems.

Mom should have been home that day when Dennis came home from school."

"Rae," my mother begins, her voice soft but clear. "We're giving him $5,000 when the house sells so that he can start his adult life in New York without us, when we move. If he mentions the money, we want you to know why. Dennis won't be coming with us. This is our time for a new beginning."

My dad chimes in: "We can't afford to give you any money. Just him. Even that's going to be a stretch. But we want you to know why, the history."

He and my mom look directly at me. *Waiting for some outburst?* I wonder. *Some huge response?* I move my chair back, away from the table so as to speak to them both. "This makes sense," I say. "This explains a whole lot."

"Are you upset, Rae? With us? Dennis? Just tell us what you're thinking. We wanted you to know before we left New York. But this is difficult, very difficult for us. You can't imagine."

"Nick and I could use some money," I say.

"I only wish we could give it to you," my mom says. "But we can't, simply can't."

"Dennis isn't quite launched yet," my dad adds. "You know that. He needs our help. We just wanted you to know why."

I stand up. "Thanks for telling me. I wish you'd told me a long time ago. But that's okay. I know now." As I rise, my chair makes a scraping sound against the ceramic tile floor. I tuck it neatly back into its place under the table top. "I'm really tired, and Cal probably won't sleep the night, so I'd better get to bed. I'm sorry about Dennis. I mean what happened."

My father remains at the table, napkin now transformed into two small orderly piles of white squares and rectangles.

My mom backs away, allowing me access through the kitchen to the stairs so that I can descend to the guestroom where Cal sleeps. I wish I had something profound or forgiving to say. But I don't. I only know that I must get out of the room, be alone. Something's still missing, a puzzle piece, a memory, one that I can't reach.

"I hear you," my mom says. "I only hope that you'll forgive us. Or understand, now that you're a parent. We couldn't tell you. We couldn't do more than we did. But you know now. That's what's important."

I'm halfway down the stairs when I hear my dad call after me, "I love you." My mom repeats, "I love you." I should call out the same: *I love you.* But the words are part of a liturgy I can't perform.

twenty-seven

Days have passed and I've written nothing. I haven't had the courage to face the page. It's been a strange silent time with little contact from Nick, Will, or Cal. The days are so hot that I keep all the window blinds closed and the air conditioning set at seventy-two.

I'm watching TV, which I've been doing a lot, and it's only midmorning. As a family, when Cal and Will were growing up, we had a policy of never turning on the TV until after dinner. Except for Saturday early morning cartoons that the kids were allowed to watch for a couple of hours.

I sit in front of some morning show, and the host, a well-dressed, good-looking generic woman in her late thirties, holds up a book and talks in an overly animated way about marriage.

"This book will change the way you relate to your spouse. Guaranteed. If men are from Mars and women from Venus, Marilyn's book will guide you both safely to the same planet. Here, you'll learn how to communicate in the same language and act with forgiveness, not grudges. I know with Brian..." she pauses slightly, turns, looks at a cameraman, then laughs are heard all around. "I know, I know," she says. "The point is that Marilyn has answers, and all of us married people need answers. Right? After the break, Marilyn will be back to give us some of her answers. Let me tell you, they work." The camera cuts to an Allstate insurance commercial in which a man assures us we're in good hands.

So, what's the problem between Nick and me? Are we still together? Why haven't I been hearing from him? Are we from separate planets? Speaking different languages? Has our marriage finally unraveled?

I snap off the show. I'd turn on *Hit and Miss,* but last night I watched the last episode. I go upstairs, through the shadowy house to my computer, having decided that I'll inventory all the important people in my life—think about and write about—my relationship with them. Then, I'll inventory all the important events in my life, sizing them up, determining their values and effects. Take stock. Get myself right.

First, though, I'll shower, get dressed, make the bed. I feel disordered, like I'm losing it. Crazy and suicidal people, I've heard, let themselves and their homes fall into disarray. They stop caring. But I won't let that happen.

Having made these decisions, I feel better, cheerful actually, as I get into the shower, let the hot water stream over me. I bring awareness to this moment—a shifting of attention—something I do when I meditate. But the challenge is to take this focused attention "off the cushion," into daily life. There's the difficulty. I breathe consciously and meditate. The water encourages this, the enclosed space of the shower stall encourages this, and I stand in the downpour, opening myself.

At the end of *Anna Karenina,* Levin, the fictional surrogate for Tolstoy, contemplates the nature of his life, of life itself.

"What is life's meaning?" Levin asks plainly. As he struggles to answer, he realizes that the peasants have something to teach him. They live their work, which is tied to the natural world—the seasons and the physical labor of tending crops. Earlier in the book, Levin joins the peasants as they scythe wheat for harvest. The rhythms of bending, cutting, collecting, and moving from swath to swath create a transcendent experience for Levin, one that frees him from intense intellectual activity yet connects him to the earth and to his physical being.

By the book's end, Levin connects this simple work to God. In sync with the rhythms of his labor, he's in sync with the rhythms of life and the seasons—which become both literal and metaphorical. And here, Levin finds God.

After my lovely shower and my brief focused meditation, I sit at my computer, about to take inventory as I planned.

People first: Nick, Cal, Will, Jesse, Suzanne. Next: family of origin: mother, father, Dennis...Lydia? Yes. Julia, their first born? Yes. Hannah, whom I've never met? Yes. Friends: Sonya, Jackie, Claudia, Elizabeth, Joel, Phoebe, Donna...and newer friends: Naomi, Diana, Stephanie...great women I've met. But my list seems short. I stop.

I think about death. Suicide. *Why?*

The next list: "things I have"—a house, many books, a computer, a car—the list here is very short.

At the end of *Anna Karenina,* Levin becomes an existentialist—to do is to be. When he finds himself doing the physical, necessary, simple work, his life has meaning. It's as if our existence is best felt in our muscles.

How would I do it? Anna throws herself under a train in a prolonged episode of desperation. She thinks she has no choice; Vronsky has lost interest in her, her husband won't give her a divorce, she can't love her daughter, and she's lost her beloved son. After she tosses her bag and jumps beneath an oncoming train, timing her jump so that she falls in between its wheels, she immediately regrets her decision. Beneath the train, she realizes her suicide is a mistake. She wants to stand up but it's too late.

I read over my inventory and think of each of the people on my list without me. Nick first. Yes, he'd miss me, feel guilty for not calling more often this summer, not realizing how desperate and depressed I'd become, but he'd move on. My death might even liberate him.

I think of Cal—he'd miss me but he's married, perhaps thinking of a family of his own. Will, well, he'd take my suicide hard. My death would open a dark door. But he'll marry one day—perhaps Suzanne—and find his way forward with his art.

My friends? Ultimately, they wouldn't be affected. A few sad months, and I'd be an interesting story.

Life goes on without us. Inventory over, computer off.

—⁂—

I'm dressed now, in Ruby, driving north on Ramsey Street, which turns into Route 401, so I'm traveling the slow road to Raleigh. Why not?

Traveling about ten miles above the posted limit, I think of having an accident, driving off the road, steering into oncoming traffic, which would be selfish, so it's a thought I immediately dismiss. I think of going home, drinking some hard liquor. We have rum in the credenza. Maybe I could overdose on my old sleep meds—I have a full vial in the cabinet. Last year I worked hard to get off them, and although successful, I've kept the entire stash, just in case. But would they kill me? Or just leave me incapacitated? Another botched suicide attempt would be the worst thing.

We have a rifle or shotgun of some kind—I don't know the difference—taken from our friend Judith when we were all in graduate school together. She kept it in the trunk of her car and was going to kill herself with it during a particularly difficult month. Her son had been fathered by the man she loved, and she didn't love her husband, her son's legal father. I don't remember the whole story, but after Judith had told us about the shotgun, Nick removed it when Judith parked at a nearby grocery story. Judith knew Nick had taken it, but they never talked about it, and Judith had never asked for it.

But I don't know how to shoot. *What am I thinking?*

In Fuquay-Varina, I see a Dairy Queen, decide to treat myself to a thick milkshake made with bits of chocolate or candy. Food therapy. Something sweet. Something to connect me to my body. And now that I've had this idea, I'm obsessed with it.

I'm in the turning lane when I burst out into sobs. But there's a lot of traffic, and I need to cross two lanes to make my turn. I wipe my face, try to get a grip. Instead, I see the faces of drivers and passengers locked in their automobile cages— blank faces, talking into cell phone faces, smoking cigarette faces, dead faces.

A guy pulls behind me in a black Ford Explorer, also to turn into Dairy Queen. Then, with a small break in the traffic, I go, and he follows. I park, but he drives to the dry cleaners next door.

I pull in between two empty parking spaces, turn off the engine. The sun is intense, and the car, without the a/c, immediately becomes unbearable. I'm no longer crying. I feel numb, blank.

I get out of the car, lock Ruby, and, before going to the Dairy Queen, a rack of colorful items on the sidewalk by the strip mall catches my attention. As I walk there, the man from the black Explorer comes out of the dry cleaners, holding a gaggle of wire hangers tied together, clothing draped in plastic, his hand lifted high to prevent dragging them. He notices me and smiles. I smile back, headed to the rack that I now see is part of the Dollar General store, attached to the narrow strip mall. It's an old, decrepit building, with racks of $1.00 tee-shirts lined up in front on the sidewalk, along with stacks of big blue baby pools, shelves of half-dead petunias in plastic tubs, and broken glass by the curb.

When I was living in New York City, after Diane tried to kill herself, I felt so alienated and disconnected that I had taken a shard of glass I'd found on the street and slashed my palm—just to feel something.

But it hadn't worked. My hand bled, but I couldn't feel it, and I pocketed the glass as a souvenir, leaving it in Diane's apartment when I moved from the city.

Now as I walk, recognizing a similar alienation, I imagine picking up a shard to see if cutting my hand might now help me feel something. But I'm older and dismiss the idea.

Looking up, I see a young White woman with a toddler in tow. She wears tiger-striped leggings and a jazzed-up gold-threaded tank top. The toddler, her son, perhaps, is dressed in superman pajamas and has a dirty face. As I stare at her, she looks at me, frowns. I glance away, deciding to walk back to the Dairy Queen.

Inside, the atmosphere is as forlorn as it was at the strip mall. This Dairy Queen hasn't been remodeled in years. The Linoleum tile floor is cracked, uneven, the few tables are shabby, seats with ripped upholstery, and even the red service counter is dull, beat-up. The side freezers, full of Dilly-bars and ice-cream cakes, have a dirty look to them, and the motor makes a shrill hum. I get in line behind an older couple with matching navy velour sweat-suits. They order two small chocolate cones. The place only has vanilla, however, as the soft-serve chocolate machine is broken. So, they reluctantly change their order to vanilla.

My turn comes, and a young man in a red Dairy Queen golf-type shirt and stained black pants asks, "Your order, ma'am?" I tell him I'll have a small Turtle Pecan Cluster Blizzard, to which he says, "Yes, I'll have that for you in a minute. Would you like to pay first?" To which I say, "Yes," and hand him a five-dollar bill. As he moves to the register, I notice his right hand is deformed and doesn't have all its fingers. He offers me change with his left, smiles, nods as he turns to fill my order.

All the details of my life are happening now in slow motion now as I bring such focused attention to each moment. *Depression,* I wonder?

The older couple leaves. Now a Black woman with a tight skimpy shirt and stretchy pants comes in. Her hair is braided into a thousand strands, a sort of medusa, and as I look into her face, I see that she's ravishingly beautiful, with chiseled features, bright eyes. She's out of breath, but when she sees me looking at her, she smiles—radiantly, naturally, with incredible warmth.

"Do you have a public restroom?" she asks the young man.

"It's out of order today, ma'am. You can use the one in the Dollar General. If you exit through the side door, you'll see it at the end of the lot." He smiles back at her, her smile obviously contagious. I notice now the young man has dimples. Sweet, I think.

"Thanks," she says, and leaves. I see her trot across the lot to Roses. No car, I observe. She's a runner.

In a few minutes, with my Blizzard in hand, I, too, walk out. But as I make my way to Ruby, I spot a concrete garden bench at the side of the store on the sidewalk that goes around the building. Probably for employees, but I sit.

As my thick Blizzard melts in the waxed cardboard cup, I dip the long-handled red plastic spoon into the ice-cream mixture, scoop some out, eat, enjoying the sweet cool flavor, its weight on my tongue, the smooth way it feels in my mouth.

I breathe deeply, look around—first, into the parking lot, then to my left, into the road traffic, still heavy. I turn my gaze closer, near the bench—noticing a large beetle making its way across the sidewalk. The beetle's thin little legs work in unison, creeping along to the asphalt lot. The back shell is iridescent green and black; the segmented, logical little body perfectly supports its action. I notice that the sidewalk is very roughly paved, and the bug struggles up the tiny concrete crevices, hills, valleys. A difficult path, a treacherous journey. Where is it going? And why? I think for a moment of putting the beetle on my hand to observe it better, but that seems too intrusive. So, I get down, onto my hands and knees, putting my Blizzard on the bench.

"Tell me something, little bug," I say. "Tell me something I don't know." My face is close to the pavement now as I ask the beetle, "How do you find your way in this great big universe?"

Obviously, I'm insane. I startle myself with the realization. Thankfully, no one is around to observe a middle-age woman almost on her belly, watching a bug crawl outside of a Dairy Queen.

Quickly, I stand up, throwing out my half-eaten, half-melted Blizzard into a dumpster behind the cement-block half-wall at the end of the parking lot. I look back to see that my beetle has successfully crawled down the enormous curb, onto the asphalt, and is making its way to who knows where and for who knows what purpose. "Goodbye," I call. "Good luck with all things."

twenty-eight

According to the latest DSM, psychologists call the psychological condition wherein the person feels "spaced out" or disconnected from his or her environment "depersonalization disorder."

People suffering with this disorder feel the world to be distorted, dream-like, and believe that reality itself is unreal, I remember from my own therapy sessions. I climb into Ruby, trying to think of where next to go. Certainly not home.

I drive out of the lot, head north, aiming for the Guardian Angel, a large thrift store supporting Alzheimer's prevention. But even the traffic seems like an animated movie with too-bright colors, and I feel like the Dairy Queen beetle crawling across difficult terrain.

At a stoplight, I peer into the white Subaru Outback next to me, where a woman, probably my age, with big, dark sunglasses, puts on lipstick. She's shifted her body from the driver's seat over to the middle so that she can see herself in her rear-view mirror. The lipstick is bright red, and the woman's hair is white-blonde, teased, hair-sprayed, in a sort of globe around her head so that it looks like a feathered hat.

The light changes to green, off we go. Her traffic lane moves faster than mine, and I try to watch her car as I did my bug. "Good luck with all things," I tell her as her Subaru vanishes.

This planet is a wobbly place. Full of odd, disturbing motion. I need to keep my balance.

The turn into the thrift store is slightly elevated, then lowers into another strip mall where the store flanks one end. Fuquay-Varina has a couple of older strip malls and then some newer ones. Like Southern Florida, I think.

I lock Ruby and head into the store, which immediately overwhelms me with its stale smells, racks of color-coded clothing, and old furniture. But I find a section of rather neatly-stacked, well-organized books and walk over to them.

No one watches me, notices anything amiss. I'm a spy in my own life—hypervigilant. I think again of slicing my hand. I look at it, imagining what might happen if I were to do this. I move to the glassware section, but then think, "crazy, crazy, crazy" and quickly return to the books.

I pick up Charlotte Joko Beck's *Nothing Special, Living Zen*, an unlikely find, walk to a nearby armchair to sit and read. The area is like a dirty little Barnes and Noble, with a rug and a few comfortable chairs where patrons can preview books they may buy.

Fate leads me to open the book to one of the many conversations, presented as interview transcripts between Beck and a student. I've read this book before, so I'm familiar with its format:

Student: Why does the pain go away when I space out?

Joko: Well, our [waking] dreams are powerful narcotics. That's why we like them so much. Our dreams and fantasies are addictive, just like addictive substances.

Student: Isn't there separation from reality involved if we feel pain?

Joko: Not if we totally feel it.

I buy the book for fifty-four cents, two quarters and four pennies, which I have in my wallet. I choose not to accept a bag and rather than continue to shop, I walk out to Ruby to read, though it's stifling hot, and Ruby's interior is even hotter, probably 115 degrees.

But there's a Chinese take-out with a few scruffy looking tables inside, and I go there, thinking I'll purchase a bottle of water and a couple of spring rolls. As I approach, however, the place looks unfriendly, with pink wallpaper peeling off one side wall, and an electric painting of a waterfall on the other wall. The painting's black cord is plugged in, but the painting's neon lights aren't working.

Back in Ruby, I continue up 401 North toward Raleigh, hoping I'll find a better place to rest, retreat, read, gather my thoughts. Then, in the distance, across the four lanes of traffic I see a Starbucks, set off in a free-standing building near Lowes, near another strip mall. I make the turn, and with book in hand, go in. The place is empty, but immediately comfortable, with low lights and delicious-looking pastries, cakes. I order a Skinny Mocha Latte Grande. I decide against food, in part because I'm still feeling the effects of the half-consumed Blizzard.

I'm finally resting, happy to have landed here, where the atmosphere feels safe, welcoming. There are photos of deserted and forlorn rural buildings on the wall, a local artist, no doubt. They're very North Carolina—places I think I've seen, reminding me how far I've come from my New York City roots. I think of the word "roots" and come up with two ideas: roots are the places we return to because they ground us to our past, and roots are the places where families currently live, where we most belong.

New York offers me neither. It's memory now. The last time I visited my old South Shelburne neighborhood so much had changed that I felt only distant connection. Now, of course, my original family lives in Florida.

My life can become memory if I let it. Then, a slip of paper falls from *Nothing Special.* On it are the typed words: *Everything you think you are and everything you perceive are undivided. Tat Vam Asi—Thou are that.*

I sit, read, and reread the words. The Mocha Latte is incredibly satisfying, and, like the words, is waking me up, offering energy.

I decide to travel up 401 and head to Raleigh, the art museum, which, I now believe, will feed my soul, help me to feel whole.

I'm turning off 401 North and onto I 40 West, accelerating as I accidentally cut off a Nissan pickup truck that must now fall behind me.

Traveling at 65, I know my exit is coming up in the next ten minutes. I can't remember the number, but there's a brown museum sign I know to watch for. I turn on the car radio, still tuned to an oldies station, rather than NPR, and leave it there to keep my spirits lifted. Soon I'm humming along to some bubble-gum pop song, the title of which I can't recall, though I know some of the lyrics.

Raleigh is a suburban, sprawling, but manageable city. Nick and I come here often, though I can't say I'm familiar with all the neighborhoods or really know my way around.

I travel awhile, further than I think I need to, then see the airport sign for RDU and remember the museum exit should be next or the else the one after that. As I think this, there's the sign. I turn onto Blue Ridge Road, soon see the museum flags and turn into the parking lot.

Inside, I see that there's a multi-media exhibition on "time" along with the regular collection, which I decide to look at first, to think about whether or not I want to pay for the exhibition; Nick and I saw it together earlier in the summer. I enjoyed it, and I'm already leaning toward seeing it again. The regular museum gallery is free.

In the open, well-lit first gallery, I stand before a huge green sculptural piece of cast glass, made in sections. I've seen it before, but now I think about Will and what he'd say about the piece. I notice many cracks, and I wonder if Will would say these are good, bad, intentional, or accidental. Will could do a piece like this, if his kiln could fit such huge pieces. But who'd purchase it? A commercial interior designer for a building's lobby? I make a mental note to ask Will about this work. In fact, I take out my phone, snap a photo, although as I look at it, I decide that the photo doesn't do the piece justice.

I move to some contemporary paintings, huge canvases, also appropriate only as museum pieces or for commercial settings. A man with a headful of dreadlocks stands beside me. His hair is mostly gray, and I think he's about my age, so as I try to figure this out, I begin to take sideway glances at him. He sees me, smiles—a lovely, honest smile, and I notice that he's wearing cool dark purple wire-frame glasses. I imagine he's an academic; he's carrying a leather portfolio, and there's something familiar about his demeanor. I return his smile, then walk to the next painting.

We're in the gallery room alone together, so as I move away, we're still connected, feel each other's presence. I think of saying something to him, and in my head try out: "Lovely day for the museum," or "I enjoy contemporary art in large spaces like this," or "Have you seen the exhibition on 'time'? I'm thinking of going," but all these things strike me as ridiculous, embarrassing, so I say nothing. My heart pounds; my body temperature rises.

Feeling stupid, as if the stranger could hear my thoughts, I walk slowly from the room. My face must be beet-red as I was about to make a fool of myself. I feel ashamed now and decide to head to the bathroom to be alone, to splash water on my face, get a grip.

Which I do, though the relief is temporary. I'm close to some edge, and in a moment of carelessness, I will step over it as Anna did. I wash my face, then stand in front of the large full-body mirror. I'm alone, so I run a brush through my hair, take off my glasses, clean them with my tee-shirt, put them on, and decide to risk looking at myself.

Okay, I think, I'm going to say aloud what I see. Be brutally honest, objective. If I can't manage the honesty, well, that's one problem identified. If I can manage the honesty but look a mess, well, that's another problem identified, but one I can tackle. Yes, I'm old, but there's still time for correction, improvement. Like writing a book, I can revise.

So here goes. My hair has turned white, a sort of blonde white, unlike the steel gray that dark hair often turns. I could dye it, which I used to do, but the color didn't take well, and I never liked the result. Friends have told me to dye my hair—my kids have, too—so maybe I should reconsider. I look at the short billowing cap my hair has become and think that perhaps they're all right. The white hair ages me. On the other hand, philosophically, I'm against the idea. My age is my age; I should own it.

Face? A disappointment. I see the girl I was, but my face sags, especially on the left side. In my forties, I had eye problems, and over the years, that side of my face suffered, perhaps from all the squinting. I could wear makeup. Again, it's a philosophical issue for me—I'm against this notion. The issue is political as well. But over the last five years I started wearing concealer—I love the word—under my eyes, across my nose when it's reddish, over a tiny mole... and do I look better? My neck is time-worn, face wrinkled. Not that such a small bit of makeup helps in the slightest.

Body—not really overweight, but not good. I'm dressed

today, as I am most days, in baggy pants, a black camisole, and an oversized, cotton-spandex button-down over-shirt. I look gender neutral—which, I'm coming to realize is my default position.

"Look at yourself, Rachel," I say. "You're a mess. A big, old mess."

It's true. I look like some past-her-prime hippie chick who refuses to live in the contemporary world. My appearance suggests that I'm attached to who I was. I feel a watery burning in my eyes. Then anger. At myself. At who I can't become.

A young mom with a toddler in tow comes into the bathroom. I move to the sink to wash my hands as if I've just come out of a stall.

"I'm hungry, Mommy," the little girl says. She is mixed-race and has a head full of springy, dark, curly hair. She wears a yellow-striped sundress, a little white cardigan, orange sandals with a tiger's face on the foam front.

"We'll get something soon." The mom's voice is gentle, lilting, and I detect an accent of some kind. She's in the stall with the little girl, so the conversation becomes muffled.

I walk out to the Rodin sculpture garden, where it's wicked hot, find a bench, sit down. I'm almost enjoying the powerful heat, knowing that I can return to the cool interior when it becomes unbearable. There is a three-figure bronze sculpture there, and my bench is directly in front of the reflecting pond, with its lily pads and lovely dark waters.

The bronze figures are in movement, bending, somehow relating to each other, but yet the cast bronze is so heavy that there's a palpable tension. Also, a tension between dark and light—the dark of the bronze, the light of the air, the afternoon sky—its white heat, a dissipating energy contributing to the piece's movement. It's shocking to see such strength in form, yet such suggestion of light. My eyes fill again. And I'm getting very hot.

I walk over to the museum's other building, to the "time" exhibition and pay the $12 admission. Entering, I'm drawn to a display of time-lapse photography of a tree through an entire year. The video loop takes four minutes to cycle through the seasons.

I sit on the bench, facing the tree. I'm not sure what kind it is because the projection is mostly abstract. It's not a maple... maybe a willow oak, judging by the leaves, but the shape of tree isn't typical for a willow oak, unless the tree is young... then again, I'm not sure.

The woman and her young daughter whom I saw in the bathroom enter the room. The little girl climbs up on the bench next to me, wiggling around, totally disinterested in the display. The mom, cross-armed, looks at the tree. "Beautiful," she says.

"Yes," I say, "death and renewal." I look at her. She's in her thirties, I'd guess, with long dark hair pulled into a single braid, and medium skin, almost olive. Mediterranean. She wears a tight neon orange tee-shirt and tight jeans.

"Mommy, look, look," we hear, turning to see the little girl in the next gallery space, an open area, where she dances in a circle of projected light. "I'm coming," the woman calls, nodding, smiling at me, walking toward her daughter.

Left alone, I remember that downstairs from the Museum of Modern Art in New York—the old one, before the museum was renovated—there was a room with a screen of projected, moving light. It must have been near the subway station because trains could be heard through the walls. There were maybe four long benches in rows in front of the screen, like a little theater, and people would come in to watch the random colors and the shapes the colors assumed—sometimes melting into one another or blotting as if they'd been spilled.

Watching the tree, then the patterns of light from a similar bench now, I'm carried back to MoMA. The tree before me is not just a tree; it's a time machine—its changing seasons taking me across decades and miles.

I'm fifteen. Henry, my boyfriend, and I have taken psilocybin on the Long Island Railroad, as we approached the city. A stupid thing to do, yes, but what did we know?

That day in particular, I'd spent a few hours in front of the screen, mesmerized by the colors and shapes choreographed to the train noise. I imagined that time stood still here and that if I stayed I'd never grow old. I wore sneakers, and one was untied. I remember thinking that if I tied my shoe, my life would change, that time would begin again. But as long as the lace dangled, I was safe. I sat like that until Henry, who'd been upstairs in other galleries, came down to get me.

"I can't move," I whispered to him as he took a seat next to me on the wooden bench. The little theater was empty, and we sat alone together.

"Yes, you can, my little swallow, my little bird. We can fly." Henry whispered, his voice coy, playful.

"My shoe," I said. "If I tie it, I'll grow old."

"Yes," Henry said. "And if you don't tie it, you'll grow old. And possibly trip on the stairs." He smiled at me.

A second later, I got the pun and laughed.

"What will happen if *I* tie your shoe?" Henry elbowed me gently.

"I don't know. I never know." The colors on the screen turned darker, in tune with my suddenly sad mood.

Henry got down on his knees in front of me and tied my shoe. "Nothing will happen to you, ever. You'll stay just as you are. So will I. We're perfect." Henry looked up at me, grinned. In the next minute, we were kissing passionately, still alone in the room.

Memories. Everyone has them. I dismiss the well of strong emotions bubbling up again, wanting to spill out at every turn.

Can I, or anyone, avoid the past? I rise from the bench, walk a few feet, but find myself tired, aching, and return, sit, try to clear my head. But now I hear Eliot, lines I inadvertently memorized from "Burnt Norton," the first poem in *Four Quartets*. I whisper them aloud:

"Time present and time past
Are both perhaps present in time future,
And time future contained in time past.
If all time is eternally present
All time is unredeemable.
What might have been is an abstraction
Remaining a perpetual possibility
Only in a world of speculation."

The tree changes from winter barrenness to a full-leafed summer display, before bright and varied leaves appear, turn brown, fall. In another minute, the buds grow, leaves appear, opening back to summer.

I take a plastic pack of tissues from my black shoulder bag and bow my head.

No one is around now, except for a guard who occasionally paces in and out of the room, leaving me to myself, head lowered as in prayer.

As I think this, my head still bowed, I find that I'm mumbling a prayer: Sh'ma Yis'ra'eil Adonai Eloheinu Adonai echad. *Hear o Israel, the Lord is our God, the Lord is one.*

During my one year of religious training—which consisted of attending Hebrew school taught by the Rebbetzin every Saturday morning for about eight months—I'd become a believer and thought I'd marry a Rabbi, maybe become a Rebbetzin myself. But even during the fervor of that early faith, I could never imagine God. Maybe that's the point.

A man comes into the gallery, sits beside me. He's Hispanic, short, and seems oblivious to my presence or that he might be intruding. He watches the tree for the four-minute year with a rolled-up museum program that he bangs nervously on his thigh. I don't look directly at him, but through the corner of my eye I can see that he's young, probably in his late twenties, has a purple streak in his black hair and a large snake tattoo crawling up his wrist onto his forearm. When I look down, I see that he's wearing canvas sneakers with the toes cut out. As he gets up to leave, he drops or puts down the rolled-up program on the bench. I say nothing.

Distracted from my sad mood, I catch myself thinking, *Yes, just like a man to leave his garbage behind. I pick it up. Litter in a museum? Rude.*

I pick up the discarded program and wander into the adjacent gallery, not the one the man has walked into, because I'm hoping not to run into him again. It's the room near the end of the exhibition, and I realize that I've lost interest in seeing the rest of the show. There I see a trash can, so I head toward it, but as I do, I unroll the program to see that it's not a program, but a glossy advertisement for low plane-fares to Europe, with flights leaving from RDU. I could fly roundtrip to Paris for $499, to London for $449, or to Barcelona for $529. I smooth out the ad, fold it, put it in my bag. A sign?

Before I exit the exhibition, I return to the last room to quickly glance at some paintings, watch a short video, and stop at a sort of light sculpture with changing projected features, but then walk out of the time exhibition completely, back to the other building, thinking that I'll visit the gift shop, then get a little something to eat in the pricey museum café.

The gift shop contains many attractive, arty, expensive items. I handle beaded earrings with Alexander Calder-ish mobile dangling pieces, handmade paper journals, a hand-knitted silk sweater for $250, batik scarves.

—⟶—

In the café, I sit at a small back table by the wall, to collect my thoughts. I've ordered a portobello mushroom sandwich on panini with potato salad and coffee.

The café is nearly empty. I see an older couple, perhaps in their late seventies, sitting at a table across the room. Also, there's a well-dressed, middle-aged man, legs crossed, reading a large unfolded newspaper. And two younger women, college-aged, leaning toward each other conspiratorially across the table, engaged in animated conversation.

I sit back in my chair, close my eyes for a moment, focus on my breath—to center myself, sharpen my attention.

But the waitress comes and delivers my coffee, presented in a white cup on a square white saucer, with a small stainless-steel milk pitcher and sugar on a separate serving plate. She's wearing tight black pants, a white shirt, both covered by a full black apron.

"Your sandwich will be out in a few minutes," she says, offering a smile.

"Thanks," I tell her, noticing that her nose and upper lip are pierced, and that she's wearing purple lipstick.

twenty-nine

God, I think, and feel something stir within me. I breathe deeply, trying to return to my thoughts in front of the tree exhibition. As I breathe, I become aware of my physical self, and that takes me to a more cognitive place. Here, I feel centered and shift my attention to my coffee, which I mindfully sip. The flavor is robust, fresh. And there's power in this moment.

I take another sip of coffee, the hot liquid energizing, feeling wonderful in my mouth, throat. For a moment, I feel more positive.

My waitress returns with a coffee carafe, smiles again, then without asking or speaking, fills my cup. Women, I think, know how not to interrupt. I'm relaxed now, better able to be with my thoughts. I think about God and faith, feeling a visceral connection to the universe. As I breathe, the universe breathes with me.

My sandwich arrives. The waitress says nothing. I look at her, say "thanks," aware that my voice doesn't want to speak. I nod my head, we smile at each other, and I notice that she's pregnant. Thin as she is, there's a definite baby bump beneath her apron.

I breathe deeply, feeling the core channel of my body hold air, then let it go. Now I'm thinking that there's some black place I've been running from.

I take a difficult bite of my portobello mushroom

sandwich, which is thick, hard to get my mouth around. A tangy mayonnaise-based sauce drips from it onto my plate. I swipe the bitten end of the sandwich into the sauce, ready for another bite. My mouth is alive with the textures and tastes of this delicious food.

Sensation—perhaps it too is sacred. The Buddhists believe that suffering can be alleviated by engaging in the present, the utter-ness of the moment, the acceptance of reality or *what is.*

My pregnant waitress, coffee carafe in hand, makes her way to me. No words again. A slight smile, pour, nod.

God in all things—even my sandwich and coffee. My present moment. I pour a dab of half-and-half into my coffee, take a sip, concentrating now on the experience of the coffee, its warmth in my mouth, its taste. I swallow, the liquid warming my throat.

I do the same with my sandwich, except that I chew it thoroughly, feeling my jaw and mouth work. The complicated tastes combine. A joy—a spiritual practice, a living practice.

Wasn't it Ignatius of Loyola who said that God is present in all things? And that spirit is found through practice?

That word again: *practice.* There's so much we call practice. As a graduate student, I studied with the poet Robert Creeley, and he'd always say that life is a dress rehearsal, but he never said for what. Maybe he was suggesting that life is our practice, that we never get it right, that nothing exists beyond the rehearsal.

I bite again into my sandwich—complex, satisfying.

My waitress is back.

"This is excellent," I say, as she stands by my table.

"I'm glad," she says. "May I get you anything else?"

"Just the check," I tell her.

Up and about in the museum, I find that I'm not quite ready to leave. I want to explore one of the permanent collections.

I stand before the African tribal collection of masks and old religious artifacts. Some masks are huge wooden things, with terrifying faces. Were they intended to scare? Does fear create obedience? Do we need consequences to behave ethically? Is it fear, that most primal emotion, that guides, controls, motivates?

In Hebrew culture class, the Rebbetzin told us that God always watched us, that whatever wrong act we committed, God would see and punish us.

I'm in front of a grouping of artifacts: a terrifying mask, a huge carved totem, a grass and textile shaman's costume. Did these items help reach God or bring people closer to the spirit realm?

No answers.

I'm walking now through some abstract modern paintings and sculpture. On one wall, a draped tapestry of used bottle caps and metal pieces cut from aluminum cans, by Ghanaian born artist El Anatsui, hangs like a glistening fabric. *Lines that Link Humanity* is its title. I stand there—first at a distance, then closer up, then at a distance again.

A couple approaches. He's probably in his seventies; she's younger, I'm guessing. They're dressed in coordinated shorts, pink tee-shirts, and white Nike athletic shoes.

The man, hunched and in pain, tries to straighten his neck to see the entire wall sculpture.

"Linda, we could do this," he says.

"Start collecting your cans," she replies, grinning at the man, who returns the grin—a pleased, intimate, knowing expression.

I eavesdrop, move closer to them.

"Yeah," the man says. "We can do anything. We just need time."

They walk off slowly to another gallery room. I hear the

thumping of his cane, the shuffling of his feet. The woman supports his other arm; they themselves look like art.

—∿—

I get it into my head to return to the other building, go downstairs to visit the Egyptian collection. Exiting, I walk slowly, mindful of the fading heat, the thick humid air. As I enter, the cool air makes me feel like I've arrived in another country. I breathe it in and walk down the large, gracious stairs to stand in front of the small, about two feet high, "Bust of the Goddess Sekmet, circa 1390-1352 B.C.E.," sculpted in granite or some hard stone, with a lion's face and women's breasts. The goddess of retribution, she and the dark forces she represents exist to take action against violence.

Yes, we want justice. When wrong is committed, we want the wrong-doer punished.

I think of Dennis and his wrong-doings—stealing, gambling, lying—and sigh.

Now in front of "Inner Coffin of Djed Mut, circa 715-525 B.C.E.," I study its painted hieroglyphs, intricate designs, intended to secure passage to the next world. Is my brother dying? Will he need passage?

Suddenly, I'm very tired and know that I need to leave. I return up the wide staircase, past the information and ticket counters, and walk out through the heavy glass doors.

thirty

Outside now, I remember to breathe, to practice. I look at the sun, lower in the cloudless sky, and walk to a bench by the entrance to the other building in a small courtyard. I sit down to ponder. *Ponder*—a good word, but almost out of diction.

Two pigeons land on the gravel near my bench. Their heads look Egyptian—stylized, erect, bobbing forward and back in staccato rhythm as they walk. Their feathers glisten, turn gray, green, blue. Then they fly off together, movements coordinated like the older couple in the gallery.

I look up at the empty sky, then down at the crushed gravel courtyard. Yes, the universe has organization and energy. God, gods, and goddesses. Direction, faith.

Thinking back to my childhood faith, I connect with something else. It's as if I'm reaching back in search of original connection. I bend forward, take my head in my hands, where I smell the flesh of my palms, with their slight acrid odor, an almost chemical smell. I breathe in, welcoming it.

Like Levin at the end of *Anna Karenina,* my intellect tells me one thing, my heart, another. Levin reconciles this contradiction by accepting faith.

I stand up, decide that I'm done. I wipe my hands, a little sweaty, on my pants. It's still hot outside, but already there's a slight evening breeze. I begin to walk to the parking lot but then decide to take the long walk around the museum grounds.

In front of *Collapse I* by South African artist Ledelle Moe, I pause. Here, the huge human form looks like a fallen colossus. Powerful yet yielding.

Deeper in, I come across another piece, *Untitled,* by the same artist. It's a low, compact boulder suggesting a person in fetal position. I stand by it, bend to touch its rough surface.

Something stirs inside me, waiting to be born. But as I think this, the feeling dissipates.

Walking, I see the sun hover over the horizon, a raised field of intentionally uncut clump grasses—wild-seeming, long-bladed. I decide not to read the botanical information on the plaque but rather to look. And as I stare, I see that it's not chaotic, random; it's ordered. I move closer. The grass is beautiful. I sink to my knees. Yellow, green, straw-colored, and red blades blaze against a darkening but open sky. Ecstatic dry energy ignites the soft light. A small insect buzzes and lands. I move closer, see its almost transparent, thin-veined wings flutter. I breathe deeply. For this moment, I'm both in and out of my body.

—⚂—

On the way home, I realize that I've turned off my phone. As I turn it on, I see that I have three messages and two missed calls. But I'm not ready yet to disturb my solitude.

I drive I-40 with no music, no radio. Traffic is light, and I set the cruise control at seventy-three, though I need to weave in and out of the three lanes to maintain the speed.

I'm thinking of Sonya, the friend I met when I was sixteen at Shimer College. We flew to Luxemburg and hitchhiked through Europe together during the summer of 1972. Now Sonya lives in Chapel Hill, so we speak to and see each other fairly often. Since that early trip, Sonya has been my sister-friend for all these years.

Now, I understand. The rolled flyer advertising fares to

Europe has reminded me of that trip. I think of Sonya and of taking another trip together, after almost forty years, back to Europe. Not hitchhiking this time, of course.

I see Sonya standing in front of Bennett Hall, the women's dorm at Shimer College, the small liberal arts college with its campus located in Mount Carroll, Illinois—a tiny town near the western edge of the state, nine miles east of the Mississippi River. Her long brown hair wraps around her shoulders. It's February; Sonya wears an Army shirt but no jacket. She and a dark-skinned girl—Cossette? Casandra?—are walking downstairs to the dorm lounge. They're laughing, chatting, and they don't see or acknowledge me. I fall in behind them, but then the memory disappears.

Sometime in February, I formally meet Sonya, in bed with a head cold. I'm bringing her some food, as a favor. She's covered with a mostly orange patchwork quilt. I don't really like her, but we talk briefly, and she tells me that she's from Key West, Florida, and is unaccustomed to the intense Northern cold.

By March, Sonya and I became friends. She stuck up for me when Billy and Eric, two boys from Texas, argued against me. We had been discussing *Hamlet,* and the boys were justifying Hamlet's lack of action. Sonya jumped in to defend me, and our friendship began.

Both loving to travel, we concocted a plan to hitchhike across America during the summer. But the plan changed. Sonya's parents didn't want her traveling across America because they felt it wasn't safe. Strangely, my own folks expressed the same concern.

So, Sonya and I decided to fly to Europe and hitchhike there. Both sets of parents agreed—believing at the time that Europe was safer than the US—and in early summer, Sonya flew to New York, where she stayed with my family for a few days before we flew out from Kennedy Airport to Reykjavik,

Iceland, then to Luxembourg.

I've bumped up my speed, now have the cruise control locked in at seventy, the speed limit on this part of I-40. I'm in the right lane, with cars zooming past on my left. The sky, mostly dark, glows dully with only a hint of light remaining. Still no radio. I'm enjoying my thoughts about Sonya and that summer. I take the metal peppermint Altoid case from my bag, remove a mint, place it on my tongue.

Adjusting myself, I realize that my back is stiff. Then I have a clear memory of Sonya and me, walking in my neighborhood and talking about the trip. We decided that taking a trip together would either make or break our friendship.

I cycle through snapshots of memory:

Sonya and I stand in a sweater store in the Reykjavik airport, the one stopover on our trip. The sweaters are beautiful, and I covet one. But they're too expensive and bulky to fit in my small knapsack, so I pass.

Sonya and I walk through Luxembourg City. Remnants of an old wall encircle the city, which goes back to Roman times when two important roads crossed at its center. At some point, those walls came down. Later, in the early medieval period, more walls were constructed, then during the Renaissance, another defensive wall went up. Walls were dismantled and built again. In fact, the history of Luxemburg could be told by its walls.

I think of "Mending Wall," in which Frost writes: "Something there is that doesn't love a wall / that wants it down." I open the Altoid tin with one hand, popping another mint in my mouth, as I slow the car into a traffic jam ahead.

At the edge of the city, Sonya and I walk a road near an open field, look down on railroad tracks, then, walking further, where buildings no longer obstruct our view, two rivers converge around what appears to be the old city. I'm moved by the stone architecture, crumbling walls, the city's visceral history.

Now, a series of linked snaps: By the end of the first day, Sonya and I are sitting in the back of a car, traveling the autobahn, zooming toward Paris. Wolfgang and Helmut, two German boys, laugh in the front seat as they offer us cigarettes, which we refuse. The boys are charming, if grotesque, caricatures. Wolfgang wears huge square-framed glasses, and Helmut has thick rubbery-looking Germanic lips.

Neither boy speaks good English, and neither Sonya nor I speak good German or French. So, we laugh, trying to communicate in three pigeon languages.

Soon, however, we realize that "Helmet-Hair" and "Wolfy," the nicknames we've given the boys, expect us to sleep with them. When we make it clear that that's not part of our plan, they abruptly let us out of the car. But by this time, however, we're already in Paris.

I remember the traffic as we enter the city. One road, in particular, part of a Parisian suburb, reminds me of Queens Boulevard. Seeing it so clearly now unsettles me, and I feel a wave of nausea. Snap. I pop another Altoid into my mouth.

There's been an accident on I-40. A Ford Explorer has overturned onto the grassy shoulder. An ambulance and two police cars attend the scene, and although both lanes of the interstate are clear, drivers are rubber-necking, causing the slowdown.

I'm interested, too. As I glance toward the shoulder, I see a young woman, an older man—her father?—and a Yorkshire Terrier on a leash. But I can't see who's hurt or how serious the injuries are.

In a moment, all the cars pick up speed, and I accelerate.

Another snap: the Paris YWCA. Sonya and I share a small room with two sets of bunkbeds. I look out the window to a spiral fire escape. Sonya, a great photographer, takes a wonderful black and white photo of the staircase—a photo I still have.

The next day, we rent Mopeds and drive them recklessly the wrong way down one-way side streets. I'm driving on a sidewalk. Sonya maneuvers her Moped up beside mine, motions with her map. We pull over on the street among parked cars, decide to find the Louvre and the Eifel Tower.

We climb up the Eifel Tower, look at the Paris beneath us. We stand in front of the *Mona Lisa* after waiting in line for about half an hour. She is small and wonderful.

Later, we sit at a café as a man approaches us and asks to join us at the table. We agree and try to speak French as he attempts English. After a few laughs, we become friendly, and question him about a good, inexpensive place to stay as we've had to check out of the YMCA because the entire place had been booked many months ago by a large group of Japanese students traveling across Europe. He replies with the suggestion that we stay at his apartment.

Sonya tells the man, "No couche," a slang, mostly literary term, roughly translated to "no bed" that Sonya's dad has taught her. He had lived in Paris for the three years following his service in World War II and thought this phrase might serve Sonya in certain situations.

"No, no, no," the man says, shaking both his head and hands, insulted that we'd mention such a thing. Sonya and I take him up on his offer and soon follow him down many sad city streets, up old stairs that lead to a depressing little apartment above a butcher's shop in a rundown area of Paris.

The man introduces us to his young son, maybe seven or eight, who is playing in his room on a bare mattress. I'm surprised that he's been left alone and that the man hadn't mentioned him. The boy looks up, smiles. Snap.

The man shows us his room, where two mattresses lie across a bare wooden floor. A bulb hangs on an electrical cord from the ceiling. The man explains that this is where we will sleep.

I-40 has been stalled with traffic twice now—once with the accident, now with roadwork splicing two lanes into one. The delay only lasts a few minutes, and soon I turn onto I-95.

Instinctively, I turn on the radio, find NPR, and listen to a rebroadcast of "Fresh Air." Terry Gross is interviewing a young female actor whose name I don't catch.

"So, tell me," Terry continues. "What made you want to act? I mean, as a child, is this the profession to which you aspired?"

"No," the actor says. "My dad was a neuroscientist and taught at university. My mother was a writer of children's books. I thought I'd grow up to be a teacher or a professor. Maybe English. I always loved books."

I turn off the radio and think back to Paris. To that night. Did I have aspirations? Did I think that I'd become an English professor or that I'd write? The actor had such smart professional parents. A real advantage, I think.

But we all have inheritances. Advantages, disadvantages, strengths, weaknesses. We do what we can.

"My parents did their best," I say aloud. And I've done mine.

"Dad," I say now. "I love you. I'm sorry that I failed you." I begin to weep. I can't remember my father's face.

Then, I'm back in Paris again. With Sonya, in that decrepit Paris apartment.

Sonya and I are in our sleeping bags on top of the bare mattresses. Snap. Neon lights from restaurants and bars blink through a window without shade or curtain. I'm sleepy, doze off, but not completely. Soon the man wakes up. I open my eyes to see that he's motioning to us and to his groin, standing there, naked, with an erection.

Sonya is awake, and we're both on high alert now. But it's the middle of the night, and the naked man is short, thin, pitiful. His dark greasy hair is combed, fitting like a cap on his head, and his feet are apart. He points to his penis as if it were a small uncaged animal he needs our help in capturing.

Sonya looks at me, and I look at her. For some reason the man has targeted Sonya and stares imploringly at her. Standing above us, he is ominous—primal man with primal needs. Sonya, elbows me, whispers, "Want to go?"

We quickly discuss. The neighborhood is dangerous. We don't know where we are or how to get back to the Paris of yesterday. And it's still dark out; although we don't know the exact time, we estimate that it's about 4:00 a.m.

"Don't know," I say, propped on my elbows, looking at Sonya, who nods. The man is small and unimposing, yet insistent.

But now the man touches Sonya's shoulder. Sonya brushes off his hand, whispering "creepy" to me, and we're totally awake. Climbing out of her sleeping bag, her long hair disheveled, wearing sweatpants and a tee-shirt, Sonya nods at me.

"Okay, let's go," I tell her, noticing the neon lights outside the bedroom still blinking in predawn gray. Grizzly, bare.

"Yes," Sonya says. And we roll up our sleeping bags, stuff our belongings into knapsacks, the man still standing there, now speaking rapid French in an increasingly loud voice. Thankfully, though, he doesn't become belligerent—upset, yes, but willing to let us leave.

On the highway, I signal to change lanes. There's a lot of truck traffic, and the right lane is moving slowly. I rev up Ruby, make my move. Successful.

Now, locking in at seventy-five, I cycle back to Sonya.

Down the rickety dark stairs, Sonya and I make our way into the predawn morning, where the Paris air is cool and moist and settles into a gray fog beneath the streetlights.

Oddly, traffic on I-95 has opened, and the sun, setting to my left, casts a last orangey glow over the landscape. I move into the right lane again, pop the cruise control back to sixty-five, slip off my sandals, and push them deep under the front seat.

We wander the Paris streets, walking out from that grimy residential neighborhood to try to find an open café.

Snap. Sonya and I find a café and meet two guys, an artist and his friend. The pair are young, hip, sitting at an outdoor table, drinking coffee, eating croissants.

They're animated, friendly, but Sonya and I eat quickly, excuse ourselves, and leave.

The streets are cobblestone. Sonya and I walk one block, then another. Paris is waking up. Cars honk, the tawdry night veneer has been peeled back to reveal another city, more charming, trustworthy. A woman in a clean gingham apron sweeps the sidewalk in front of her shop. A man straps a briefcase onto the back of his Vespa. Two school girls in short plaid skirts, starched white shirts, bobby socks, Oxford shoes, knapsacks on their back, walk by us, giggling and holding hands. I look at Sonya, put my arm around her waist. She turns her face to me, smiles, and I realize that I love her. Snap.

A road sign announces that I'm back in Cumberland County. Four more exits now until the I-295 connector and I get off.

I've had such a busy mind, this drive home, I think. *But I'm not done.*

Later in our trip, Sonya and I split up for a few days. Sonya wants to visit a friend in Germany, a girl who studied as a foreign exchange student in Sonya's high school. I decide to hitchhike to Amsterdam, mostly to see the city and also to give Sonya time with her friend.

On my second ride across Belgium, a businessman picks me up in his newer model Volvo. I get into the front seat, and the man, dressed in a dark suit, only speaks Dutch and French. I peel an orange on my lap—breakfast—and as I do, the man pulls the car abruptly onto the shoulder. Cars zooms past us at a hundred kilometers an hour.

The man tries to rip open my blue work-shirt. I scream, grab his jacket lapels, thrust him against his door. "No," I yell. "No!" Snap, snap, snap.

He releases me, and as I unlock the door, I fall backwards out of his car, knapsack tumbling out with me. The man throws my half-peeled orange at me, as I sit stunned, heart racing, by the side of the road. He takes off, leaving skid marks on the asphalt shoulder.

Snap. I sit there for maybe five minutes, my heart thumping against the cage of my chest, before a I hear an air horn and look up to see a large commercial truck has stopped for me, maybe seventy-five feet ahead.

Gathering my knapsack, I toss the half-eaten orange into the nearby undergrowth, find my legs, walk to the truck cab. The driver, a bit grizzly, with a long auburn beard and plaid flannel shirt but a lovely smile, welcomes me. We drive uneventfully into Amsterdam.

It's dark out now, nearly 9:00, and I turn on my car lights. I'm ready to be home.

thirty-one

I pull into the driveway. I fish out my house keys, and when I open the door, Jake is there to greet me. I bend to pet him, both of us making our way into the kitchen. I put my bag on the table, turn on the light.

"Food, Jake?" I pick up his bowl, and he follows at my heels until I feed him. Exhausted, I recheck my phone to find that it's remained on mute. I place it on the counter.

In the sunroom, I sit on the couch in darkness. Something, a memory, stirs. I get up, go upstairs to my study, switching on my bronze serpent lamp, a leftover from my father's furniture store.

In an instant, I'm back there, and see my dad working at his office desk. "Hello, Rae." he turns to me to say, flashing a brief smile, and I now see his face.

The room is alive. I sit at my laptop, open the file I've been working on—twenty-two pages—and read what's there. A beginning, perhaps, or maybe a throwaway.

I drill down to see if I can continue. Jake struggles up the stairs to join me. I wait a moment as he enters the room and jumps up to nap on my futon.

I draw a lifeline on a blank sheet of paper. I write my birth year at one end and the year of my death at the other end, an optimistic ninety-two, barring suicide or fatal accidents.

I add other dates: college graduation, marriage, Cal's birth, first graduate degree, Will's birth, second graduate degree. I think of my book publications but don't add them. I think of my suicide attempt. No. My European trip, maybe.

I crumble the paper, toss it into the garbage, and open up a new Word document. A memory stirs, and I think back to my Queens apartment, to my shared bedroom, sensing something there.

I close my eyes: I'm in bed, under my pink winter quilt; my brother stands next to me. But the room smells bad, has a stuffy, almost acrid odor. I breathe into it.

Then stop. I know this moment; I've been here before. I close my eyes and press.

"Dennis," I say, and now recognize that the smell is his. "Tell me the secret before you die."

—⁂—

The room is dark, and we're back in our shared bedroom in Queens, in twin beds along opposite walls. I open my eyes, and Dennis sees I'm awake. The window blinds are open slightly, letting in the faint glow of streetlights, illuminating the gray space between Dennis and me, between me and memory.

Dennis throws back his covers. It's early morning, and hours before our parents rise. Dennis leaves his bed and approaches mine. He's touches the front of his pajama bottoms and strokes my cheek, telling me to relax. My jaw clenches and relaxes.

Through the gauze of time I see him standing by my bedside—an eight-year-old boy, skinny, in baggy cotton pajamas that have a cowboy theme. They're brown and beige, printed with a checkerboard pattern. Images of lassos, pointed boots, and cowboys on bucking horses fill blocks in the grid like cells in a cartoon.

Dennis is with me, inside one of the cells. Like a cowboy himself, he has drawn a gun from some hidden holster, and he's forcing it into my mouth.

"Don't shoot," I whisper.

But Dennis smiles at me, and his gun is aimed and steady, and then, suddenly, I've become his horse, choking on my bit, and he's urging me to gallop. Which I can't, because he's holding me down, and his grip is tight. I want to scream, but I'm choking. I want to breathe fully, but I can't.

In the next moment, we're back in our separate beds.

"Dennis," I say, summoning him now. And as I do, two faces appear—the boy's and the dying man's. But are they smiling or grimacing?

The ghost-child groans as if in pain, looks up imploringly at me, but says nothing. Somehow, in this act of terrible intimacy, Dennis and I have traded places, and he is no longer the victim.

"Dennis, I understand," I say to my dying brother, who hovers so closely that I can smell his cancer.

"Don't forget me," he says, and blows me a foul-smelling kiss.

—⁕—

I pace the upstairs—walk from my bedroom to Cal's old bedroom to Will's old bedroom and back. I'm remembering an enormous fight I had with my mother before Sonya and I left for Europe. Although my mom had agreed that hitchhiking in Europe would be far safer than traveling in the U.S., she had reservations.

And even at that late moment, even after she had given me her permission and Sonya and I had already bought our tickets, she was nervous about letting me go. We fought for hours. I kept insisting that Europe wasn't dangerous and I'd be fine.

"Mom," I tell her now. "You were right. Europe was dangerous. But the real danger was in my bedroom in Queens."

She stands before me, vaporous, dressed in 1970s black

pants with a royal blue pull-over sweater, too warm for the weather. She's thirty-five years old, younger than Cal is today.

"Did you know what Dennis did, Mom?" I ask her shadow-self.

"No," she replies. "I knew absolutely nothing. How could I have known?" And balancing a cigarette between long slender fingers, she takes a drag. Her cheeks suck in and her red-lipped mouth puckers. When she exhales, a large cloud of smoke surrounds her, and she's gone.

I try to find my anger—at her, at Dennis, on behalf of the victim-child I was, but it's a lost thing, misplaced in the chaos of years.

We were all victims, I think. And perhaps Dennis was hurt the most—by his assailant, by his gambling, and by now the cancer that will kill him.

—m—

"Does fire have a shelf life?" Does rage burn out? I imagine being consumed by fire, burned alive by it, like the Vietnamese monks of the sixties and seventies, who set themselves aflame, in protest. *And what for?*

My mom has suffered and Dennis has suffered. And I, too, have suffered. I think of firearms, of guns, the gun that was pointed at my brother's head when he was raped. And the gun that appeared in my dream. Perhaps my confusion about gender has its origins here.

I'm in Cal's old room, and I sit on the futon, turning my hand into a gun that I aim at the ghosts of my mother, my father, my brother—as I challenge them to come, be present with me. But they won't appear. I'm alone. I point the gun at my own head and say "bang."

thirty-two

It's Saturday. I wake to another hot, sunny summer morning. I've not responded to my missed calls or messages; in fact, I've turned my phone off. I've been on silent retreat. No words except for those I've spoken to myself or written.

For breakfast, I eat a piece of whole wheat toast with homemade apricot jam that a student gave to me as a present last semester. I eat only that and sip coffee. I sit at the kitchen table, thinking I'll take a short walk along the Cape Fear Nature Trail before it gets too hot.

I put on my Capri yoga pants, a black camisole, over-shirt, socks, sneakers, and I'm off in Ruby, driving the short distance to the trailhead.

Rape. Silence. Writing. Faith. That ought to be my mantra. I walk the paved trail down the first big hill. Not a soul out. One bird sings, a long trill, followed by another bird, whose call is twittery, sharp. In the distance are muffled road sounds. A waist pack I'm wearing jiggles with loose change and keys against my right hip.

At the bottom of the hill, I notice a side path into a wooded area and take it. Yes, ticks are bad this time of year, but I'll take my chances.

The path is sandy. Many of the border trees are longleaf pines, with thick rough bark, few lower branches, and tall majestic profiles lifting to the sky. *Lifting.* I breathe in the warm heavy morning air. I see filtered light as if broken into atoms and molecules. *Matter.* Stuff of the universe. And what *"matters."* I think back to the museum, to Rodin's heavy bronze sculptures. To El Anatsui's sculpture with cut metal cans draped on the wall. Creation. Connection. With the world, the universe, the self. God in all things, connecting us like thought to action.

Leaves crunch beneath my feet. On a fallen tree off the path, I sit in the cathedral of pines, oak, and trees I can't identify. My heart pumps hard as I look back at the trail to realize that I've been walking uphill.

Staring through the underbrush, I spot a deer, then two, three, four. Two are fawns. The large one looks directly at me, swishes its tail. I think it smells more than it sees. I breathe deeply to catch its wild, gamey scent. Its spirit is untamed, untamable.

The four deer stand only ten feet from me—animal spirits, representing the eternal energy to meet life's challenges with grace. Deer totem, I recall, is associated with gentleness, strength, regeneration.

Finally, the deer move. Slowly at first, then trotting into the woods. I watch them until they all disappear. The path now is straight, level, no longer uphill.

—⁓—

Jake sleeps on the couch and doesn't see or hear me when I come in. Such an old dog, I think; he won't be with us much longer. I pet him as he wags his tail a couple of times, opening his ancient eyes—deep down in their sockets—bloodshot, struggling, before closing them to return to heavy sleep.

Walking upstairs to shower, I first turn on the radio to break the silence. I peel off my sticky clothes, tossing them into the laundry basket. I find a cool cotton-knit sundress, take it off the hanger and lay it out on the bed as Jake lumbers up the stairs to join me.

I shower, the water forceful and warm against my skin—a celebration. Out of the shower, I towel off and catch a glimpse of myself in the bathroom mirror—sad, worn, old, undesirable. No, I correct: *beautiful.* Go with that.

I find my scar. I touch it. The uneven, pulled skin feels like a soft, embedded centipede. Then I feel my mother's lips kissing it, hear her voice assuring me that it's beautiful. I think of the fawn in the woods, its spirit totem: grace to meet challenges.

"Live with it," I say aloud. "Live with it all."

Recognizing the "it" as a vague or broad pronoun, I try to find a noun replacement. But I'm not an academic paper. I'm more poem than scholarship.

I close the closet door and see my cell phone on the dresser. I pick it up and turn it on. I've had more messages: three calls from my mom, two from Nick, two from Cal, and one from Will. I sit with Jake, who has joined me on the bed.

I can't call Nick, so I'll have to wait until he calls me. But I can call my mom, Cal, and Will. I check the time—10:45 a.m., certainly acceptable. So, I try Cal. No answer. I leave a message. I try Will, and he answers.

"Hey, Mom," he says.

"Catching you at an okay time?" I ask.

"On my break. Just taught an early class. Have a few minutes though. What's up?"

"Nothing. Saw I missed your call."

"Yeah. Called the other night. Just wanted to tell you that I sold some wine glasses and a vase. To a couple from Fayetteville. The woman said she knew you from the Arts Council or something. But I don't remember her name."

"Cool. Congrats about the sales. How are you?"

"Good. Real good. Went climbing last Wednesday. Day off. But have you heard from Dad?"

"Yeah, he called, but I missed him."

"Well, when you talk, tell him to call me. I have a question about my truck."

"Problem?"

"No, I just need to change the oil, want to ask him something. No hurry, really. Listen, I got to go. Get back. I'll talk to you later. Will you be around?"

"Yes," I say. "Call when you have some time. We'll catch up. And I'll tell Dad to call you."

"Love you, Mom."

"Love you, too, Will. Bye."

—⁂—

By afternoon, I'm working. Ideas come to me. I write about my junior high school walkout and give my female protagonist the name Anna, in honor of Tolstoy's Anna. My book, I've decided, though autobiographical, will be third-person limited, and Anna should be about five years older than I am so that she's more caught up in the sixties. So much to say. I'm writing again.

When the phone rings, I'm inclined to ignore it, but I've missed calls for too long, and I know I need to answer.

"Hello," I say, hit, and save my work.

"Rae?" Mom asks. "Where've you been? I've been trying to reach you for days."

"Sorry, Mom." Then, turning off my laptop, I lean back on my chair, hear my mother's deep, familiar sigh—the cigarette sigh without the cigarette—and ask, "What's wrong?"

"Bad news. Very bad. Where are you?"

"I'm home, Mom. Sitting in my study. What's going on?"

"He's dying." She says this in a matter-of-fact voice, her in-control voice.

"Where are *you*, Mom? Are you home, at the hospital?"

"I'm home. Lydia took me and the girls to the hospital

today very early, and we stayed there for about three hours. He had a procedure and tests yesterday. Not good. Julia had to work, so we came home. Hannah's inside, watching TV. Lydia's getting ready for her shift this afternoon. I'm down in the laundry room, catching up with our wash."

"Tell me what happened." I look out the window, onto the summer morning.

"The other day, no, two days ago. Rae, I can't keep track of time. I haven't been working. I'll probably get fired. It's okay. I don't need that stupid job. Dennis got sick, was in terrible pain. We went to his doctor, who immediately sent him to the hospital. The cancer's metastasized to his liver. They want to do more chemo, but it doesn't make sense." Long sigh again. "He's given up. I don't blame him."

I'm quiet, staring at the large Bradford pear tree, the shape of its branches, a near perfect oval. "I'm sorry," I say.

"What should I do, Rae? He's going to die." I hear my mom's loud, awful sobs, punctuated with "It's not right. Not right, not right..."

"How long does he have?"

"They don't know or won't say. Best guess, maybe a few months." My mom blows her nose. "Every day, it's been the same thing. Hannah changing his stoma bandage. Dennis getting out barely, seeing friends some nights when he feels well enough. But mostly he's been on the couch, in terrible pain. Down to 135 lbs. Didn't want to go back to the doctor, but finally the pain was so overwhelming that we had to bring him in."

"Are you going to try to go back to work?"

"Yes, I'm supposed to go on Monday. We'll see. I don't know. I don't know what to do." She blows her nose again. "I'm sorry to burden you with all this."

I'm silent for a few minutes, thinking about whose burden

it is, then ask, "How are the girls doing?"

"Hannah's a joy, so smart, helpful. Julia...well, is Julia. She's working and going to school. But I don't think she'll finish." My mother sighs again.

"Keep me posted, Mom. I'm sorry. So sorry. Let me know if anything changes."

"I will. I will. Love you," she responds. "But answer your phone."

"Okay, Mom. Love you, too." We hang up.

—⁕—

I open my laptop, think about doing more work, but I close and unplug it, begin pacing again—first, to Cal's old room over the garage, and next, into Will's old bedroom, with the two old dressers that came from our South Shelburne house, from Dennis's childhood bedroom. They're mid-century modern; I touch the white laminate top and burst into tears. My weeping is loud, and I give myself permission to let go. Like in childbirth, I moan along with my sobs.

"Dennis, Dennis, Dennis," I call out. "What's happened to you?"

But as I ask this, I already know. Dennis has played out the drama that's defined his life, and he has hurt the people he's loved most—our parents, his wife, his daughters, and me. My parents were in denial, about his gambling, about dealing with his rape. My parents could have insisted that Dennis see a therapist—especially when he was young—but they never did. They could have discouraged his stealing by preventing easy access to their money, jewelry, and bank accounts, but they never did. They could have given him consequences for his actions, but they never did. And Dennis? He was driven by forces greater than he could manage. And soon, he'll be dead.

Late afternoon sun throws gray shadows across the wood floor of my study. I sit, lean forward on the futon, shake my head, feel by brother's presence.

"Dennis," I say to the child he was, "I'm sorry for you." Then I breathe and say to the dying man I no longer know, "I'm sorry for you, too."

—⁓—

I feel very old. My kids are grown. Their bedrooms are guestrooms. Tears well up again. Our lives happen in slow motion, speed up, then they're over.

I walk to the hall bathroom for some toilet tissue, dry my eyes, blow my nose. Out the bathroom window is our backyard, and I imagine my boys playing there with Byron, our previous dog. We had a fort and a sandbox. Had I known how quickly they'd grow up, I would have given them more. More of my time, my heart, my self.

I'm sitting now on the closed toilet seat lid, weeping for everything that's lost or will be lost. I can't stop. I cup my face in my hands, let grief overtake me. Then, I walk to my bedroom, pull back the quilt, get into bed, decide to sleep, and quickly free-fall into fitful memory-dreams, cascading, colliding.

It's 1969 again. I'm in the hallway of Lawrence Junior High, but I'm sixty years old. I'm listening to a transistor radio, hearing Neil Armstrong's voice: "One small step for man, one large step for mankind." Then, I'm sixteen, at the Madison Square Garden Rolling Stones' concert, then in Kevin's bed, losing my virginity. In Washington Square Park, under the arch, I smell the city summer air as two men dispute a chess move on the public concrete chessboard under a mimosa tree.

My mother slaps my face, asks, "What were you thinking?" I've just spilled another glass of milk on the wobbly kitchen table in Dunhurst, Queens. My father kisses me as I sit on his lap. Men smoke cigars, play poker at the dining room table, and my father shows me how to hold cards, fan-shaped, in a single hand. I walk slowly down the aisle toward Nick on my wedding day. My dad walks by my side; my tears fall as everyone looks on. I'm twenty-one. I'm marrying Nick, promising not *till death do us part*, but rather for *as long as love shall last.* He pulls back my veil. We kiss.

I'm in my dorm room at the University of Bridgeport, reading in bed, evening light fading from the narrow window over my desk. It's a paperback edition of *To Bedlam and Part Way Back*, Anne Sexton's first book of poems, the one she wrote as therapy at her psychiatrist's suggestion. On the book's back cover is a photo of Sexton, who looks like my mother. I hear a woman's voice Mom? I ask. Anne? Could that be you?

And we are magic talking to itself,
Noisy and alone. I am queen of all my sins
Forgotten. Am I still lost?
Once I was beautiful. Now I am myself.

thirty-three

My cell phone is playing a song; it's singing me awake.

I turn over in bed, my left hand finding the phone on my night-table. I don't check the caller-ID, just answer.

"We have news," I hear. "Jess and I. Big news." Cal's voice is loud and bright.

I'm sitting up now, looking out the bedroom window at a pale black sky gently ending the day. It's probably 8:30 at night, I think, which means I've been sleeping for hours. I immediately feel awake.

"Hey, Cal," I say. "Good to hear from you. News? Great. What is it?"

"Jess is pregnant!"

The words are like starbursts of light in my head. I stand up.

"Wow!" I say. "Double wow!" I pace the bedroom, then run down the stairs, looking for space. I need space.

"How far along?" I'm cradling the phone, in the sunroom, then stepping into our backyard and onto our patio. The dark sky is soft, welcoming.

"We wanted to wait until the doctor told us everything is okay. She's about eleven and a half weeks. We're really happy, Mom."

Tears well up. But I'm grinning, too—and somehow enabled, ready to accept myself as mother, grandmother, gender-neutral or gendered enough. I sit on a webbed lawn chair. Jake has come through his dog door and is standing beside me. I put my hand down, stroke his back; he wags his tail.

"You there, Mom?" I hear.

"Yes. I'm totally here. Just happy. No, thrilled. Really thrilled." I feel a shift. Continents have drifted apart, then together. Time has stopped. A breeze passes, lifting the branches of our weeping cherry.

"Where are you?" I ask.

"I'm walking to the pizza place. Jess is at home."

We chat about his work—he has a new client in Connecticut, and he'll be able to visit his uncle and grandmother while he's there. He'll tell them the news in person, he says, "So don't you tell them."

"I won't," I promise as I drift from tears and memories of my own pregnancies to incredible presence. The earth stops shifting for a moment, and I'm mindfully attentive. A new baby. A first grandchild. A reason to forgive, a reason to continue.

"Well, I got to go, Mom. Can you tell Dad to call me? Give him the news. But I want to talk to him myself. Soon. Please."

"I love you so much, Cal. And Jess. Give her my love."

"You coming up to Boston before school starts, right?"

"That's the plan. A quick trip when Dad gets back. Probably next month. Can't wait."

"Jess and I will call again. Wanted to give you our news as soon as possible. Love you, Mom. Oh, tell Will for us. And Sonya. Everyone but Grandma and Uncle John can know."

"Okay, sweetheart. This is fabulous. I love you so much."

"Bye, Mom. Love you, too. Got to go."

"Bye, Cal. Love you." I hit the screen's end-call button. But as soon as I do, the phone rings again, and this time, it's Nick.

"Well hello," I say. "How are you?"

"Where have you been? I was worried. Been trying to reach you for days. You okay?"

"Great," I answer, standing up, walking up the back steps to enter the sunroom, where I sit down on a comfortable chair, put my feet up on the coffee table.

"I can't talk for long. Just wanted to check in, make sure you're okay. I've been calling and couldn't get you. Where have you been?" Nick's words spill out. I can't tell if he's angry or just concerned.

"Look," I say. "I'm great now. I wasn't, but I am now. I have big news."

"Okay," he says. "What's up?"

"Jess is pregnant. Cal just called a minute ago."

"Wow. You're kidding!" his words are so present that I can feel him, as if he's beside me, almost as if he is me. *Nick loves me*, I now recognize.

"Yeah," I say. "No, not kidding. She's about twelve weeks. We're going to be grandparents."

"I love you," Nick says.

"I love you, too." Tears again. For the millionth time. I wipe them with my hand.

"Look," he says. "I'm coming home soon. Can't wait to see you. Just another week."

"Yes," I say.

"I'll call Cal and Jess tomorrow. But this is so good. So good." I hear people in the background.

"Yes, call them. Also call Will. He wants to talk to you about his truck. And tell him the news. But go now. Enjoy."

"Speak with you tomorrow. Yes? And I'll call Will."

"Yes. Bye."

"Bye."

Then I'm off the phone, and alone again with Jake in the

sunroom. I look out at the black sky and notice a half moon sitting low, illuminating the eastern horizon. I hear cicadas. And I'm hungry.

But as I rise to enter the house, I see Dennis's shadow—his young face, his mad-glad face—beside me.

"I've been thinking about you," I tell him.

"I know," he whispers. "Do you forgive me?"

But as I turn toward him, finally ready to say "yes," his shadow dissipates and steps aside.

acknowledgments

I want to thank the following individuals whose love and friendship sustained me through the writing of this novel: Michael, Dan, Ben, Jen, Jenna, Ruth, Cristina, Emily, Joe, and, Barbara. Additionally, I want to thank my granddaughter, Lilly, whose light and love offer me a quality of unmatched joy. And, finally, I want to thank Pat, my friend who left this earth a better place.

the author

Robin Greene is a Professor of English and Writing and the Director of the Writing Center at Methodist University in Fayetteville, NC, where she held the McLean Endowed Chair in English from 2013-2016. Greene has published two collections of poetry (*Memories of Light* and *Lateral Drift*), two editions of a nonfiction book (*Real Birth: Women Share Their Stories*), and a novel (*Augustus: Narrative of a Slave Woman*).

Greene is co-founder and editor of Longleaf Press, Methodist University's literary press, co-founder of the Sandhills Dharma Group, a Buddhist sitting group, and a certified yoga teacher. Every year, Greene leads an annual women's writing retreat in Oaxaca, Mexico, where she enjoys combining yoga and contemplative practices with her teaching. Greene is a past recipient of a NEA/NC Arts Council fellowship in writing, and has won teaching awards. She has published over eighty pieces of poetry, fiction, and nonfiction in literary journals and magazines. Originally from New York City, Greene makes her home in Fayetteville, NC. She holds a M.A. in English from Binghamton University and a M.F.A. in Writing from Vermont College of Fine Art at Norwich University.

Robin Greene is available for readings and workshops, and encourages readers to connect with her through Facebook at robingreene.author and her website at robingreene-writer. com.

You might also enjoy
these other books about strong women

Healing Maddie Brees
Rebecca Brewster Stevenson
"A gorgeous meditation on broken bodies, fractured faith, and the soul-wrenching path to serenity." –*Kirkus Reviews*

In the Midst of Innocence
Deborah Hining
"An endearing ballad of the struggle for existence and understanding." –*Booklist*

The Particular Appeal of Gillian Pugsley
Susan Örnbratt
"memorable—feisty, unexpected" –*Kirkus Reviews*

A Theory of Expanded Love
Caitlin Hicks
"...enough charm to fill the corridors of Vatican City twice over" –*Foreword Reviews*